M000303031

MAGAZINE

Tin House

Volume 14, Number 4

"I almost wish we were butterflies and liv'd but three summer days—three such days with you I could fill with more delight than fifty common years could ever contain."

—JOHN KEATS

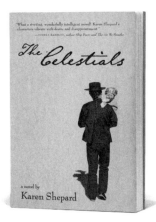

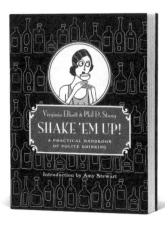

THE CELESTIALS

a novel by Karen Shepard

In June of 1870, seventy-five Chinese laborers arrived in North Adams, Massachusetts, to work for Calvin Sampson, one of the biggest industrialists in that busy factory town. Combining history and fiction, Karen Shepard's *The Celestials* beautifully reimagines the story of Sampson's "Chinese experiment" and the effect of the newcomers' threatening and exotic presence on the New England locals. When Sampson's wife gives birth to a mixed-race baby, the infant becomes a lightning rod for the characters' struggles over questions of identity, alienation, and exile.

"What a riveting, wonderfully intelligent novel! Karen Shepard's characters vibrate with desire and disappointment, so obdurately individual that a whole world springs to life around them and the past becomes completely present."

—ANDREA BARRETT, author of *Ship Fever*

Available Now

SHAKE 'EM UP

by Virginia Elliott and Phil D. Stong

Introduction by Amy Stewart,
author of *The Drunken Botanist*

As the authors say: *Shake 'Em Up* is "for People Who Fling Parties, People Who Go to Parties . . . People Who Don't Really Drink but Feel That a Cocktail or Two Enlivens Conversation—in short, for the American People," and that's as true today as it was upon the book's original publication, "in the twelfth year of Volstead, 1930."

Virginia Elliott and Phil D. Stong created a handbook for polite—if not entirely legal—drinking during the height of Prohibition, but the advice remains sound, the voice charming, and the cocktails strong.

Available June 2013

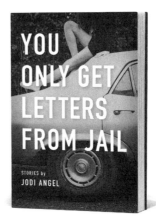

THE VIRGINS

a novel by Pamela Erens

It's 1979, and Aviva Rossner and Seung Jung are notorious at Auburn Academy. They're an unlikely pair at an elite East Coast boarding school (she's Jewish; he's Korean American) and hardly shy when it comes to their sexuality. *The Virgins* is the story of Aviva and Seung's descent into confusion and shame, as reimagined in richly detailed episodes by their classmate Bruce, a once-embittered voyeur turned repentant narrator.

"Now that James Salter is in his twilight years, his considerable fan base will be ecstatic to encounter his heiress apparent, Pamela Erens, whose erotically charged prose reaches for naming the ineffable, honoring the elusive, and celebrating the bodily majesty of life. An extraordinary novel."

—ANTONYA NELSON, author of *Bound*

Available July 2013

YOU ONLY GET LETTERS FROM JAIL

stories by Jodi Angel

Jodi Angel's story collection *You Only Get Letters from Jail* chronicles the lives of young men trapped in the liminal space between adolescence and adulthood. Haunted by unfulfilled dreams and disappointments, and often acting out of mixed intentions and questionable motives, these boys turned young men are nevertheless portrayed with depth, tenderness, and humanity. Angel's gritty and heartbreaking prose leaves readers empathizing with people they wouldn't ordinarily trust or believe in.

"Jodi Angel writes like an angel—in the full sense of the designation—which is to say someone fallen out of the armpit of a restless deity—sharp-eyed, ruthless, and tender at the same time."

—DOROTHY ALLISON, author of *Bastard Out of Carolina*

Available July 2013

MFA at PSU

Fiction | Nonfiction | Poetry

Diana Abu-Jaber

John Beer

Paul Collins

Charles D'Ambrosio

Michele Glazer

Michael McGregor

A. B. Paulson

Leni Zumas

Jon Raymond, visiting

James B. Norman, *The Portland Bridge Book*

Announcing for 2013

TIN HOUSE WRITER-IN-RESIDENCE: Joanna Klink

TIN HOUSE MASTERCLASS AND VISITING WRITER: Maggie Nelson

www.pdx.edu/mfa-creativewriting

Application deadline for 2013: January 3, 2013

Portland State
UNIVERSITY

BRENDA SHAUGHNESSY
Our Andromeda

$16 PAPERBACK

"*Our Andromeda* ... is a monumental work."
—*The New Yorker*

In Brenda Shaughnessy's *Our Andromeda,* playful musicality and deadpan humor meld with blunt questions and a plea for an alternate galaxy in which merciful do-overs are possible. Throughout her remarkable poems, Shaughnessy blasts apart our typical expectations while she maintains the familiar and consoles sufferers in the real world of hostile truths.

"In *Our Andromeda,* Shaughnessy has imagined a universe, and in it, real love moves, quick with life."
—*Publishers Weekly,* starred review

Human Dark with Sugar

WINNER OF THE JAMES LAUGHLIN AWARD

$15 PAPERBACK

"*Human Dark with Sugar* is both wonderfully inventive and emotionally precise. Her 'I' is madly multi-dexterous—urgent, comic, mischievous—and the result is a new topography of the debates between heart and head."
—Judges' comment, James Laughlin Award

"In *Human Dark with Sugar,* poet Brenda Shaughnessy, mistress of eclectic diction and erotic wordplay, brazenly bends language to her will."
—*Vanity Fair*

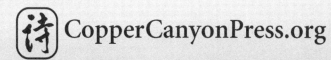

Tin House MAGAZINE

EDITOR IN CHIEF / PUBLISHER
Win McCormack

EDITOR	Rob Spillman
ART DIRECTOR	Diane Chonette
MANAGING EDITOR	Cheston Knapp
EXECUTIVE EDITOR	Michelle Wildgen
POETRY EDITOR	Matthew Dickman
EDITOR-AT-LARGE	Elissa Schappell
POETRY EDITOR-AT-LARGE	Brenda Shaughnessy
PARIS EDITOR	Heather Hartley
ASSISTANT EDITORS	Desiree Andrews, Lance Cleland, Emma Komlos-Hrobsky

CONTRIBUTING EDITORS: Dorothy Allison, Steve Almond, Aimee Bender, Charles D'Ambrosio, Brian DeLeeuw, Anthony Doerr, CJ Evans, Nick Flynn, Matthea Harvey, Jeanne McCulloch, Christopher Merrill, Rick Moody, Whitney Otto, D. A. Powell, Jon Raymond, Rachel Resnick, Peter Rock, Helen Schulman, Jim Shepard, Karen Shepard, Bill Wadsworth

DESIGNER: Jakob Vala

INTERNS: Daniel Casto, Erin Gravley, Veronica Martin, Allyson Paty, Janet Matthews and Devon Walker

READERS: Susan DeFreitas, Polly Dugan, Megan Freshley, Ann-Derrick Gaillot, Mark Hammond, Bryan Hurt, Aaron Kroska, Alina Labrador, Louise Wareham Leonard, Sarah Marshall, Shannon McDonald, Maya McOmie, Lisa Mecham, Cynthia-Marie O'Brien, Hannah Pass, Stacy Heiney Perrou, Elizabeth Pusack, Jeremy Scheuer, Annie Rose Shapero, Neesa Sonoquie, Lee Steely, Jennifer Taylor, J. Toriseva, Christie VanLaningham, Linda Woolman

DEPUTY PUBLISHER	Holly MacArthur
CIRCULATION DIRECTOR	Laura Howard
DIRECTOR OF PUBLICITY	Nanci McCloskey
COMPTROLLER	Janice Carter

Tin House Books

EDITORIAL ADVISOR	Rob Spillman
EDITORS	Meg Storey, Tony Perez, Nanci McCloskey
ASSOCIATE EDITOR	Masie Cochran
EDITORIAL ASSISTANT	Desiree Andrews

Tin House Magazine (ISSN 1541-521X) is published quarterly by McCormack Communications LLC, 2601 Northwest Thurman Street, Portland, OR 97210. Vol. 14, No. 4, Summer 2013. Printed by R. R. Donnelley. Send submissions (with SASE) to Tin House, P.O. Box 10500, Portland, OR 97296-0500.

Basic subscription price: one year, $50.00. For subscription requests, write to P.O. Box 469049, Escondido, CA 92046-9049, or e-mail tinhouse@pcspublink.com, or call 1-800-786-3424. Additional questions, e-mail laura@tinhouse.com.

Periodicals postage paid at Portland, OR 97210 and additional mailing offices.

Postmaster: Send address changes to Tin House Magazine, P.O. Box 469049, Escondido, CA 92046-9049.

Newsstand distribution through Disticor Magazine Distribution Services (disticor.com). If you are a retailer and would like to order Tin House, call 905-619-6565, fax 905-619-2903, or e-mail Melanie Raucci at mraucci@disticor.com. For trade copies, contact Publisher's Group West at 800-788-3123, or e-mail orderentry@perseusbooks.com.

The best writers not only create worlds beyond our imagination but also lead us into places we'd never dare venture alone. Over their long careers, Stephen King and Margaret Atwood have continually surprised us with their dark worlds. In his new short story "Afterlife," King transports us into the mind of a man at the white-light moment of his death. And Atwood, master of speculative fiction and a fervent conservationist, talks about dystopian societies and vanishing species with *Tin House* editor-at-large Elissa Schappell. Critic Parul Sehgal explores issues of race, class, and gender politics, as well as the significance of African and African American women's hair, in her interview with Orange Prize—winning novelist Chimamanda Ngozi Adichie.

But discovery isn't always about darkness, especially in the summer, when thoughts turn to sun and vacation. In this issue, poet Tom Sleigh, who has seven collections of poetry and numerous awards to his credit, continues to burn bright with two new poems; Katie Arnold-Ratliff writes about eating her way through Disneyland; and Jennifer Gilmore chronicles her attempt to make a meal with her Greek mother-in-law on the island of Naxos.

For us, it is always exciting to publish our heroes, but it is equally invigorating to discover new heroes who take us to new worlds. We were so excited when we first read Jodi Angel's haunting stories about rural, wrong-side-of-the-track teens that next month we're publishing her second collection, *You Only Get Letters from Jail*, and include here the story "Firm and Good."

We hope you'll follow us to both our dark and our light places, and we appreciate you taking us along—to the mountains, to the beach, to the backyard hammock.

CONTENTS

ISSUE #56 / SUMMER READING

Fiction

Poetry

Interview

Features

Afterlife

William Andrews, an investment banker with Goldman Sachs, dies on the afternoon of September 23, 2012. It is an expected death; his wife and adult children are at his bedside. That evening, when she finally allows herself some time alone, away from the steady stream of family and condolence visitors, Lynn Andrews calls her oldest friend, who still lives in Milwaukee. It was Sally Freeman who introduced her to Bill, and if anyone deserves to know about the last sixty seconds of her thirty-year marriage, it's Sally.

"He was out of it for most of the last week—the drugs—but conscious at the end. His eyes were open, and he saw me. He smiled. I took his hand and he squeezed it a little. I bent over and kissed his cheek. When I straightened up again, he was gone." She has been waiting for hours to say this, and now that it's out, she bursts into tears.

Stephen King

Her assumption that the smile was for her is natural enough, but mistaken. As he is looking up at his wife and three grown children—they seem impossibly tall, creatures of angelic good health inhabiting a world he is now departing—Bill feels the pain he has lived with for the past eighteen months leave his body. It pours out like slop from a bucket. So he smiles.

With the pain gone, there's little left. He feels as light as a fluff of milkweed. His wife takes his hand, reaching down from her tall and healthy world. He has reserved a little bit of strength, which he now expends by squeezing her fingers. She bends down. She is going to kiss him.

Before her lips can touch his skin, a hole appears in the center of his vision. It's not a black hole but a white one. It spreads, obliterating the only world he's known since 1956, when he was born in the small Hemingford County Hospital in Nebraska. During the last year, Bill has read a great deal about the passage from life to death (on his computer, always careful to erase the history so as not to upset Lynn, who is constantly and unrealistically upbeat), and while most of it struck him as bullshit, the so-called "white light" phenomenon seemed quite plausible. For one thing, it has been reported in all cultures. For another, it has a smidgen of scientific credibility. One theory he's read suggests the white light comes as a result of the sudden cessation of blood flow to the brain. Another, more elegant, posits that the brain is performing a final global scan in an effort to find an experience comparable to dying.

Or it may just be a final firework.

Whatever the cause, Bill Andrews is now experiencing it. The white light obliterates his family and the airy room from which the mortuary assistants will soon remove his sheeted breathless body. In his researches, he became familiar with the acronym NDE, standing for near-death experience. During many of these experiences, the white light becomes a tunnel, at the end of which stand beckoning family members who have already died, or friends, or angels, or Jesus, or some other beneficent deity.

Bill expects no welcoming committee. What he expects is for the final firework to fade to the blackness of oblivion, but that doesn't happen. When the brilliance dims, he's not in heaven or hell. He's in a hallway. He supposes it could be purgatory, a hallway painted industrial green and floored in scuffed and dirty tile could very well serve as purgatory, but only if it went on forever. This one ends twenty feet down at a door with a sign on it reading ISAAC HARRIS MANAGER.

Bill stands where he is for a few moments, inventorying himself. He's wearing the pajamas he died in (at least, he assumes he died), and he's

PREVIOUS: SEE PAGE 217 FOR PHOTO CREDITS

barefooted, but there's no sign of the cancer that first tasted his body, then gobbled it down to nothing but skin and skeleton. He looks to be back at about one-ninety, which was his fighting weight (slightly soft-bellied, granted) before the cancer struck. He feels his buttocks and the small of his back. The bedsores are gone. Nice. He takes a deep breath and exhales without coughing. Even nicer.

He walks a little way down the hall. On his left is a fire extinguisher with a peculiar graffito above it: *Better late than never!* On his right is a bulletin board. Onto this a number of photographs have been pinned, the old-fashioned kind with deckle edges. Above them is a hand-printed banner reading COMPANY PIC-NIC 1956! WHAT FUN WE HAD!

Bill examines the photographs, which show executives, secretaries, office personnel, and a gaggle of romping kids. There are guys tending a barbecue (one wearing the obligatory joke toque), guys and gals toss-

> Bill feels the pain he has lived with for the past eighteen months leave his body. It pours out like slop from a bucket.

ing horseshoes, guys and gals playing volleyball, guys and gals swimming in a lake. The guys are wearing bathing suits that look almost obscenely short and tight to his twenty-first-century eye, but very few of them are carrying big guts. *They have fifties physiques*, Bill thinks. The gals are wearing those old-fashioned Esther Williams tank suits, the kind that make women look as if they have not buttocks but only a kind of cleftless bulge above the backs of their thighs. Hot dogs are being consumed. Beer is being drunk. Everybody appears to be having a whale of a good time.

In one of the pictures, Richie Blankmore's father is handing Annmarie Winkler a toasted marshmallow. This is ridiculous, because Richie's dad was a truck driver and never went to a company picnic in his life. Annmarie was a girl Bill dated in college. In another photo he sees Bobby Tisdale, a college classmate back in the early seventies. Bobby, who referred to himself as Tiz the Wiz, died of a heart attack while still in his thirties. He was probably on earth in 1956, but would have been in kindergarten or the first grade, not drinking beer on the shore of Lake Whatever. In this picture the Wiz looks about twenty, which would have been his age when Bill knew him. In a third picture, Eddie Scarponi's mom is baffing a volleyball. Eddie was Bill's best friend when the family moved from Nebraska to Paramus, New Jersey, and Gina Scarponi—once glimpsed sunning herself on the patio in filmy white panties and nothing else—was one of Bill's favorite fantasies when he was still on his masturbation learner's permit.

The guy in the joke toque is Ronald Reagan. Bill looks closely, his nose almost pressing against the black-and-white photo, and there can be no doubt. The fortieth president of the United States is flipping burgers at a company picnic.

What company, though?

Where, exactly, is he?

His euphoria at being whole again and pain-free is fading. What replaces it is a growing sense of unease. Seeing some familiar people in the photographs is disorienting, and the fact that he doesn't know the majority of them makes it worse. He looks behind him and sees stairs leading up to another door. Printed on this one in large red block letters is LOCKED. That leaves only Mr. Harris's office. Bill walks down to it, hesitates, then knocks.

> His euphoria at being whole again and pain-free is fading. What replaces it is a growing sense of unease.

"It's open."

Bill walks in. Beside a cluttered desk stands a fellow in baggy, high-waisted suit pants held up by suspenders. His brown hair is plastered to his skull and parted in the middle. He wears rimless glasses. The walls are covered with invoices and corny leg-art cheesecake pix that make Bill think of the trucking company Richie Blankmore's dad worked for. He went there a few times with Richie, and the dispatch office looked like this.

There's no window. According to the calendar on one wall, it is March of 1911, which makes no more sense than 1956. To Bill's right as he enters, there's a door. To his left is another. There are no windows, but a glass tube comes out of the ceiling and dangles over a Dandux laundry basket. The basket is filled with a heap of yellow sheets that look like more invoices. Or maybe they're memos. Files are piled two feet high on the chair in front of the desk.

"Bill Anderson, isn't it?" The man goes behind the desk and sits down. There is no offer to shake hands.

"Andrews."

"Right. And I'm Harris. Here you are again, Andrews."

Given all Bill's research on dying, this comment actually makes sense. And it's a relief. As long as he doesn't have to come back as a dung beetle or something. "So it's reincarnation? Is that the deal?"

Isaac Harris sighs. "You always ask the same thing, and I always give the same answer: not really."

"I'm dead, aren't I?"

"Do you feel dead?"

"No, but I saw the white light."

"Oh yes, the famous white light. There you were and here you are. Wait a minute, just hold the phone."

Harris breezes through the papers on his desk, doesn't find what he wants, and starts opening drawers. From one of them he takes a few more folders and selects one. He opens it, flips a page or two, and nods. "Just refreshing myself a bit. Investment banker, aren't you?"

"Yes."

"Wife and three kids? Two sons, one daughter?"

"Correct."

"Apologies. I have a couple of hundred pilgrims, and it's hard to keep them straight. I keep meaning to put these folders in some sort of order, but that's really a secretarial job, and since they've never provided me with one . . ."

"Who's *they*?"

"No idea. All communications come via the tube." He taps it. The tube sways, then stills. "Runs on compressed air. Latest thing."

Bill picks up the folders on the client's chair and looks at the man behind the desk, eyebrows raised.

"Just put them on the floor," Harris says. "That'll do for now. One of these days I really am going to get organized. If there *are* days. Probably are—nights, too—but who can say for sure? No windows in here, as you will have noticed. Also no clocks."

Bill sits down. "Why call me a pilgrim, if it's not reincarnation?"

Harris leans back and laces his hands behind his neck. He looks up at the pneumatic tube, which probably *was* the latest thing at some time or other. Say around 1911, although Bill supposes such things might still have been around in 1956.

Harris shakes his head and chuckles, although not in an amused way. "If you only knew how *wearisome* you guys become. According to the file, this is our fifteenth visit."

"I've never been here in my life," Bill says. He considers this. "Except it's *not* my life, is it? It's my afterlife."

"Actually, it's mine. You're the pilgrim, not me. You and the other bozos who parade in and out of here. You'll use one of the doors and go. I stay.

There's no bathroom here, because I no longer have to perform toilet functions. There's no bedroom, because I no longer have to sleep. All I do is sit around and visit with you traveling bozos. You come in, you ask the same questions, and I give the same answers. That's *my* afterlife. Sound exciting?"

Bill, who encountered all the theological ins and outs during his final research project, decides he had the right idea while he was still in the hall. "You're talking about purgatory."

"Oh, no doubt. The only question I have is how long I'll be staying. I'd like to tell you I'll eventually go mad if I can't move on, but I don't think I can do that any more than I can take a shit or a nap. I know my name means nothing to you, but we've discussed this before—not every time you show up, but on several occasions." He waves an arm with enough force to cause some of the invoices tacked on the wall to flutter. "This is—or *was*, I'm not sure which is actually correct—my earthly office."

"In 1911?"

"Just so. I'd ask if you know what a shirtwaist is, Bill, but since I know you don't, I'll tell you: a woman's blouse. At the turn of the century, I and my partner, Max Blanck, owned a business called the Triangle Shirtwaist Company. Profitable business, but the women who worked there were a large pain in the hinder end. Always sneaking out to smoke and—this was worse—stealing stuff, which they would put in their purses or tuck up under their skirts. So we locked the doors to keep them in during their shifts and searched them on their way out. Long story short, the damned place caught on fire one day. Max and I escaped by going up to the roof and down the fire escape. Many of the women were not so lucky. Although, let's be honest and admit there's lots of blame to go around. Smoking was strictly verboten, but plenty of them did it anyway, and it was a cigarette that started the blaze. Fire marshal said so. Max and I were tried for manslaughter and were by-God acquitted."

Bill recalls the fire extinguisher in the hall, with *Better late than never!* printed above it. He thinks: *You were found guilty in the retrial, Mr. Harris, or you wouldn't be here.* "How many women died?"

"A hundred and forty-six," Harris says, "and I regret every one, Mr. Anderson."

Bill doesn't bother correcting him on the name. Twenty minutes ago he was dying in his bed; now he is fascinated by this story, which he has never heard before. That he remembers, anyway.

"Not long after Max and I got down the fire escape, the women crammed onto it. The damn thing couldn't take the weight. It collapsed and spilled two dozen of 'em a hundred feet to the cobblestones. They all died. Forty more jumped from the ninth- and tenth-floor windows. Some were on fire. *They* all died, too. The fire brigade got there with life nets, but the women tore right through them and exploded on the pavement like bags filled with blood. A terrible sight, Mr. Anderson, terrible. Others jumped down the elevator shafts, but most . . . just . . . burned."

"Like 9/11 with fewer casualties."

"So you always say."

"And you're here."

"Yes, indeed. I sometimes wonder how many men are sitting in offices just like this. Women too. I'm sure there *are* women, I've always been forward-looking and see no reason why women can't fill low-level executive positions, and admirably. All of us answering the same questions and sending on the same pilgrims. You'd think that the load would lighten a little each time one of you decides to use the right-hand door instead of that one"—he points to the left—"but no. *No.* A fresh canister comes down the tube—*zoop*—and I get a new bozo to replace the old one. Sometimes two." He leans forward and speaks with great emphasis. "This is a shitty job, Mr. Anderson!"

"It's Andrews," Bill says. "And look, I'm sorry you feel that way, but Jesus, take a little responsibility for your actions, man! A hundred and forty-six women! And you *did* lock the doors."

Harris hammers his desk. "They were stealing us blind!" He picks up the folder and shakes it at Bill. "You should talk! Ha! Pot calling the kettle black! Goldman Sachs! Securities fraud! Profits in the billions, taxes in the millions! The *low* millions! Does the phrase *housing bubble* ring a bell? How many clients' trust did you abuse? How many people lost their life savings thanks to your greed and shortsightedness?"

Bill knows what Harris is talking about, but all that chicanery (well . . . most of it) went on far above his pay grade. He was as surprised as anyone when the excrement hit the cooling device. The proof of his essential innocence, it seems to him, is that he is the pilgrim and Harris is stuck sitting in this office. He's tempted to say there's a big difference between being beggared and burned alive, but why rub salt in the wound?

> Twenty minutes ago he was dying in his bed; now he is fascinated by this story, which he has never heard before.

"Let's drop it," he says. "If you have information I need, why not give it to me? Fill me in on the deal, and I'll get out of your hair."

"*I* wasn't the one smoking," Harris says in a low and brooding tone. "*I* wasn't the one dropped the match."

"Mr. Harris?" Bill can feel the walls closing in. *If I had to be here forever I'd shoot myself,* he thinks. Only, if what Mr. Harris says is true, he wouldn't want to, any more than he'd want to go to the toilet.

"Okay, all right." Harris makes a lip-flapping sound, not quite a raspberry. "The *deal* is this. Leave through the left door and you get to live your life over again. A to Z. Starting gun to checkered flag. Take the right one and you wink out. Poof. Candle-in-the-wind type of thing."

At first Bill says nothing to this. He's incapable of speech and not sure he can trust his ears. It's too good to be true. His mind first turns to his brother Mike, and the accident that happened when Mike was eight. Next, to the stupid shoplifting thing when Bill was seventeen. Just a lark, but it could have put a hole in his college plans if his father hadn't stepped in and talked to the right person. The thing with Annmarie in the fraternity house . . . that still haunts him at odd moments, even after all these years. And of course, the big one—

> "She put her legs around me when I got on top of her, and if that doesn't say consent, I don't know what does."

Harris is smiling, and the smile isn't a bit pleasant. Okay, so his ears *did* deceive him. Or maybe Harris was just getting back at him for suggesting that Harris deserved to be here, in this limbo of bureaucracy.

"I know what you're thinking, because I've heard it all from you before. About how you and your brother were playing flashlight tag when you were kids, and you slammed the bedroom door to keep him out and accidentally cut off the tip of his pinky finger. The impulse shoplifting thing, the watch, and how your dad pulled strings to get you out of it—"

"That's right, no record. Except with him. He never let me forget it."

"And then there's the girl in the frat house basement." Harris lifts the file. "Her name's in here somewhere, I imagine, I do my best to keep the files current—when I can find them—but why don't you refresh me."

"Annmarie Winkler." Bill can feel his cheeks heating up. "It wasn't date rape, so don't get that idea. She put her legs around me when I got on top of her, and if that doesn't say consent, I don't know what does."

"Did she also put her legs around the two fellows who came next?"

No, Bill is tempted to say, *but at least we didn't light her on fire, smartass.*
But still.

He'd be teeing off on the seventh or working in his woodshop or talking to his daughter (now a college student herself) about her senior thesis, and he would wonder where Annmarie is now. What she's doing. What she remembers about that night.

Harris's smile widens to a locker-room smirk. It may be a shitty job, but it's clear there are parts of it he enjoys. "I can see that's a question you don't want to answer, so why don't we move along. You're thinking of all the things you'll change during your next ride on the cosmic carousel. This time you won't slam the door on your kid brother's finger, or try to shoplift a watch at the Paramus Mall—"

"It was the Mall of New Jersey."

Harris gives Bill a who-gives-a-shit flap of the file folder and continues. "Next time you'll decline to let your friends fuck your semicomatose date as she lies on the sofa in the basement, and—big one!—you'll actually make that appointment for the colonoscopy instead of putting it off, having now decided—correct me if I'm wrong—that the indignity of having a camera shoved up your ass is better than dying of cancer."

Bill says, "Several times I've come close to telling Lynn about that houseparty thing. I've never had the courage."

"But given the chance, you'd fix it."

"Given the chance, wouldn't you unlock those factory doors?"

"Indeed I would, but there are no second chances. Sorry to disappoint you." He doesn't look sorry. Harris looks tired. Harris looks bored. Harris also looks meanly triumphant. He points to Bill's left. "Use that door—as you have on every other occasion—and you begin all over again, as a five-pound baby boy sliding from your mother's womb into the doctor's hands. You'll be taken home, wrapped in bunting, to a farm in central Nebraska. When your father sells the farm in 1963, you'll move to New Jersey. There you will cut off the tip of your brother's little finger while playing tag. You'll go to the same high school, take the same courses, and make exactly the same grades. You'll go to Boston College and commit the same act of semirape in the same apartment house rec room. You'll watch as the same two guys—your friends—then have sex with Annmarie Winkler, and although you'll think you should call a halt to what's going on, you won't quite muster up the moral fortitude to do so. Three years later you'll meet Lynn DeSalvo, and two years after that you'll be married. You'll follow the same career path, you'll have the same friends, you'll have the same deep disquiet about some of your firm's business practices . . . and you'll keep the same silence. The same doctor will urge you to get a colonoscopy when you turn fifty, and you will promise—as you always do—to take care of that little matter. You won't, and as a result you will die of the same cancer." Harris drops the folder back on his cluttered desk. "Then you'll come here, as you always do, and we'll have this same basic discussion all over again. My advice would be to use the other door and have done with it, but of course that is your decision."

Bill has listened to this sermonette with increasing dismay. "I'll remember nothing? *Nothing?*"

"Not quite," Harris says. "You may have noticed some photos in the hall."

"The company picnic."

"Every client who visits me sees pictures from the year of his or her birth and recognizes a few familiar faces amid all the strange ones. When you live your life again, Mr. Anders—presuming you decide to—you will have a sense of déjà vu when you first see those people, a sense that you have lived it all before. Which, of course, you have. You will have a fleeting sense, almost a surety, that there is more . . . shall we say, *depth*? . . . to your life, and to existence in general, than you previously believed. But the feeling will pass. And why not? It's an illusion."

"If it's all the same, with no possibility of improvement, why are we even here?"

Harris knocks on the end of the pneumatic tube hanging over the laundry basket, making it swing. "*CLIENT WANTS TO KNOW WHY WE'RE HERE! WANTS TO KNOW WHAT IT'S ALL ABOUT!*"

He waits. Nothing happens. He folds his hands on his desk.

"When Job wanted to know that, Mr. Anders, God asked if Job was there when he—God—made the universe. I guess you don't even rate that much of a reply. So let's consider the matter closed. What do you want to do? Pick a door."

Bill is thinking about the cancer. The pain of the cancer. To go through all that again . . . except he wouldn't remember he'd gone through it already. Assuming Isaac Harris is telling the truth, that is.

"No memories at all? No changes at all? Are you sure? How can you be?"

"Because it's always the same conversation, Mr. Anderson. Each time, and with all of you."

"*It's Andrews!*" He bellows it, surprising both of them. In a lower voice, he says: "If I try, really try, I'm sure I can hold on to something. Even if it's only what happened to Mike's finger. And one change might be enough to . . . I don't know . . ."

To take Annmarie to a movie instead of to that fucking houseparty, how about that?

"Mr. Andrews, there is a folk tale that before being born, every human soul knows all the secrets of life and death and the universe. Then, just before birth, an angel leans down, puts his finger to the new baby's lips, and whispers, *Shhh.*" Harris touches his philtrum. "According to the story, this is the mark left by the angel's finger. Every human being has one."

"Have you ever seen an angel, Mr. Harris?"

"No, but I once saw a camel. It was in the Bronx Zoo. Choose a door."

As he considers, Bill remembers a story they had to read in junior high: "The Lady or the Tiger." This decision is nowhere near as difficult.

I must hold on to just one thing, he tells himself as he opens the door that leads back into life. *Just one thing.*

Then the white light envelops him.

The doctor, who will bolt the Republican Party and vote for Adlai Stevenson in the fall (something his wife must never know) bends forward from the waist like a waiter presenting a tray and comes up holding a naked baby by the heels. He gives it a sharp smack on the bottom and the squalling begins.

"You have a healthy baby boy, Mary," he says. "Congratulations."

Mary Andrews takes the baby. She kisses his damp cheeks and brow. They will name him William, after her paternal grandfather. He might do anything, he might be anything. The idea is intoxicating. In her arms she holds not just a new life but a universe of possibilities. Nothing, she thinks, could be more wonderful. 🜚

PALMS FACING OUT AND AWAY FROM THE BODY

After my mother said do not come back
Until he gives you good money I went
To the place of men in jackets waiting

For the bell, the trade, what might make
Enough to sell. How did they come to be first,
Able to leave before break of day the sleeping

Who depend as if somewhere is written
Redemption can be had. Managing excess
Is what the market does and in the open

Outcry and face to face will be a few
Who walk away with much. I look for one
Who will buy what I owe among the many

Who take from each other what I cannot
Understand until everything being profit
Or loss is a promise of someone on the other

Side. And then to be nimble for he
Who drives out risk does not look back;
I will let him borrow when his hand

Is where I can see it. The bull does not
Die easily, runs up and down the fence
And wants you near when there is talk

About distress and what could be done
When found. Closing in on that which is the same
And that which has strayed, the bid

And the ask. And I who wonder
Does she wait for me to round the bend
Come home with a brochure instead—

I search for the one who leaves with less,
I shadow him with something to change
Quick before the close of day, before the pit

Grows quiet, empty, each terminal dark
With how today is not tomorrow,
The floor strewn with paper:

Husks broken into radiance,
No longer static inside the sleeve, gold
Let loose, grain for the cow, field, and city—

And into the lavish night goes the chosen,
Hungry to seek what is capable
And for the unleashing it cannot wait.

AS DISCIPLE

I was first to believe and gave
My mouth, anything I could find
To be in front of whoever wandered in

And wanted to watch. Still, whatever
The exchange from tongue to tongue becomes
My doubt, realm which cannot be worked out,

Which keeps turning in order to see
Itself and more territory where much uprising
Is used as part of the story

Told one to the other. And into the night
Of your hair I bring what cannot be
Helped even if it accumulates

Into how much I wanted you
To fill my hands with all you know of me.

Shy-Shy

Liz Moore

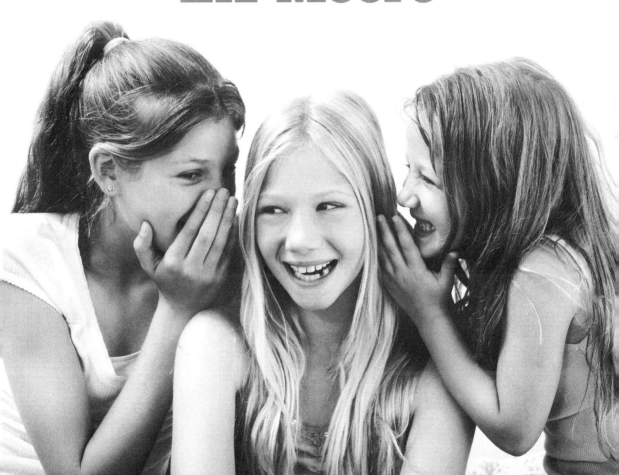

Here are the things you know surely about yourself: you are ten years old; you have two Siberian hamsters; you have perhaps three-hundred books; you have had chicken pox but have never broken a bone; you're bad at sports; you're good at school and you wish, often, not to be; you have parents who are unlike the parents of your schoolmates, the young funny parents who drink beer and hug their children fiercely and tell them to quit doing things your parents wouldn't notice, like picking their noses and skidding in socks down a hallway; you're fat; and you're shy.

The penultimate item on your list is important to you, something you spend a great deal of time thinking about. Your fatness. Your childish body, the weight of it, the softness, and the trouble it causes you. The places you don't fit into. A cardboard tube that your teacher uses as a prop in gym class. Half of a tractor tire that forms a hollow arc on the playground, into which other children your age fit neatly as a pocketknife.

But the ultimate item is essential: something you'd have to work very hard to change. You've been told it all your life. At school you have no friends. There's not much malice in your friendlessness—just fact. You are the shy one. You are not reviled like Karen Babbitt, and you are not gossiped about like Laura Hughes. You are simply ignored. To lunch you bring a book. To recess. On the school bus. Everywhere you go you have a book. You have nothing to say to your classmates, and they have nothing to say to you either. Every person in your fifth-grade class knows who you are, and many have known you since you were five, and when it is your birthday, every person will sing "Happy Birthday" to you, inserting your name, led by your teacher, Mrs. Hall. You will not look at anyone; you never do. You are not happy with your shyness—it is something you wish would go away, and you have elaborate fantasies about becoming famous for something outside of school, thus forcing your classmates to take notice of you. But until this happens, you think, there is nothing to be done. Your classmates know who you are and who you are is the shy one. Your shyness is a part of you the way your lungs are, the way your heart is.

You have a monumental crush on a boy named Paul, and Paul is a year older than you, in the sixth grade. Paul has the opposite of a crush on you, which is to say he does not know who you are. Later in life you will remember Paul distinctly and you will ask yourself: what was it about this Paul that so moved you, that sent you gazing after him down hallways and up stairways, that caused you to dream about him nearly every night, that caused you to look up his number in your parents' telephone book and then, shamefully, call his house once a day, every day, for two months? And you will give an answer to yourself: it was his beauty. Simply, simply. It was his eleven-year-old beauty, which you at ten found nearly unbearable to look at, something very cold and hot at once, like frost. It was his doll-like face, his glassy eyes, his resemblance to a certain teenage singer whom the girls in your class adored, and whom you, too, adored, only you never said anything about it to your classmates or your parents, who would have made fun of him for his terrible songs. It was Paul's beauty, nothing more, and your obsession with it, your value of his beauty, that made you love him.

In the middle of your fifth-grade year you turn eleven and your parents decide, abruptly, for the first time, to send you to sleepaway camp.

Your mother tells you. You are lying facedown on the carpet in the living room, the way you like to do in the late afternoon, when the light comes in, dappled, and warms you. The rug has a pattern of vases along its edges and it's nubbly and rough as a man's afternoon chin. You're a cat. You're a cat on a carpet. When your mother enters the room you can tell she has something serious to say from the way she sits on the love seat, straight-backed, with both hands on her knees.

You spend the two months following your mother's announcement bargaining. You will entertain yourself this summer, and you will help around the house. You will be their housekeeper. You will work hard to make friends, and you will read less. All of these arguments, you lose. The camp will be good for you, your parents think. They found it in a catalog. The name of it is Camp Dowling, and according to the pamphlet they received, which they give to you, it's nestled in the Adirondack Mountains of upstate New York, and it offers fifty different activities to its campers, from weaving to soccer to acting to chess. You are to choose two. You can choose whatever activities you want, your parents say. As long as one is a sport, your father says. But you have to go. They have put a deposit down already. They have signed you up. They have signed themselves up, simultaneously, for a two-week vacation in Montreal.

In July, you and your parents fly to Albany Airport, where your father rents a car. The three of you drive up the roads that lead into the Adirondacks, where your parents will leave you and then continue over the border.

You are in the backseat, examining your legs in their pink shorts. You are determining the width of them, measuring them with your hands and then bringing your hands up, stiff-armed, into the air before you. You are nervous in a way that makes you sick.

But you have decided, since you have been forced to follow the will of your parents, to make the best of it. You will never again have to see the girls in your cabin. You should practice being brave. You are entering middle school in a year and it will be a chance to start over. *I won't be shy,* you tell yourself. *I won't be shy anymore.*

The houses along the way, sparse at first, increase in number as you near the town. Still, there is alarming space between them, and each is ruined in a different way—some yards harboring junked cars and homemade aboveground swimming pools, some overgrown with weeds, some houses or barns beginning a slow collapse toward the ground.

The contrast between the terrible houses and the landscape—beautiful, mountainous, dappled with light and shadow from ancient, generous trees—is unsettling, and you begin to be afraid that your parents have made some mistake, and worst of all you fear that they, too, are wondering this.

"Isn't it pretty," your mother says, dubiously. She keeps putting one hand on the dashboard of the rented car to brace herself when your father takes a turn.

"This road is like a dromedary," you say, because you have just learned the word in school.

Your father misses the turnoff for the camp twice: once on his left and once on his right, after he has turned around. *Camp Dowling,* says a tiny wooden sign, underscored by a finger pointing down a dirt road. The second time he misses it he curses, puts the car into reverse, and backs up the road, despite the hairpin turn that blocks his view of oncoming cars.

Your mother sucks in her breath and folds her arms tightly around her rib cage, a second seat belt, and holds them there until your father has safely turned off the main road.

"Why on earth is the sign so small?" says your mother, and your father says, "Probably so the perverts can't find it."

Now you are turning down a driveway, shaded into dusk by heavy trees. At the end of it there is a much bigger sign, an upside-down horseshoe like the entrance to an amusement park. *Welcome to Camp Dowling!* says the sign. Below it, in smaller letters, *Where Lifelong Friendships Are Made.* Beyond the sign there are cars parked in a line along a sloping lawn. Your last name begins with *M.* You are scheduled to register at three o'clock. It is one o'clock. Your father says this doesn't matter. Your mother disagrees. You agree with your mother.

> You should practice being brave. You are entering middle school in a year and it will be a chance to start over.

There are various folding tables set out on the lawn with signs on them that say *7–8, 9–10, 11–12, 13–14, 15–16.* All the tables are manned by attractive teenagers in shirts that say *Camp Dowling.* Boys and girls. They have no chewing gum. They are practicing the skills they have been taught by parents and employers: politeness, attentiveness, helpfulness, patience.

Your father walks toward the table marked *11–12.* Your mother follows. You follow.

"We're early," your mother says to the girl at the table, and laughs.

"No problem," says the girl. "I'm Polly." And she sticks out her hand to you, and you shake it—the first time you've had your hand shaken by someone younger than your parents. "I'm your counselor," says Polly.

"Don't be shy," says your father. "Say your name."

You say it, and you feel your teeth retract into your gums, and you feel your gums retract into your head, which you duck from the shame of hearing your name aloud—and the strange way you've said it. You've never said it like that before, so loudly.

"Nice to meet you," says Polly. Her name enthralls you and she herself enthralls you, with her Farrow haircut and her breasts, the fact of them, and her thinness, and the tiny glamorous mole on her cheek and the one earring she wears, a dreamcatcher, and her lack of another earring, and her chipped nail polish and the ways, you imagine, it gets chipped, with her teeth, and her long neck and her short feet in their boat shoes, and her pegged pants, and her fashionableness in general, and the way you can tell she is both popular and unique, very unlike the popular girls in your school, who are all, you tell yourself, the same.

"Let me show you the cabin," says Polly. "Follow me."

You're on the end of things, and suddenly it seems important to be in the middle.

Now you are walking to the top of the sloping lawn, passing a large structure built of dark logs, with a wraparound porch. Polly says it houses the mess hall and the infirmary and the administrative offices, where people are sent when they misbehave.

There is a lake that shoulders the place, a small unimportant lake named after a woman who was important to somebody. Lake Joan. There's a small beach and several floating lines that separate the shallow water from the deep and a Peg-Board with tags for every camper. There's a small boathouse on the bank of Lake Joan that houses small boats. There's a lifeguard stand. Lake Joan is always cold, Polly tells you, even on the warmest days.

There is a boys' side of the camp and a girls' side. Each is separated into cabins and each cabin is for a different age group. From the outside, the cabins are not like cabins you have ever pictured. They are more like little houses, shingled, curtained. The curtains have pine trees on them. Each cabin has a small porch with a rocking chair and a line of hooks for towels.

But on their insides they meet your cabinly expectations. Your cabin is mainly one big room, with a flimsy little partition at the back that forms a sort of cubicle: this is for Polly and the counselor-in-training, whom you have not yet met. The walls and the ceiling and the floor are all made of light unfinished wood—plywood, your father says—and the ceiling has been signed by so many hundreds of campers over the years that only a few empty spots remain. What will happen, you wonder, when the ceiling is completely full? Will there be a new ceiling?

There is rough unfinished furniture, dressers and shelves. There are eight twin beds. Four on one side of the room and four on the other. None have been claimed. You are the first one there. "Choose a bed," your father says, but you don't want to. You want to wait for everyone else to choose a bed first. "Go on," your father says, "choose a bed. Don't be a martyr." And when he says this, it is Polly he looks at, expecting her to laugh. You place your things on the very end of the least desirable-looking bed, and then walk out onto the porch. You put your hands on the railing of the porch. Inside you can hear your mother asking Polly where she goes to school. "I'm taking a year off," says Polly—an answer your mother won't like. There is a cabin to your left for younger girls and a cabin to your right for older ones. Aside from these cabins you can see nothing but trees.

Now your parents are leaving. You love them. You will know nobody. When you were smaller you would press your face hard into your mother's pant leg and you have the urge to do this again, to wrap your arms around her tightly.

"You'll have such a good time," says your mother. "This will be so fun."

Your father says to Polly, "Don't let her get away with being shy."

After they have left you look at Polly, and then away, not wanting her to feel obliged to talk to you.

But she sits down on your bed, unprompted, and folds her legs up beneath her, and looks at you as if you are a friend. "You'll like it here," she says to you. "I promise."

Now your cabinmates are arriving. They are claiming beds with vigor and you wish you'd chosen differently. You're on the end of things, and suddenly it seems important to be in the middle. Most of them seem to know each other in ways you can't determine. They hug each other and speak in high familiar voices. Some of them, the twelve-year-olds, look much older than you—more like Polly than like you. None of them greets you. You sit on your bed, legs folded like Polly's were, and take out a book to give yourself something to do. *Get up*, you tell yourself. Walk toward each one of them. Introduce yourself. But your cabinmates don't return your gaze, and you take this as proof of their hostility or disdain. At the very least, their uninterest. You stay on your bed, pretending to read.

All of the parents are gone now. Only your cabinmates remain, and Polly, and a girl named Carly who will be your cabin's counselor-in-training.

Polly claps her hands once to get everyone's attention.

"Circle," says Polly, and she draws a hoop around her waist, telling you all to sit on the floor.

She wants you to play an introduction game that involves choosing an adjective to describe yourself. The adjective has to start with the same letter as your first name. And you have to make a hand motion to go along with it. You wonder what Polly will say. You would choose *pretty* for Polly, but you know that she wouldn't say this, couldn't possibly.

Instead, when it comes her turn, she says, "I am Pugnacious Polly," and makes fists with her hands. *Pugnacious.* It is a word you don't know, despite the fact that you have recently read *Jane Eyre* and *Pride and Prejudice* and *Oliver Twist*, and have packed *Emma* for your stay at camp. The fact that Polly has outsmarted you impresses you further and reaffirms your conviction that she is a kindred spirit.

Carly says she is charismatic and gives a thumbs-up, and a girl named Stacey says she is sassy and makes three snaps in the air. Robin, sitting next to Stacey, says she can't think of a word. *Rambunctious,* you think. *Redundant. Ridiculous. Raucous.*

"How about *rambunctious?*" says Polly, and you look at her with wide eyes.

When your turn comes you say the word that you have been storing up, repeating in your head.

"Loud," you say, softly.

"What's your hand motion?" asks Robin.

You put your hands up to your mouth as if you are calling out. "Loud," you say again.

That evening there is a ceremony that everyone goes to. The ceremony is held on a sloping lawn overlooking Lake Joan, and several rows of logs in a semicircle function as a small amphitheater. There is a campfire at the base of the hill. You want to sit next to Polly on the log reserved for your cabin, but Robin and Stacey sit down on either side of her, so you sit next to Robin.

You think of several things you might say to her, things that are disparaging of the camp or the situation in general, for you feel that these are the things that are easiest to say. But before you can say anything she is leaning forward and shouting to a friend from another cabin.

Another girl sits down to your right. She is the least appealing member of the group. You noticed her earlier, when you were playing your introductory game. "Beautiful Barbara," she had said, and she isn't. And she shouldn't have. She says nothing to you, and you are grateful. Distance yourself from her, you think. This is what you must do to practice being popular.

The camp director comes out of the woods to your right wearing some sort of giant feathery headdress. He carries a spear, which he uses like a walking stick. He stands on a log in front of the fire so that he appears in silhouette. He is a short, muscular man with a hairline that would be receding if a razor hadn't already made him bald.

"Campers," says the camp director, "welcome to Camp Dowling!"

It is only then that you realize that you have been mispronouncing the name of the camp, you and your parents, mispronouncing it for weeks, for months, since they signed you up. Until now you have not noticed, though surely you must have heard it said correctly by someone who knows. It is not pronounced to rhyme with *howling*. It is pronounced *doe-ling*, like a little female deer, like a fawn. This is further evidence, to you, of the utter mistake of your being there. It is definitive evidence that you are an outsider and it is fuel for your loneliness, which takes hold of you suddenly sometimes, especially in crowds.

> Distance yourself from her, you think. This is what you must do to practice being popular.

Everyone is cheering. "Camp Dowling, Camp Dowling, no place better in the world" is the song they are singing. Even Beautiful Barbara is singing. Only you are not.

You look over at Polly, expecting her to be reserved like you, to be smiling and watching the campers. Instead you see that she is singing loudest of all, clapping her hands, taking the hands of Robin and Stacey, beside her, and clapping their hands too.

Your loneliness increases: you miss your parents and you miss your home, and the patterned carpet, and the feeling of pressing your face against the roughness of it, and closing your eyes tightly into it, and so you do this now. You screw your eyes shut tightly and keep them like that for a moment or two, and when you open them you see Robin and Stacey watching you, leaning forward slightly to turn their heads toward you. And then you see Robin look at Stacey, and you see Stacey mouth one word to her slowly and distinctly: *Weird*.

You learn the camp's routine quickly and you follow it quietly. You get up at seven and shower, bringing all of your clothes into the stall with you so you don't have to change in front of anyone; you go to breakfast at eight;

from nine to eleven you do your preselected morning activity, which for you is drawing; from eleven to noon you have an hour of free time, which you spend on your bed, reading; from noon to one there is lunch; from one to two there is free swim; from two to four there is your afternoon activity—soccer—a mistake; then another hour of free time; then dinner; then a campwide evening activity, including a stand-up comedian, a play, a series of trust-building exercises, several campfires, and a talent show.

> You imagine all of your future boyfriends, who will fight over you because by then, surely, you will be beautiful.

Despite your best intentions, you speak rarely. When you are spoken to you sense an abruptness, an abbreviation. When you were small you had a friend, quiet like you, who moved away, and you make a show of writing to her nightly, licking the envelope with a flourish, using a pen filled with pink ink. You walk next to Polly and Carly on the way to and from meals. At the table you work to look involved in others' conversations; you change your expression to match theirs. This is in case anyone at a different table is watching. Usually you are on the end. Usually whoever is sitting next to you is leaning away from you in eager engagement with someone else. You lean in as well. You prop your elbow on the table and laugh when everyone else laughs. At meals, you are not spoken to.

You begin to notice particular habits others have that you do not: that they brush their teeth for longer than you do. That they sleep with two pillows. That they end their sentences with question marks. That they hug each other upon greeting, even if they've been apart only for an hour. That they listen to music you've never heard of. That they own Discmans. That they shave their legs on the front porch. That they shave their legs at all.

Every morning, you will yourself to follow your own instructions. To break out of the shyness you have lived inside for all of your life, from the time you were small. But because all of the girls have been coming here for years, the cabin's social order has been established for as long, and you find this daunting. At the top of course is Polly, who is older but still the benevolent leader of all of you. After her comes Carly, the counselor-in-training. She seems quieter than Polly and is addressed differently by your bunkmates, the princess to Polly's queen, but she is beautiful in a different way, a ballet dancer with long dark hair that she puts up only for exercise.

Everyone likes her because Polly likes her, and because you can all hear Polly talking to her at night in their little separate room, just low enough so you can't make out the words, but you imagine they are confessions, and you wonder desperately what they might be. Carly, as the vessel of Polly's secrets, acquires some of her glamour. Carly is seventeen, and Polly is nineteen, and the two numbers appear in your head whenever you see them, and you measure them, all the pros and cons of being each. You compare them as you once compared your dolls. You imagine yourself at both of their ages, and imagine all of your future boyfriends, who will fight over you because by then, surely, you will be beautiful.

Of the campers, Stacey and Robin come first. One is dark and one is light. Both are wiry and can run gracefully and do handstands and somersaults and springy cartwheels. Both of them sing, but you think you can sing better. And after that come Karen and Jessie and Jenny and Jocelyn and Georgina, who has a funny name but a rich father, and all of them are somewhat interchangeable and all of them rise and fall in the rankings depending on their affiliation with Stacey and Robin, and after that there is you—invisible—and after you there is Barbara, who called herself beautiful, but who is in fact fatter than you are and who doesn't shower with any frequency at all and who sometimes forcibly inserts herself into conversations in a way that makes the other girls crowd even more tightly into whatever circle they are standing in, their backs to Beautiful Barbara.

Barbara has a habit of cursing like a middle-aged woman. "Hell's bells," she will say. Or "Damn it all to hell." And to your embarrassment she reads a great deal, just like you. And like you she detests physical activity; unlike you, she is obvious about it, and cries on the hike that your cabin takes. And, worst of all, she can be asked questions about herself that she will answer with alarming honesty.

"Who's your best friend from home, Barbara?" asks Georgina.

"My dad," says Barbara.

"How much do you weigh?"

"Like a hundred and eighty pounds," says Barbara.

"What's your favorite movie?"

"*Snow White*."

"Are you pretty?"

"Heck yes."

"Have you ever kissed a boy?"

"No."

"Who do you like, Barbara?"

"I like you guys."

"No," says Robin. "Who do you *like*,"

And Barbara thinks a moment and then says, "John Price."

And Robin claps a hand over her mouth and a high-pitched sound comes out from between her fingers and the rest of the girls do the same.

"Want me to tell him?" says Stacey.

Barbara says, "No way," very emphatically, and it is the first correct answer she has given, the first indication that she understands anything about the way the world works.

Everyone likes John Price. You like John Price. The only benefit of signing up for soccer as your afternoon activity is that John Price also signed up for soccer. He is thirteen and as beautiful as Paul from your school, or maybe even more beautiful, and he is fair and fine-boned, with blond feathery hair that he wears longer than what's popular, which makes him, in your eyes, a rebel of the sort that inspires you. If you had to categorize him you would call him a hippie, but the word doesn't really do him justice. He wears rough gray-and-blue ponchos most of the time and when he is playing soccer he wears checkered Adidas shorts and Adidas cleats, and sometimes he doesn't wear shin guards, and when this happens the counselors yell at him but still let him play, because he is the best of anyone. He listens to many kinds of music. You have never been interested in music before knowing John, who plays guitar and has hangnails and nubby fingernails that he bites in between sentences while he is waiting for his turn to talk.

When you are on the soccer field, you try your hardest not to move. You try your hardest to position yourself so that you are on the opposite side of the field from the ball. You try your hardest never to be open. You try to be invisible to your opponents and to John Price alike.

But because he is different from the popular boys in your school—who are athletic, polo-wearing, jocular boys, boys who play football and baseball—you harbor a secret hope that maybe your crush isn't as absurd as it seems to you in low moments. Maybe, you think, he will recognize you as his soulmate. Maybe his oddness, like Polly's oddness and your oddness, means that all of you are kindred.

Yet you have never spoken to him. Some days, during free periods, he goes from cabin to cabin confidently and sits on porches and plays his guitar. You have listened to him play song after song and you have stood at the back of the porch, behind the other girls in your cabin, peering out from between the heads of Stacey and Robin. One day, amazingly, he uses your name—you had not thought he knew it. "Sorry," he says, after brushing past you on his way to the stairs. And then your name.

You coast on this for days. Your crush becomes an obsession. You have had other crushes before, on Paul from your school, on other boys from your hometown whom you knew better than to love, boys who weren't nice to you in the least. But John Price sometimes returns your gaze when he is playing guitar, and you force yourself to hold it, which at eleven is the most erotic thing you've ever experienced. *Hold it, hold it*, you tell yourself, and you grip the railing you're leaning against to steady your heartbeat.

> The only benefit of signing up for soccer as your afternoon activity is that John Price also signed up for soccer.

During your second week of camp, you begin to despair: you have not enacted any part of your plan, have not tested your own limits, the way you promised yourself you would do. Only Beautiful Barbara talks to you, and when she does you answer her quickly and quietly, hoping no one else will notice.

On Wednesday, you walk back from soccer and you climb the stairs to the porch and, through the window, see Stacey and Robin sitting on your bed. No one else has returned from afternoon activities yet. You pause for a moment and let your heart pound. What if they have found one of the postcards that your mother has sent you—embarrassing missives that all begin "Dear honey," and end with "Plates of poutine, Mommy"? Or, worse, what if they have found your diary? In it you have drafted elaborate fantasies about you and John Price, fully plotted short stories involving professions of love that he makes to you in a variety of ways.

But when you enter the cabin you see that their hands are empty. They are just talking; they are just sitting on your bed.

"Hey," says Robin, casually, and you try your best to replicate the way she says it exactly.

You aren't certain what to do. Normally you would lie down on your bed. Now your bed is taken. You shift your weight to one foot and put the other behind your calf.

"Come join us," says Stacey, smiling, patting the space on the bed to her right, which you aren't sure will accommodate you.

Nevertheless, you go to her, making yourself as compact as you can be, keeping some weight on the balls of your feet where they rest on the floor.

"Stace was just saying," says Robin, "how we feel like we don't know you at all. I mean, we've been here for like two weeks. How does that happen?" she asks, and she laughs, and you feel nervous.

"I'm not sure," you say, too quietly.

"You're really shy," says Robin. "You're, like, *shy*-shy."

You open and close your mouth. Here it is, here it comes: a sensation so familiar to you that it's nearly comforting. A feeling of being frozen, of being incapable of motion or speech; a burning in the gut so physical that it stops the tongue from moving.

> The friendship of Stacey and Robin makes you feel sort of invincible, as if it is a shield of armor.

But this is your chance. This is where you transform. You turn your face away from Stacey and Robin so they can't see, and you close your eyes briefly to gather courage, and then you open them and turn your face back toward them and out of you comes a monologue that has been stored inside you so deeply that you never noticed it forming.

Mostly it is lies: about how camp has been weird; about how you're really loud at home, loud and funny; about your group of five best friends whose names all start with C or K; about the boy who likes you whom you don't like back; about how you got in trouble last year for writing notes in class and had detention for like a month; about how your teacher is lame; about being on the travel team for soccer; about Barbara from your cabin—in the end you talk mostly about Barbara from your cabin, who in this monologue becomes the avatar for all of your hate of yourself, who becomes the victim of an outrageous slew of insults.

You end with "I mean, does she shower?" and Stacey and Robin burst into laughter in precisely the same way: their right hands over their mouths, their left hands slapping their left thighs once.

"*I'm Beautiful Barbara*," you say, tilting your head to the right and left, affecting the voice of someone disabled. "Who *says* that?"

Stacey and Robin double over.

"Who even says that?" you ask them, and yourself.

For the next two days you are friends with Stacey and Robin and you are not yourself. You feel this almost physically: like you are disembodied, like you are watching yourself from outside yourself, watching yourself as you walk down the mulched paths of Camp Dowling with Stacey and Robin, watching yourself as they sit on either side of you at the center of the bench at dinner, watching yourself as you lie on the porch with them on Thursday and Friday evening and talk with them until lights-out. You have invented another life for yourself and you tell all three of you stories about it: your father is a musician, and you've moved all over the world, and your favorite place that you've ever lived is Singapore. You are not certain where Singapore is but you like the sound of it. You tell them that you have three dogs and that you have an older brother whom all your friends have a crush on and then, in a terrible moment, you tell them your mother is dying of cancer. It isn't true. That night you have a dream that she's gone and you wake up crying.

Saturday is the last day of camp and Saturday night there is a farewell dance. Afternoon activities have been canceled, and you spend the time before dinner preparing. Now you join your cabinmates when they shave their legs on the porch. You tell no one that you have never shaved your legs before. You mimic what they do, dipping a razor you have borrowed from Jenny into a soapy bucket, running the metal over your legs, praying that you will not cut yourself and bleed. When you've finished you feel disappointed—you had expected that the act would be transformative in some essential way, but your legs still have their baby fat, and your toenails are still unpainted, unlike the toenails of the other girls, which are pink and gold and neon green.

You look around at all of your friends and marvel that you can use that word. All of you there, on the porch. *The girls*, you think. *We're the girls.*

Only Barbara is inside, lying on her bed, reading.

Maybe you'll dance with someone tonight. Maybe, you think, you'll dance with John Price. You wouldn't put it past yourself. The friendship of Stacey and Robin makes you feel sort of invincible, as if it is a shield of armor. And you have borrowed a shirt from Stacey. And it fits.

Polly and Carly come out from behind their partition and tell you that you all look beautiful and Polly claps her hands once and says, "I have to take a picture!"

You all line up and you sling your arms around one another and you smile very widely and your face is flushed with heat and confidence and later, when you look at this picture, it will be hard to recognize yourself. You will have to look at yourself for a very long time to know it's you.

The dance is held in the mess hall, which has been cleared of benches and tables and dressed up with streamers and lights. It's hot inside but all of the windows are open and if you stand by one you can feel the night outside.

You have never danced before.

Stacey and Robin each take one of your hands and make their way onto the dance floor before anyone else is on it and in your other life you would die, actually die, because everyone on the periphery is watching you, but here you're someone new, and you watch how they dance and mimic them, moving your feet from right to left and left to right, holding your hands up on either side of you as if you're about to snap. It's not even hard. It's not hard at all. Eventually, people join in.

Earlier, before leaving for the dance, you all signed the ceiling of the cabin with your names in a little spot in a corner picked out by Polly. You and Stacey and Robin signed it last and each wrote "Slur" beneath your name. It is a near acronym made up of all of your initials. It is your inside joke. When Polly saw it she frowned a little but didn't say anything. You remembered how you felt when you arrived and saw the names above you, like heroes who came before, like immigrants arriving in a new land. Now you look around the dance floor and find each of your cabinmates in turn and give each a little wave and think, *We all look ridiculous.* No one looks good dancing. And you feel as if you've stumbled upon some secret about life.

You have to use the bathroom, so you go, and when you look in the mirror you smile widely and don't mind the hair that has escaped your ponytail or the red that has crept into your cheeks. Robin has let you use her lip gloss and you press your lips together to bring it out, the way you have seen your mother do. Then you turn and leave the bathroom, snapping your fingers on the way.

A slow song is on and the dance floor has cleared somewhat, but you don't immediately see Robin and Stacey. You walk around the periphery of the floor completely, trying to look casual. You pass Jenny and Jessie and wave hello but they are in a tight little circle with the girls from another cabin and you're not sure they see you. You keep moving.

Eventually you spot Stacey and Robin in the middle of the dance floor. Each one is dancing with a boy. Each one has her hands on a boy's shoulders and has a boy's hands on her waist. Each one is laughing at something a boy is saying.

You go back to the bathroom and lock yourself in a stall until the slow song is over; this time you don't look at your reflection.

When you go back to the dance the music has sped up but Stacey and Robin are still dancing with boys. You know you should try to join them but some spell has been broken. Your feet won't move. You stand at the edge of the dance floor and think of the word *wallflower*, and of how your mother explained it to you once, the meaning of it. It is you, now. You at your first dance are a wallflower.

You get a cup of soda. You get a cookie. You do one lap and then another. You go outside to a designated area that you're allowed to be in. You edge toward the outskirts of it, until a counselor admonishes you to stay inside the ropes. You come back inside. You get a cup of soda. You get a cookie.

> No one looks good dancing. And you feel as if you've stumbled upon some secret about life.

Stacey and Robin, at last, come off the dance floor and over to where you are.

At the same time you notice Beautiful Barbara to the left. She is reading a book, at a dance. She is leaning against a wall with three cookies in one hand and reading.

Stacey and Robin are talking to each other. Suddenly, you feel invisible to them. You want to speak to them but you don't want to insert yourself into something you're not invited to. It is this feeling that has stopped you all your life.

Stacey looks at you and smiles briefly and tightly and it is your chance, and you take it.

"Hey," you say to them, the same way that Robin said it, four days ago, sitting on your bed.

They say it back, and then Robin whispers something to Stacey and nods toward the boys that they were dancing with and they look as if they're about to leave again, so you put a hand on Stacey's shoulder. She looks at you.

"Barbara," you tell her, tilting your head to the left.

The three of you turn to look and it's better than you could have hoped for: Barbara is still holding the book and the cookies and leaning against the wall, but now she's also singing along to the song that's playing and sort of moving her head in circles, maybe to the beat. Her hair is in a high ponytail that you can tell she has constructed out of a sense that she should dress up for the occasion. Her T-shirt says *Boston, Massachusetts*, with an emblem of a ship below the words. Around her ample waist is a neon-pink fanny pack, in which she keeps ChapStick, chewing gum, a few dollars for candy, a whistle her mother gave her in case of attackers, and several small porcelain figurines of animals, the meaning of which you have never discerned.

"Oh my God," mouths Stacey, and presses her head into Robin's shoulder, and sort of dissolves into laughter.

Later you will wish you hadn't seen him in this moment, but now you consider it great good luck that John Price appears in your line of sight, for it gives you a terrible and powerful idea. There he is, in his beauty, in the midst of a group of boys his age, clearly the leader of them all. They are moving oddly and you realize they are playing with a hacky sack. The confidence you have in your other self returns, and it is with a calm certainty that you turn to Stacey and Robin and say, "Watch this." Watch *this,* watch *this,* watch *this.* The phrase, the pattern of stress and intonation, echoes in your head for days afterward.

> You can't hear her but you know what she is saying. Everyone watching her knows what she has done.

You walk toward Barbara, and Stacey and Robin follow you. The three of you are a triangle and you are the prow or the point. Barbara notices you and stops singing and lowers her book and her cookies so that her hands are at her sides. She smiles at you warmly.

"Some night!" she says, a phrase your grandmother would use.

"Barbara," you say, loud enough so that Robin and Stacey can hear over the music, "guess what we just heard."

You tell her that John Price has a crush on her and watch as her face changes from open to closed, a sort of contraction in her chin, her eyebrows furrowing. Behind you, Robin grabs your wrist and squeezes it in muted incredulity.

"How do you know?"

"His friend Peter just came over and told us," you say, now expert at lying. You have been lying for days. "He thinks you're hot. He wants to dance with you."

"With me?" asks Beautiful Barbara, placing one finger on her sternum.

You nod solemnly. "Swear," you say.

"What should I do?" asks Barbara, and Robin says, "Go ask him!"

"The dance is almost over," says Stacey. "They'll play a slow song last."

Barbara looks down at her three cookies and her book and makes a stack of them, and then places the stack on the table next to her. She turns her fanny pack around from front to back and again Robin squeezes your wrist. All four of you look out onto the dance floor at John Price, still playing with the hacky sack in a circle of boys, and then, just as Stacey promised, the music changes and the DJ, a burly bearded counselor named George, says into the microphone, *Let's slow it down for one more song, Camp Dowling*, and it sounds like the voice of God.

"What the heck," says Barbara. "What the heck."

She breathes deeply in and out and suddenly you recognize her as yourself, and as she is leaving, you put out one hand to stop her but she mistakes your purpose and gives you a high-five, which makes Stacey and Robin double over as soon as she is gone.

"Oh my God," say both of them in unison, and in unison they each put a hand over their mouths, and watch, and watch.

You watch too.

There is Beautiful Barbara, the wide back of her, wading into the crowd as if it is the sea, lifting her feet up higher than they should go, willing them to move. All around her are streams of campers: some leaving the dance floor if they can't find partners, others walking onto it, hand in hand. But John Price and his group of boys don't move. They are still playing their game, their backs to the world, until Barbara reaches them and taps John on the shoulder. He is much taller than she is and when he turns around he doesn't immediately notice her. He has to look down.

Then you see it on his face: a look of surprise, a lack of recognition, and the rest of his group stops and watches. The hacky sack falls flat on the floor.

You can't hear her but you know what she is saying. Everyone watching her knows what she has done.

John Price stands for a moment with his long arms at his sides. He seems much older than you now but he is only a boy, you realize later, which therefore makes his next decision unthinkably valiant, a moment of bravery that you will recall forever as evidence of the fundamental good of human beings.

Sure, he says. You can see the word as it leaves his mouth, like the *weird* that left Stacey's mouth at the start of last week, like the couple you once saw fighting through the glass of a grocery store window. *You terrible bitch*, the man's lips had said. And that phrase, too, has stayed with you.

John Price offers his left hand to Barbara as if he is from another time. He puts his right hand on her waist, and you realize then that John Price's mother must make him take ballroom dancing lessons, and you drown where you stand.

He waltzes her.

Barbara gazes up at him as if she isn't sure what's real. Her feet in their sandals are small, much smaller than the rest of her, and she moves better than you would have imagined, certainly better than you could do in her place, and you wonder what goals she came here with, what she told herself to work on, what she wants to change about herself, what she loathes about herself. And the answer comes back to you: maybe nothing. Maybe nothing.

There is real goodness in the world, and, despite what you have always tried to tell yourself, it is clear to you now that it does not include you. You are part of the badness, capable of cruelty, most at home alongside those whom you have always imagined to be your persecutors. You know that you're going to cry.

You say nothing to Robin and Stacey but leave to walk outside, into the area designated by the staff as a safe place for campers, and you walk to the edge of it and look longingly at a nearby grove of pine trees, thinking how cool and inviting it looks, thinking if you could quickly run to it you might have a moment to yourself. You're crying hard and silently but you know that in a moment you will sob. It is all you want, now: to be alone.

But when you turn around to check if anyone will notice, you see that Polly is watching you, and she comes toward you now and puts her arms around you. You thought she was like you but you were wrong.

"Poor kiddo," she says to you. "Poor kid."

You lean into her.

"What happened?" she asks you, but you're not entirely sure.

MOTH ORCHIDS

If you are ill or can't sleep,
you could lie on the couch
and watch them spread their wings—the hours
it might take for a baby to be born—
the furled sepals arching, until
the petals splay like a woman stretched, flung
open, blood blooming through her veins.
And then stillness, the white fans glisten
day after day like new sunlit snow
tinged with the greeny kiss,
intricate, curved labellum like bones
of a tiny pelvis and the slender tongue reaching out
to the air as though the parts of the body
could blend: mouth fused to hips, face to sex,
the swollen pad where the bee lands.
Here they float:
eleven creamy moths, eleven white egrets
suspended in flight, eleven babies in satin bonnets,
eleven brides stiff in lace, the waxy pools
of eleven white candles, eleven planets
burning in space.

ODE TO THE FIRST PEACH

Only one insect has feasted here,
a clear stub of resin
plugs the scar. And the hollow
where the stem was severed
shines with juice.
The fur still silvered
like a caul. Even
in the next minute,
the hairs will darken,
turn more golden in my palm.
Heavier, this flesh,
than you would imagine
like the sudden
weight of a newborn.
Oh what a marriage
of citron and blush!
It could be a planet
reflected through a hall
of mirrors. Or
what a swan becomes
when a fairy shoots it
from the sky at dawn.

At the beginning of the world,
when the first dense pith
was ravished and the stars
were not yet lustrous
coins fallen from the
pockets of night,
who could have dreamed
this would be curried
from the chaos.
Scent of morning and sugar,
bruise and hunger.
Silent, swollen, clefted life,
remnant always remaking itself
out of that first flaming ripeness.

THE END OF THE WORLD
AS WE KNOW IT

Elissa Schappell

A Conversation with Margaret Atwood

Margaret Atwood is a force of nature. A cross-genre, shape-shifting fiction writer, Atwood glides with preternatural grace from realism to science fiction, from the speculative to the historical, exploring the depths of issues such as the suppression of female power and sexuality, the unreliable nature of memory, and the fall of society and the aftermath, while lacing her tales with mythology, fairy tales, and scripture. She is also a poet, critic, and essayist, as well as an outspoken human-rights and environmental activist (as anyone who follows her on Twitter knows), and she is, it would seem when one looks to her darkly comic dystopian novels, a prophet.

Last year, the Republican Party's assault on women's reproductive rights sent sales of Atwood's 1985 masterpiece, *The Handmaid's Tale*, soaring. This chilling novel is an examination of women's status under a totalitarian regime of radical Christian white men who have suppressed female sexuality and reproductive freedoms, dividing the female population into wives, sex workers, and handmaids—women designated for breeding. The most often quoted line, one fans have had tattooed on their bodies, "Nolite te bastardes carborundorum" (Don't let the bastards grind you down) became one of my personal mantras during the last election cycle.

While the struggles between men and women also occupy Atwood's realistic works, novels such as *Cat's Eye*, *The Blind Assassin*, and *Alias Grace* deal more with female friendships and the wars women wage against each other.

However, the real battle being fought by both genders front and center in Atwood's work today consists of the high winds of change—literally—shaping our planet. This fall she will publish *MaddAddam*, the last in a trilogy that began with *Oryx and Crake* and continued with *The Year of the Flood*— novels in which Atwood divines a future society ruled by merciless multinational media and technology-based corporations whose reckless genetic engineering of animals and humans contributes to a global environmental catastrophe, a "waterless flood" that leaves only a handful of survivors. Among the living are an eco-religious cult referred to simply as "God's Gardeners," Adams and Eves led by the mysterious Adam One; and MaddAddam, a bioterrorist group headed by one-time gardener and full-time bad boy Zeb.

Atwood has shared little about what readers can expect in the final volume, although she offers this teaser: "How could I not write a book about MaddAddam and their leader Zeb?" As Atwood explains, "That is the one element of this world that has not been fully explored. Who are these people? Why did they decide to break off from the pacifist God's Gardeners and become actively resistant to the regime? And what happened to them next?"

Active resistance? Is Atwood calling for an uprising?

I for one would follow her into battle.

This interview was conducted on the go, with Atwood constantly on the move between readings and prepublication appearances, the proceeds of which— Atwood being an honorary president of BirdLife International's Rare Bird Club— are largely directed into various conservation organizations.

ELISSA SCHAPPELL: I read that you are related to Mary Webster, who survived being hanged for witchcraft in Massachusetts in the seventeenth century. (I hear some rumblings from the radicalized right wing of the GOP that that sort of thing may be coming into vogue again here in the States.) Did having such an apple on your family tree influence you in any way?

MARGARET ATWOOD: *The Handmaid's Tale* is dedicated to Mary Webster, along with Perry Miller, the father of American studies and an expert on the Puritans. Just before the Salem events, Mary Webster was accused of witchcraft, dragged to Boston, tried, and acquitted. The townsfolk strung her up anyway, but she didn't die. I've long been interested in her, and in what the experience of having been not entirely hanged might have been like. I did try to write a novel about her, but it came to nothing. The poem suite "Half-Hanged

I believe women are human beings. Pretty radical, that. I don't believe women are angels, or that every woman is morally superior to every man.

Mary"—in *Morning in the Burned House*—is, however, about her.

My grandmother's maiden name was Webster; it's the same family that includes Governor John Webster of Connecticut and—later—Daniel and Noah. On some days my grandmother would say we were related to Mary Webster, but on other days she would think better of it. I've been unable to discover whether or not Mary had any descendents, or what became of them.

ES: Right now in the States, the GOP is waging a "War on Women." *The Handmaid's Tale* has never seemed more relevant. From the beginning of your career with *The Edible Woman*, you have often questioned the status of women in your work—the ways in which patriarchy dominates women's lives on both the political and the personal level, as well as the sexual oppression and exploitation women endure. Do you consider yourself a feminist writer? Is it possible to be a writer and a feminist, without being a feminist writer?

MA: I've never liked pigeonholes and labels. "Communist writer" would imply that the Communism is the important thing in that

writer's work, and the writing just a means to bring about the Communism. Similarly "right-wing writer." Or "Christian writer." And similarly also "feminist writer." When you ask people what they mean by any of these terms, they often flounder around. So how can you put up your hand for something that is so fuzzy in the minds of those who are asking the question?

I believe women are human beings. Pretty radical, that. I don't believe women are angels, or that every woman is morally superior to every man (see *Cat's Eye* and *Life Before Man*, among others). Women come in as many different varieties as men do, and are as subject to circumstance. In some parts of the world they are also subject to various kinds of bullying—including institutionalized rape and genital mutilation—that are gender related. But different kinds of societies treat women differently. And class and income and race play their parts.

As a writer, and indeed as a citizen, all these things interest me. Men interest me also. I suppose Hilary Mantel is a "feminist" insofar as she is a writer, and some think that women should not do anything so active as writing. But her subject—of

This kind of question was devised by generations younger than mine. I don't think anyone can "control" the "stories" of entire genders or groups of people.

late—is Thomas Cromwell. Gender is not the only important thing for writers.

All that said, the antiwoman situation in the United States is a throwback to the country's Puritan foundations. If the U.S. imposes state control over women's bodies, as all totalitarianisms do, it will suffer the consequences.

ES: It's hard to believe that there is still this notion of female characters needing to be likable when one of the objects of fiction is to present the complexity of human nature. Female characters who resist the roles society presses on them are often seen as unsympathetic; they make readers and critics uncomfortable (or maybe it's the authors themselves who make them uncomfortable). This seems to be more the case in realistic fiction than in speculative or science fiction. Why do you think that is?

MA: Notwithstanding Cathy in *Wuthering Heights*, and Scarlett O'Hara in *Gone with the Wind*, and, and . . . those who kick against the pricks make rambunctious neighbors. We like rowdy women better on other planets, rather than as our roommates. Real answer:

I don't have the foggiest; but go back and read the early reviews of Alice Munro and Margaret Laurence and you find a lot of that sort of negative commentary about outspoken females. However, sometimes people are just stupid about reading fiction. They think it should be entirely about well-behaved, decorous folks leading happy routine lives—Hobbiton without the wizards and the Eye of Sauron. Fiction seldom is about such jolly folks, unless you use them as the core protagonists and then add hostile vampires or rabid dogs or a financial crash or some other source of threat and conflict. Even *Cranford*, that bucolic English village chronicle, dumps a financial crash on a dear old lady.

ES: In *The Handmaid's Tale*, and *The Blind Assassin*, you have two women writing their versions of their life histories. Obviously, male writers can write female characters and vice versa, but how important is it for women to control their stories?

MA: This kind of question was devised by generations younger than mine. I don't think anyone can "control" the "stories" of entire genders or groups of people. They can write the stories. But they can't control them. Stories get out into the world and take on a life of their own.

ES: Your speculative novels seem to spring from a sense of *This is what will happen if society continues down the path it appears it is heading down.* That path always leads to terrible darkness and destruction and your politics are made very clear. Does writing for you ever feel like going into battle, or waging war?

MA: I was born in 1939, two months after Canada entered World War II. I grew up in real, global wartime. Writing books is not like war. If you mean do I steel myself, call on inner grit, et cetera—yes, I sometimes do that. Maybe more in my comics and my newspaper pieces, however.

ES: Do you feel as George Orwell that "no book is genuinely free from political bias" and that all writers feel a "desire to push the world in a certain direction"?

MA: I love much about Orwell but he is not always right about everything. He lived in the midst of political turmoil. He was not a lyric poet.

That strain of thinking leads to people being put in the gulag for writing poems about daffodils.

ES: What about the process of writing itself—is it a battle for you? Have you ever had to wave the white flag in surrender and take a break from a book, or admit defeat completely and throw a book away?

MA: I've thrown away two, have one that was completed but unpublished (praise be!), and had to start over with several of them. You have a feeling about things—whether they're "working" or not. Sometimes you have to pause, and retrace your steps. Sometimes you have to jump the tracks.

ES: It's become very popular for authors to publish books on the craft of writing. Your book *Negotiating with the Dead* would, at first blush, appear to be just that, but it's not.

MA: No, it's not an instruction book. It's a *What Is This?* book. What is this "writing" of which you speak, Earthling? How is it different from the other arts, and from oral storytelling? Who do writers think they are? Like that.

ES: There is the notion today, perpetuated by writing programs of all stripes, that anyone can become a writer. Do you believe this is true?

MA: Of course anyone can become a writer. You do that by making legible marks on a piece of paper. You can easily become a published writer now, too, through self-publishing. But can you become a good writer? An interesting writer? A well-read writer? A rich writer? Are those all the same? Ah. Different questions.

ES: There are some who believe that the author has a moral obligation to society, to write books that are instructive. Do you agree?

MA: Everyone has a moral obligation to society. Insofar as we can define "moral." Insofar as we can define "society." But the chief "moral" obligation of the writer is writing to the best of one's ability. The first loyalty of any serious writer is to writing itself.

Or, put it this way: Beethoven had a brother called Bob. Bob Beethoven was deeply serious about his moral obligation to society. He wanted to express this moral obligation through his music. But he couldn't play any instruments, and he had a tin ear.

ES: With the publication of *MaddAdam* this fall, you will complete the MaddAdam trilogy that began with *Oryx and Crake* and continued with *The Year of the Flood.* While it's speculative fiction, satire, do you believe there is a real and present danger that man in his quest to create a perfect society could destroy the earth?

MA: We have all the tools necessary to do a fairly thorough job of destroying ourselves, or at least our present civilization. It's less certain that we could put paid to all of nature, and there are thousands of lifeforms tucked away in places we'd be hardpressed even to reach. But as for us, the range of conditions we can tolerate (heat, cold, wet, dry, food supply, fresh water) is limited, and our requirements have become increasingly demanding. Our ability to live and breathe depends on a balance. Is it like a bank balance? Have we overdrawn it? 🛡️

MY MOTHER SAYS

Your father drinks weak coffee.

Vacuum the dead moths from behind the window screen.
Their powdered wings look like ghosts against the glass and you know how I'm
superstitious.

I talked with the cat this morning.
She's upset with you.
She said you'd know why.

My morning got away from me.

We live in a fucking zoo.

I couldn't stand your father at first.
He drove a motorbike and had long, brown hair.
And he never read anything longer than a magazine article or a menu page.
But he took me to the airport on our first date.
We parked in a field and lay on the hood of his car, watching the planes take off
and land.

Kelly, Kristen, Kimberly, Kimberly, Kimberly.

When I go to church, I want to feel something moving above me.

The garden smells like tomatoes ripening.
Your father gave me a tomato on our second date that I ate over the sink while
he watched.

Whore.
I love the way that word feels in my mouth.
Whore, whore.

Try to keep up with me.

I kind of have a knack for these things.

I used to tell the dog to play in traffic.
But then I stopped, because I knew it would be my fault if he actually did.

Who put a wet towel down the laundry chute?
I will have your head.

I woke at dawn to feed the birds.
Have you seen them all?
I sat with a book and pretended to read and sometimes there are so many of
them, I have trouble breathing.
This morning chickadees and swallows swarmed me.
The closest I've been to flying.

Where is my boy? Oh where, where is my boy?

DEFINED CONTRIBUTION

I'm in the room without my glasses, wondering
why the room doesn't feel more betrayed.
If I were that sign over there I'd be angrier.
If I were that sign I don't know what
I would say. Everyone in this room has thoughts
about what everyone else should be doing
while I push food around on my plate
until it spells out *I dare you to take off my shirt.*
It's true that I only want to feel it on my neck
until it covers my whole face. I don't care what
happens after. It's true too that sometimes I want
to stop looking altogether but I can't, I'm waiting
for those moments when a city rising clearly up
out of the ground is so beautiful I think
that it must have been a part of the earth
until God or something like it shook it—
the earth—until its lesser parts just fell away.
I know what's built is built by people. I know
that to call this kind of knowing knowledge isn't.
As a container fills, it tilts toward being made
more of what it's made of. Sometimes it won't
stop until it's made something like itself of us.
Today I'm putting it all toward counting
on the nearby trees, how without permission
they grow ever outward, to convince me.

PEOPLE WITH NOTHING TO SAY SAY PLENTY TO THE DOG

Today the trees fill the space
I might fill saying *today the trees*.
A whole stand of them laps

at the horizon. It's a morning
I have a feeling we keep walking
into the same morning

or that I meant to say *waking*
and we must always say
we say what we mean.

The dog's bowl empties at a speed
that's alarming. The dog empties
its bowl and who cares how fast.

This won't be the same as what
we want to say or trees, so say
today's when we say what we can

on a day with weather or in a room
with a dog, then put whatever's left
out in a box I can keep on making

boxes out of. The dog has its blank dog-
thoughts we feel free to put a thing or two
inside of, like *look at me being a dog*

*I'm a dog dog dog I have some teeth I'd like
to show you* is one way we can throw
our voices. Away toward trees is another.

FICTION

Firm and Good

Jodi Angel

M e and Elbow Ritchie took the corner from Monroe to Jefferson at an easy forty-five and Elbow went deep with his right foot and dropped the Hurst shifter down a gear so the engine turned to a tight whine as the back end slipped out from under us and we fishtailed onto the other side of the street until Elbow led it back to our side with a relaxed left hand and we spit pavement under fifteen-inch radial slicks. Elbow was just showing off and I knew it, but his birthday had been two weeks ago and he had every right to brag, since his father had bought him a '71 Mach 1 and I was driving a Schwinn. He had pulled up to my house the night of his birthday and hit the horn and the gas and I heard nothing but a 351 four barrel blow exhaust at the curb and I knew that fucker had worn his father down to nothing but a wallet who had spilled out the cash it took to put Elbow behind the wheel of too much car and not enough brakes and we had barely been home since. Now we were twenty minutes out of school that didn't end for another sixty-five and Elbow had the short end of some backyard green he had paid thirty bucks an ounce for and I was so high I didn't know if our tires were touching the street as we drove through the neighborhood and took the shortcut to get us home. Elbow had this big-ass smile on his face but everything else about him was sharp concentration and competence, because if there were things about Elbow that I didn't trust, his driving wasn't one of them, and he had a way of cocking his arm out the window, holding a cigarette and the wheel, and cranking up the stereo volume all at one time that looked like some ritualistic form of dance. I almost told him that, had my mouth open and was forming the words over the top of Black Sabbath doing "Fairies Wear Boots," when we hit the cat—nothing more than a black-and-white stone in the street—

and I jerked my head out my open window to watch it rebound and spin into the curb and Elbow pulled the cigarette from the corner of his mouth, exhaled, squinted toward me, said something about the paint job, and the Mustang went sixty to zero in a long burn of Goodyear rubber.

It was March and the weather had turned bleak. The sky was milk and there was no warmth in the air even though there had been the threat of sunshine, and we had the windows down mostly because the passenger side didn't roll up all the way and we both got tired of hearing the heavy slapping sound of tire echo if the driver's window wasn't down to match. There were white and weak pink blossoms in the trees, which still seemed as naked as November, and everything was poised on the edge of a spring that just was not coming. The only movement was the sharp wind that bit through our T-shirts, and the trees, and darker clouds that came in from the west and were the color of heavy aluminum and depression, hammered together above us.

Without the ramair hood vibrating across the top of the engine, we were suddenly dumped into more quiet than I had expected and for a minute I wondered if I had seen the cat get hit, or if maybe it was just my imagination and we were still moving forward and blowing back miles.

"We hit that fucking cat," Elbow said, and there were many things I did not trust about Elbow, but what he said around his cigarette was not one of them, and in the empty seconds as side one faded out on the tape deck and there was the quiet pause before side two, I knew that we had killed that thing in the road and I wasn't that high anymore and it would be impossible now to fake it and forget.

"What do we do?" I said. My mouth was as dry as the air that came in through the window, and I could smell burning wood, a distant fire leaking out someone's chimney. For a minute I was reminded of fall and away games when I had played basketball and the team had traveled by bus to a distant town and me and Lonnie Howard would leave the gym when we were supposed to be doing homework while the varsity team played, and we would walk foreign sidewalks of cities we did not live in and there was always a smell that October carried with it—dank and dark and full of smoke and cold and fire and rotten vegetables waiting to be upturned by garden rakes on blustery Saturday afternoons when there was no sun and no heat. But now it was March and Lonnie Howard had transferred schools after freshman year and I was with Elbow Ritchie and I did not play basketball anymore and there was a dead cat behind us and a few months of senior year in front of us and beyond that nothing but the sputter and hiss of dead air like the end of our own tape.

"Well," Elbow said, "we probably have two choices." He shifted his weight in the seat and I could see his right foot rise up from the floor mat and strain toward the gas pedal, and I knew that choice, so I pulled the handle on my door and spilled myself into the street and made choice number two. I heard Elbow make a noise behind me and then I had my legs underneath me and I was headed back along the gutter to the shape and the mess. Elbow gunned the car's engine and I thought maybe he might punch it and run but then the motor cut and there was silence in the street and in thirty feet I was looking down at what we had done. It wasn't as bad as I thought it would be. Other than the unnatural angle of the cat's head and the way that the glassy eyes stared in opposite directions, it looked like it could be picked up and petted. I had seen a squirrel hit by a station wagon one time when I was walking home from school and it had exploded. Crunch and poof. It had looked as if the squirrel had decided to turn itself inside out and go empty in the process.

But the cat was intact. I looked down at it and it looked sideways at me and it said to me five words that I would not forget even after the last of the cheap weed wore off. "It should have been you."

Then a woman in the yard beside the gutter was screaming and Elbow was beside me and the cat continued its accusation and I wanted to reach down and lift it from the thin stream of water it was lying in, but it told me to just step away, leave it alone, let it be. I looked at Elbow to see if he had heard the cat's decision, but Elbow was lighting a cigarette and squaring up against the woman, who was yelling, "Toby, my God you killed Toby," and I shoved my hands deep into my jeans pockets and decided to go as limp as the cat.

She wasn't a tall woman, but she crossed the yard in quick strides, and then the sidewalk, and she was on us before Elbow even had a chance to exhale. Elbow squinted at her and raised both hands in a gesture of accepted defeat. "It was an accident," he said.

"You," she said. "You ran right over him. You didn't even try to stop."

"Ma'am, I didn't even see him. He ran right in front of my car." He hooked his thumb up the street toward the Mustang, which was parked at a decidedly drunken angle in our lane. I could still smell the faint burn of new tire and by now other neighbors had left the warmth of their houses to stand on their porches with their hands on their hips or folded across their chests in a gesture of conviction and I knew that Jefferson Street had found us guilty of the crime and we would never get a jury of our peers.

"I want the names of your parents. Both of you." She said this matter-of-fact, and I realized that she was not hysterical or crying, but her face was flushed and she kept wringing her hands in front of her as if they might escape and do something on their own if she didn't hold them back.

"Everything okay over there, Marianne?" a guy called from two houses down. He was wearing an unbuttoned mechanic's shirt over a white T-shirt and he had a can of beer in his hand.

"These boys ran over my cat."

I heard a woman gasp and suck in her breath and a quiet murmur ran up the street like a wave. We were surrounded on all sides now. There were kids standing on the sidewalk, and crowds forming in driveways. "You want me to deal with them?" beer-can mechanic called. A siren started up in the distance and I wondered if someone had already called the police.

"It's okay, Randy. Everything is under control." She looked at both of us, and Elbow just kept smoking and staring down the street at his car and I kept looking for a place to put my eyes, but in the end they just met hers and I couldn't break away and she wouldn't let me.

> I went home and the evening stretched out in front of me in one long inhale and I choked on my heartbeat every time the telephone rang.

Eventually the woman made us write down our names and phone numbers on a piece of binder paper I pulled from my backpack, and then beer-can mechanic came down the sidewalk with a pillowcase and a pair of gloves and everyone watched his performance of pulling the cat from the gutter, dripping water and wrappers, its limbs already stiff, and some of the kids cried and some of the women covered their own eyes from the sight and Elbow grew bored and started taking small steps back toward the car while the cat was bagged and carried away. "Your parents will be hearing from me," Marianne said.

I went home and the evening stretched out in front of me in one long inhale and I choked on my heartbeat every time the telephone rang. The air was cold and my eyes itched from too much weed and the fact that I couldn't seem to close them and rest even though I wanted to.

I had only pushed my dinner around on my plate and when the obligation was over, I went to my room and shut the door and lay on my bed in all of my clothes, right down to shoes and socks, and watched the light leak from my windows and the shadows shift and change on my ceiling. She still hadn't called, and I figured maybe the woman had been all threat and no follow-through—it was an accident. Even Elbow had been saying that the entire way back to my house—"What is the bitch *really* going to do to us? It was an accident. I mean, we weren't driving around trying to kill fucking cats."

When my clock ticked past nine, my eyes finally felt like they could close and I had put it all into justification and perspective and even decided that we hadn't really been that high and it couldn't even be proven that we had actually hit the cat when you got right down to it, and even if she called tomorrow or the next day, there was no way my parents would bust me for being a passenger in a car that had hit a cat—even if we had been cutting school and were stoned and I wasn't supposed to be with Elbow Ritchie in his *too much car for a kid like him* without permission. Those were details—unimportant compared to the fact that it was an accident. Perfectly innocent. Perfectly faultless.

> "I don't know how yard work is going to pay her back for her dead cat," I had said.

I heard the phone ring the second before it actually did and I heard the television mute in the other room and I kept my eyes shut and pretended that I was blind. I wondered if losing your vision really does increase the strength of your other senses and if my eyes were closed would food taste different or better, could I feel my way from my bedroom to the end of the block, could I hear somebody strike a match in the house next door? With my eyes closed right then on my bed in the darkness of my room I could taste my own fear and smell my own sweat and hear my father's voice on the phone and the sound of my name.

Elbow got his dad to pay her off. He wouldn't tell me how much or how the conversation went, but I figured it was more than a C-note, maybe more than two, and Elbow skated right out of punishment and my parents found another reason to think he was a bad influence on me, and come that Saturday morning I was standing in front of her house, 477 Jefferson, ready to serve three weekends of my time as penance for being high, for cutting school, for being with Elbow, for riding shotgun in a cat-killing machine. Three weekends of work, yard care, house painting, trash hauling, hammering broken stairs, gutter cleaning. Elbow's dad threw her some money and

I got to serve the time. "Take this weed with you," Elbow said Friday after school as we headed out to the parking lot and I got relegated to the backseat because guys who didn't have the money to pay to stay out of trouble didn't get to ride shotgun in a cat-killing machine anymore, and now Brock Irwin was in my spot and I was in back like the hired help. Elbow handed me a Ziploc bag with a handful of joints at the bottom, all of them rolled like perfection. "It will make you forget that you're doing work project." Brock held up his hand and Elbow gave him a hard high five and I rested my head against the back of the seat until the music came tearing out of the speaker behind me and I realized how much I hated that song.

My father woke me up on Saturday morning, five minutes before my alarm was set to go off, and he followed me around while I got ready, monitored my time, supervised my routine, and when he dropped me off in front of her house, he waited at the curb to make sure that I didn't bolt, which is exactly what I wanted to do. She opened the door after the first weak knock and invited me to step past her and into the half-light of her living room. Her house smelled like flowers and cooking and things I could not name but recognized. "You can call me Marianne," she said.

I stood there awkwardly looking down at my old pair of Converse I had worn to work in, and she did not break the silence that followed and relieve me of my shame. I could hear the heavy tick of a large clock coming from a room I could not see, and I wondered if that sound ever got on her nerves, woke her up in the night, made her have to turn the television louder in order to hear her shows. I looked around to see what kind of television she had. I didn't see one at all.

"So?" she said. I shifted my weight and scratched a place on my cheek that did not itch. "You want some coffee?"

I thought about it for a second. The agreement was that I would work for her from eight to five every Saturday and Sunday until the time was served. "It's a good lesson for you, Marty," my dad had said. "And it's a good gesture. She lives by herself. She needs the help."

"I don't know how yard work is going to pay her back for her dead cat," I had said. "I mean, the last time I checked, you can't mow some lawns and bring back grandma if she dies."

"Keep at it, Marty," my father had said. "You want to make it six weeks?"

So the deal was nine hours a day, Saturday and Sunday, all the way into April. It was about serving the time, not the amount of work I got done, and the way I figured it, if she wanted to offer me a cup of coffee, that big loud clock ticking off the minutes was reminding me that for every tick and sip, it was less time I had to haul and scrape and hammer and cut.

"Yeah," I said. "I'd like a cup of coffee. That would be great."

She led me into her kitchen and there was a small table under a window and the room was full of early morning sunshine that was already warm, and I could smell cinnamon and baked sugar, and the table was set with two cups painted with little blue designs, and there was a pot of coffee on a beaded potholder and a white cream pitcher and a cup with sugar and little silver spoons. She pointed me toward a chair and she went to the oven and lowered the door and pulled out a braided loaf of bread, and she set it on the counter while she drizzled icing over the top and then cut it into thick slices, and I could see steam rise out of the bread each time the knife pulled away from it.

"I hope you don't mind raisins," she said.

She took a slice of the bread and lifted it onto a blue painted plate that matched the cups and the saucers, and she drizzled more icing over it and set it in front of me and then took the other empty chair at the table and poured coffee into each cup. When she was finished, she lifted her coffee, sipped at it, added a spoonful of sugar, and then sat back and stared at me. I realized that I had never sat in a stranger's house by myself, never sat and eaten food in front of someone I did not know without the presence of my parents or a friend from school. I had never been alone with a stranger in a stranger's house, and I wasn't sure what to do with my coffee other than to just drink it even though it tasted hot and too bitter, but the thought of adding things to it and having her watch me seemed like too much to go through.

"You don't want cream?" she said.

"It's good," I said. "I'm fine."

"That bread was my mother's recipe," she said. "It was my favorite when I was a girl."

I picked up a small silver fork and held it in my hand, unsure whether I should cut off a piece and take a bite, or drink the coffee, or just pick up the slice of bread and eat it that way. I realized I was sweating and for the first time in my life I couldn't wait to go outside and work.

"Don't be nervous," she said.

I swallowed a too-hot mouthful of coffee and followed it up with another one. "What should I do today?" I asked.

She reached out and before I could pull my hand back or pretend I was cutting into the bread on the plate, her hand was over mine, and it was dry and warm and light. "You haven't even had some food and finished your coffee yet," she said. "Don't be in such a hurry."

In the other room I could hear the clock ticking, tight and hollow and solid, as the sun filled the room. I felt sleepy and wished I was spending this Saturday morning like I had spent the last one—warm in bed, wasting time, surfacing at some point past noon when I got too hungry to sleep. Instead, here I was eating a stranger's cinnamon bread and drinking black coffee and sweating. On the floor in the corner was a small plastic dish of water, and I realized it was a cat's dish, Toby's, and it was still there, still full of water, waiting for the cat that would not come. I wondered if it was the same water that had been in it when he had died, or if she had changed the water since then, refilled it with fresh water out of habit.

"I'm really sorry about Toby," I said. "Really."

"Who?" she said.

> I realized that I had never sat and eaten food in front of someone I did not know without the presence of my parents or a friend from school.

In the other room the clock began to chime and it went on for a full ten seconds while it played out the half hour, and I knew that if I had to hear that much noise every thirty minutes I would chop the clock to pieces and burn it up within an hour.

"Your cat," I said. "Toby. I'm sorry."

Marianne poured more coffee into her cup and followed it with cream. "Oh," she said without looking at me. "I know."

I ate quickly and she offered me more but I wanted out of that sunny kitchen, out from under her staring at me. She finally walked me to her backyard and showed me the project for the day. I immediately wished that I had milked more time with a second piece of too-sweet bread and another awkward cup of coffee. Her yard was at least three feet high in overgrowth—grass gone to seed that had withstood the winter and was committed to its takeover; vines crawling over anything that stood still—a birdbath in the corner, decorative rocks, the walls of the house; rosebushes reaching out from the perimeter of the fence; trees, bushes, shrubs. The entire thing looked as if it belonged in a South American movie scene—something from *Romancing the Stone*.

"I guess you can start here," she said. "This will probably take you most of the day."

This will take me most of my life, I thought. "Okay," I said.

She pointed me toward a shed that had yard tools in it, and after wrestling the door from the grips of the grass and vines, I was able to go inside and figure out what to use and where to start. I was hoping she might disappear back into the house and her bread and her smells and her clock, but instead she just made her way to the elevated cement slab attached to her back door, where the grass had to relent its march, pulled a wicker chair forward, and sat down to watch me work.

When I saw the first snake, I was grateful I had started with the lawn mower. The grass was so high that the lawn mower kept getting bogged down and I had to push it forward and backward, forward and backward in a rocking motion until it could chew through the grass and take on the next section. When it nudged the snake free and sent it sidewinding into the deeper grass, I was thankful for the noise of the motor because I was pretty sure I had let out a small scream, and I hoped Marianne hadn't heard. I felt all of the hair on the back of my neck stand up, and a shiver of disgust ran up my arms and slid down my back with the sweat. I hated snakes.

> Everything smelled green and wet and alive. I was suddenly thirsty but I didn't think it was a good time to ask for anything.

The sun was high in the sky and it felt as if the spring that had been holding its breath had finally exhaled and we were going to take a quick jump over spring and land somewhere in the middle of summer. After two more push-and-pull paths with the lawn mower, an entire tangle of snakes scattered in front of me and the blade caught a small one that hadn't made the quick decision to go forward and right and instead had gone back and left and there was a thick sound from the lawn mower, the churning of the snake, and then it was spit into the grass beside me, the yellow and black stripes now ragged and red. I looked away quickly and pushed the lever down on the handle and the yard went quiet. There was sweat under both of my armpits and I pulled my sweatshirt over my head and walked toward the fence, careful to take only the path that was mowed and not the deeper grass, where the snakes had retreated. I didn't even want my shoes to touch the ground.

I hung my sweatshirt on the fence. "You have snakes back here," I said.

Marianne shielded her eyes from the glare of the sun. "Water snakes, I know. They love that deep grass." She didn't seem the least bit upset by it. Of all days to forget to wear my watch, today was the worst and I had no idea what time it was or how much time was left. I looked up at the angle of the sun and wished I had been a Boy Scout and knew things like how to tell time by the level of the sun or how to rid a lawn of snakes before mowing them down. The one I had hit was sitting on top of the fresh grass.

"I accidentally ran over one," I said.

Marianne stood from her chair and looked down at the grass where I was pointing. She crossed her arms over her chest and shook her head. "The casualties keep adding up," she said.

I lifted the collar of my T-shirt and rubbed the sweat from my face. I could feel pieces of grass sticking to me. Everything smelled green and wet and alive. I was suddenly thirsty but I didn't think it was a good time to ask for anything.

I heard the back door slam and I figured I had finally done enough to piss her off and make her retreat, and in a way I was sorry it had to be over a dead snake, but I wasn't that sorry. I wouldn't be sorry if I ran over all of them, and if she wasn't sitting back there watching me, maybe I would. Just rake up all the shredded bodies with the grass clippings, bag them, and put them at the curb.

I went back to the lawn mower, pushed the lever, and was just about to pull the cord when the back door opened and I looked up and Marianne was standing there with two green bottles in her hand. "You look thirsty," she said. "Take a break."

I went to the cement slab and she handed me one of the green bottles. There was no label on it, no identification. It was just dark green and full and cold. I looked down at it and tried to guess the contents by the color.

"It's beer," she said. "You like beer, don't you?"

For a second I thought it was a test—something to see just how far I would go, but she had already sat back down in her chair and was sipping from her own bottle while staring out across the half-mowed lawn, and not looking at me at all. I took a small sip. It didn't taste much like beer, at least not any that I had ever drank, but maybe it was imported.

"My husband brewed it," she said. "What do you think?"

I took another swallow, this one bigger, and it felt good going down, cold and a little spicy, something like tea. "It doesn't taste like beer," I said.

"Cardamom," she said.

"What?"

"Cardamom. He liked spices. I'm more like you, though. I like herbs."
She gave me a knowing look. I had one of Elbow Ritchie's joints of perfection tucked into the front pocket of my jeans.

"Where is your husband?" I said. "My dad said you lived alone." The beer was going down easily and I was down to half a bottle in another swallow.

"He died," she said. "It's been a while."

I wished there was a label on the bottle and I could pick at it, fixate on it, do something so that I didn't have to look at her and apologize, but I was out of luck and the glass was smooth green, the same color as the lawn, and I watched a trail of ants wander into a crevice in the cement. "I'm sorry," I said. I didn't know what else to say. In the movies they always say, "What happened?" and then there is an awkward and personal moment when maybe too much has been said but there is always some kind of relief in the telling of the story. I didn't ask her that question.

"You want another one?" she asked, gesturing toward my bottle.

I nodded.

We drank the next one in silence, and by then the sweat had dried from my back and the sun had shifted and the wedge of shade that held the cement porch had pulled back and slipped down to the grass. I looked at her from the corners of my eyes, saw the way her hair was so black that it threw off its own glare, and I could remember how in science class we had learned that on the visible color spectrum, darker colors absorb rather than reflect, but her hair was breaking that truth. I could feel my shoulders tightening up and the thought of dragging that mower around the rest of the snake habitat made my arms ache. My Converse were grass stained and my ankles itched.

"Why don't we go inside," she said. "It's actually getting to be hot out here."

"I should finish the yard," I said. The two empty bottles sat beside me on the cement and I could hear other lawn mowers in the neighborhood, the Saturday chorus, and I knew that with the sudden warmth there would be hoses running and cars being washed and phone calls for impromptu barbecues.

"I have been in a battle with Mother Nature for many years, Marty. She always wins."

She stood up and opened the door and waited for me. I picked up my bottles and went in.

The kitchen was warm but not uncomfortable, and at some point she had cleared the table because the coffee cups were gone and I didn't know what to do, so I sat down at the table and folded my hands in front of me. She stepped into the utility room, and I heard a refrigerator door open and then she was back with two more beers. My head felt a little fuzzy from drinking and I figured it was because I wasn't used to working outside. Me and Elbow could put away a twelve-pack together without so much as a stuttered step and I was only on two and already buzzed. I had to remind myself to drink slowly.

"It's the worst kind of sun out there," she said. "It's when the sun is hot but the air is cold that people get sunburned. You don't feel the heat, but it's there—it's just not how it appears and you think if you're not too hot, then you're not getting burned. Then you come in out of the sun and find out you were wrong. You look a little red, Marty."

"This beer tastes different," I said.

"Comfrey," she said. "He was always experimenting."

"It's not bad," I said.

"He died in a car accident," she said.

> I wished there was a label on the bottle and I could pick at it, fixate on it, do something so that I didn't have to look at her and apologize.

She had taken the other chair at the table and she was watching me drink. "He swerved to avoid something in the road. An animal, a piece of something—no one knows—it was dark and he was on a back road coming home from one of his trips. He liked to disappear sometimes. Drive to nowhere."

The table was made out of grainy wood, natural looking, and I could see small knots in it, trace the raised grain with my finger.

"He left me a lot of money," she said. "I have shoe boxes full of it in my closet."

I looked up at her. She met my eyes and I didn't pull away. I took a long swallow from the bottle.

"I didn't need your friend's money," she said. "When he showed up here with that girl, I had already given him two choices, but I knew which one he would take."

Elbow hadn't told me anything about this. What he'd told me was that Marianne had called his house that night after we hit the cat, and his dad had offered her money, made a deal, and paid her off the next morning.

He never said anything about going over there himself, and he sure as shit didn't say anything about bringing a girl. I looked at her like I didn't believe a fucking word she said.

"Oh he came up my driveway in his loud car and that girl was with him and he practically shoved the money in my hands. I'd told him on the phone that he could work one Saturday with you, do those things for me, and that would be enough of a gesture of apology—that's what it's about, isn't it. A gesture. A show of remorse. One day of work and the both of you would be free from obligation." She stood up and opened the back door. The smell of cut lawn was thick and heavy and sweet.

"Or he could pay me one hundred dollars for every weekend he chose not to work and you did the work instead. And he came here, handed me the money. Three one-hundred-dollar bills and that girl holding on to his arm and giving me a look."

I told him that I was going to ask Alyson to prom because the only thing I wanted to remember senior year by was ending it with her.

"What girl?" I asked.

"The skinny girl. He should let me have her for a month. I could fatten her up."

"Did she have kind of dirty blond hair?" I asked. "Kind of tall, with pretty lips?"

"Exactly," she said. "Kind of tall with pretty lips."

Elbow Ritchie had brought Alyson with him. Alyson had three classes with me—history, English, and biology—and I knew every freckle on her arms and the way she wore her hair depending on the mood she was in and one drunken Friday night right after Elbow got his car I told him that I was going to ask Alyson to prom because the only thing I wanted to remember senior year by was ending it with her.

I felt hot suddenly, cold and hot, and when I reached out to take a drink from my beer, my hand couldn't close around it and I knocked it on its rounded edge, and for one quick second I thought it might regain its balance but it tipped and spun and everything that was left in it spilled out across the table and into my lap. I just sat there and let it, didn't even make the attempt to jump back, move, avoid what was happening.

"I knew that was the choice he would make," Marianne said. "I knew you were different. I could tell that even before he stopped the car that day."

My jeans were soaked in the front and everything smelled like strange flowers and the heavy grass and I realized that all I had eaten was that thick slice of sweet bread and my stomach did a slow turn and I stood up and asked Marianne where the bathroom was and she pointed me down a hallway and I was gone.

I ran cold water into the sink and rinsed off my face and small flecks of grass fell into the water that was pooling around the drain. The cold water made me feel better and I was able to breathe again, and breathing made my stomach drop out of my throat and I knew I was going to be okay. Elbow would explain. It had to be getting late. I could finish up the day here and walk to his house and knock on his door and just say, "Hey, you know what that lady told me?" and I knew he would say, "Man, Marty, not only is she a bitch, but she's a crazy fucking liar, too. Let's egg her house tonight," and everything would be okay.

"Marty, is everything all right in there?" Her voice was close against the door and I tried to picture her on the other side, maybe leaning against it, maybe pressing her ear against the wood to hear if I was sick or crying or still alive.

"I'm fine," I said, and I thought maybe I would have to convince myself of that fact, but I realized that I was. I was just fine.

"I brought you a change of jeans," she said. "You can't go home smelling like beer. I don't think your parents would be too happy about that. Why don't you just open the door a crack and I can hand them in to you."

"I'm fine, really," I said. "I can just rinse them off here in the sink. It's not that much. They will dry out."

"Marty, don't be ridiculous. I can wash your jeans. You can wear a pair of my ex-husband's."

Something in her voice made me realize that she wasn't going to let it go until I at least took them from her, and then I could just tell her that the jeans didn't fit and rinse mine off and go back out to the yard and the sun and finish up this shift so I could go find Elbow and laugh about the bullshit story she had told me. I opened the door a little and she reached around the edge and handed me a pair of faded jeans that were folded so tightly I could see the crease line in the knees. "I'm giving you a T-shirt, too. Just give me all of your clothes. You've been working. If I'm going to wash your jeans, you might as well go home in clean clothes."

"Really, it's fine," I said, but she shoved something else in my hand and then I pushed the door shut and stood in the silence of the bathroom.

There was a basket on the back of the toilet with small circle-shaped soaps of different colors, and the towels were deep red, and I could smell lilac or jasmine or one of those scents that you always associate with your grandma or your mom.

I set the jeans down and unfolded a black T-shirt. There was a picture on the front, a beaver with wings, and I tossed it aside. I opened up the jeans and looked in at the waistband. They were 33x31s. I preferred 34s, depending on the cut, but these were damn close, and I thought about folding them back up and setting them on the edge of the bathtub and thanking her anyways, but they were too small, and instead I found myself dropping my own jeans to the floor and kicking off my shoes and sliding out of my pair and into a dead guy's pants. I remembered Elbow's joint in my pocket and fished out the wet and ruined paper that was unraveling and spilling green. I thought about flushing it, but I knew half the time that shit didn't work in movies and I could just imagine it never going down with the water and Marianne back in the hallway, asking if everything was all right through the door.

I pulled off my T-shirt and was surprised to feel how sticky it was and how much it smelled like gas and grass and fumes and sweat. It felt good to get it off my skin and for a minute I stood shirtless in my socks and borrowed jeans and looked at myself in the mirror. I ran more water and splashed it across my chest and scooped it under my arms and leaned forward and let myself drip into the sink, then I took my dirty shirt and rubbed my body off and ran some more water through my hair and when I was done I felt like another person and I pulled on the beaver T-shirt, gathered up my things, and left the room.

Marianne was sitting at the table and there was a full beer in front of my empty chair and the mess had been cleaned and the back door was closed and I could hear the clock ticking in that other room. I found myself wishing that it would go into its overachieving chime to mark a moment of time I could identify, but it did nothing but tick and tock, and I could picture the pendulum swinging. Getting sleepy, very sleepy. I smiled and sat down and Marianne took the wad of clothes out of my arms and went back to the utility room and I heard a washer kick on, the familiar sound of water filling the machine, and I heard dials turning and then she was back and she picked up her beer and looked at me.

"I knew those clothes would fit. I just knew it."

"They're not bad," I said.

"Do you like music, Marty?" she asked. "I have a stereo. We should turn on some music." She clapped her hands together and stood up and left the room. I looked around for a clock, anything to let me know how much time was gone in the day and how much remained. The sun was still bright outside and the shadows did not seem to be lengthening in that way they always do when someone needs to mark the hour.

I heard music, and I could recognize the song, something my parents listened to, something with a lot of guitar, but not the right kind. Acoustic. It wasn't terrible, but it wasn't anything I would ever reach to turn up. "How's this?" she called from the other room.

"I like it," I said. I stood up from my chair and walked around the kitchen. I bent down and looked at the dials on the oven—no clock, just a timer. There wasn't a clock anywhere in the room.

> I'd had too much beer, and there were snakes, and maybe it would be best if I came back first thing in the morning.

"Do you need something, Marty?" She was standing in the doorway. I could see that she was barefoot and her pants fell over the tops of her feet. Her toenails were painted a bright and glittery purple.

"I was just wondering what time it is," I said. "My dad wants me to call him when I need to be picked up."

She stepped into the room and she smelled different. Sweeter, cleaner. For the first time I noticed that she was wearing hoop earrings, simple and silver, and her hair was tucked behind her ears and I could see her cheekbones and how they held the color up high near her eyes.

"It's one of those days," she said. "One of those days when it feels like it's so much later than it really is. We still have hours. I promise." She sat down and picked up her beer and started drinking again. "You're not anxious to get back out there and work, are you, Marty?"

In all honesty, I wasn't, and part of me was hoping that maybe she would just let me leave early, call it a day; I'd had too much beer, and there were snakes, and maybe it would be best if I came back first thing in the morning, but now I realized I had made the mistake of letting her hold my clothes hostage and I was standing in her kitchen in a dead guy's jeans and winged-beaver T-shirt and I wasn't going anywhere until she gave me back my clothes, returned me to myself, and set me free.

"You remind me so much of Ben," she said.

"Ben?"

"My husband. Who died. Your friend?"

"Elbow," I said.

"Elbow—that's such a strange name."

"When he fights he swings with his elbows. Not with his fists. His real name is James."

"Your friend James, he didn't remind me of Ben at all. Too big, too broad. Too much of something in his eyes. But you? It's like I told you. I could tell even before you got out of the car that you were the one."

I couldn't wait to tell Elbow this conversation. And I would tell him about it as soon as I told him about the first one and asked him some questions and got him to tell me just how full of shit Marianne was.

I smiled. "The one?"

She had to be drunk. I was buzzing on those beers and Elbow and I weren't lightweights. I wondered if home brew had more alcohol and I figured it probably did, since there was no government regulation to control what went into the bottle.

> I rubbed harder at the glass and then I realized there wasn't anything there to see. There were no hands on the clock. No numbers.

"I knew you were someone I could count on, that's all, Marty. I knew that if you were like Ben on the outside, you were probably like him on the inside and I wasn't wrong."

I ran my finger over the pattern in the table. All those lines counting off the stages of development in the tree, tracing the pattern of growth, etching the passing of time. I finished my beer and stood up from the table.

"I really have to see how late it is," I said. I walked past her and toward the room I had not been in before she could stop me. Even over the too-quiet tinny guitar I could hear the clock and I followed the sound.

The room was dark, the curtains pulled, and there was only a thin sheet of light that made the journey past the drapes and it seemed as if it wore itself out in the process and died just beyond the window. The room had the smell of disuse, dust, and forgetting. I could see the red light on the stereo and the light from the dials and I could make out the shapes of furniture, things on shelves. The clock was one of those big upright grandfathers, solid wood and brass and glass, and the ticking was so loud that the window vibrated a little bit every time the pendulum connected with the full extent of its arc—left to right tick, right to left tock. The face of the clock was behind a pane of glass and I could not read it in the faint light so I looked around for a lamp or a switch and found nothing. I walked to the window and pulled back the curtain.

I pulled back the curtains far enough to let in the struggling light and I realized that the room was full of dust, dust settled on everything, everything hidden. I stretched out my left hand so I could keep the curtain pulled with my right, and I wiped my palm across the face of the clock. I couldn't see anything. I rubbed harder at the glass and then I realized there wasn't anything there to see. There were no hands on the clock. No numbers. Just a blank face and the pendulum swinging beneath it marking the passing of absolutely nothing at all. I let the curtain drop and went back through the darkness.

"Marianne, do you have a clock that works?" I said.

Marianne wasn't at the table and the kitchen was empty. I checked the utility room and the only sound was the washer spinning the water from my clothes. "Marianne," I called.

The refrigerator was in the corner across from the dryer, so I pulled the door open and reached in to get a beer. The refrigerator was empty except for rows of green bottles on the top shelf and underneath it stacks of sheets. I took a bright green bottle and bent down to look at the sheets and then I realized that they were not sheets at all and the one on top looked familiar, like a pillowcase, like something I had seen before, and even though I didn't really want to, I lifted back the open end and he was in there, there was no mistaking the black-and-white hair, Toby, only this time he had nothing to say to me like he did the first time we had met, and I remembered that moment, too high and thinking he had given me a message, and now I pulled my hand back as though he had bit me, and then I thought about it and lifted the open ends of the other pillowcases, three of them altogether, black-and-white Toby, a dark silver and gray, a tabby marked just like the one my sister had when we were kids. I returned the bottle to the shelf and quietly shut the door so that it did not even make the comforting noise of a click.

The door to the backyard was not closed all the way and I opened it just enough so that I could look out onto the lawn. Marianne was out there with her back to me, and she was bent over and there was a stick in her hand, a broom handle, the bristles stuck out in a stiff row behind her. She was bent over, poking at something, pushing it around in the mowed and dead drifts of grass I had not gone back to rake, and I realized she was tapping at the snake I had run over, lifting it slightly, rolling it over, letting it fall back to the ground.

There was laughter out on the sidewalk, kids playing, and I remembered that there was a world beyond the yard. I heard the steady clip of a sprinkler and I could smell wet pavement, that unmistakable scent of wet dirt and cement. I had not applied to college, my parents didn't have enough money, and I had none at all, but maybe that would change, and part of me wished that I was going to be someplace else next year and maybe I would be—there was still plenty of time for anything to happen. In the distance I could hear a muscled-up car go by, loud and strong like a 351 Cleveland hitting 5400 rpm and blowing dual exhaust, and somewhere closer, in that same direction, I could hear brakes lock up, the unmistakable squeal of rubber leaving tread across asphalt, and maybe something or someone getting hit.

Rich Smith

FOR SARAH IN HER BLUE JUMPSUIT

Even in her blue jumpsuit Sarah hates love poems.
If you leave a poem in her drip pan
she will wheel out from beneath the Ford and say,
I came to this town without so much as a virginity.
If she finds a poem in the pockets of her blue jumpsuit
she will tell you, *I cannot sustain another thin body*
displeased with the way his chest hair is coming in,
and if you read a poem to her while she wears her blue jumpsuit
she will say, *What I need is a Franklin*
to barrel through my cabin in his trolling flannels
with a generation of squirrels dangling from his trap,
or she will say, Spare me your love poems;
hand me that wrench. You can see why I want to write
a love poem for Sarah in her blue jumpsuit.
In it, I would like to include her blue jumpsuit,
the wrench, and the Ford. I would like to include
the oil smear on her cheek, and her pronunciation of *croissant,*
as when she said, "To a Jiffy Lube you bring a *croissant?*"
Because she says it in the way of our people,
whom only friction moves.

HOW I MET
MY WIFE

Robert Boswell

Alternate Methods of Characterization

"Writing is like getting married. One should never commit oneself until one is amazed at one's luck."

—IRIS MURDOCH

A few years ago, in an introductory fiction workshop, my students and I witnessed a young man make relentless awkward attempts to get to know a young woman in the class. He was passionate and clumsy and his efforts were wholly transparent. When the time came for him to turn in his story, he submitted a piece about a young man much like himself who is hopelessly in love with a young woman much like the young woman in the class, and the two characters are in a creative writing workshop together. One night the male character shows up tipsy at the young woman's house to ask if she will stroll with him in the warm night air and hold his hand, but the door is opened by her boyfriend, who answers for her with a punch to the jaw, sending the character flying and leaving a scrape on his chin—much like the scrape on the chin of the young man in my workshop.

Undaunted, the character retreats to his dorm to write a story about yet another character who is much like the first character who is much like the author, with the idea that a female character who is much like the first female character who is much like the girl in the workshop will read the story and understand that this literary version of himself represents his real self and that he is in love with her.

In the final scene, the girl suddenly understands—during workshop, no less—that the boy is in love with her, and she is powerfully moved by this knowledge. Everyone in the real workshop knows that the real girl would have to be blind and deaf and witless not to understand that this boy was in love with her, but this public declaration—this tender, ridiculous, marginally grammatical, potentially humiliating public declaration—nonetheless moves us.

The girl in the story is described as dark and astonishingly beautiful, while the actual girl is dark and pleasantly ordinary. But her youth holds to her powerfully and perhaps also holds an inclination to embrace men willing to make fools of themselves for that passing vitality—willing to punch people or write absurd stories—and wouldn't she be a fool herself not to let them fight over her while she has the skin and the light in her eyes that distinguishes her for such a brief time (in this case, just twelve and a half double-spaced pages)?

We workshop witnesses like the story. Sort of. We're interested, anyway, but we're unable to have much of a conversation about craft or other such trivial matters, waiting until the girl decides to comment. When she raises her hand to speak, we grow quiet, the only noise the spring wind beyond the windows. Finally, she says, "The character is convincing . . . but kind of pathetic."

Our hearts drop. We cannot help it. We are rooting for the boy. We hold our collective breath while she pauses, and it seems that even the weather outside the window ceases.

Then she adds, "But it's hard not to like him." She smiles at the young man, and the class relaxes. We even offer a trickle of laughter.

But the young man isn't laughing, and his smile is sad, as if he understands that he is now entering the remainder of his life and it will be an effort to live up to the gesture that started him on this path. Not that he could ever articulate this, at least not for years, and only then if he continues to take creative writing. All he knows at the moment is that he will not, after all, have to live without the girl.

Everyone in the class is happy that he gets to indulge his foolish love at the expense of the punching boy and to the possible detriment of the smiling girl, who is smarter and a better writer, and who will be young and irresistible exactly once.

Why are we drawn to stories about people falling in love? There are likely a host of reasons, but here's a good one: marriage, when observed from a place of solitude, has the power of dream. Solitary people fall in love with couples, imagining their own lives transformed by such a union. And once the transformation finally happens, people need to talk about it, telling not only their families, friends, and strangers on the bus but also *themselves*—repeating it to make it real, to investigate the mystery of marital metamorphosis. And they get good at the telling. People who cannot otherwise put together an adequately coherent narrative to get you to the neighborhood grocery will nonetheless have a beautifully shaped tale of how *he* met *she* (or *he* met *he*, or *she* met *she*) and became *we*.

Such stories often have many literary qualities. They rely, almost by definition, on the revelation and transformation of character—the same elements that are the backbone of literary stories. The narratives have a mystery at the beginning: how the characters begin loving each other before they understand they're doing it, the way sleep enters our bodies before we're actually asleep; and like sleep, we *fall* into love, and fall deeper as we go. The narratives also have something like a built-in ending. A wedding, after all, is the traditional conclusion for comedies, and it is meant to indicate that the transformation has transpired. Passing through the ritual of the wedding ceremony, the bride and groom are irrevocably changed.

It seems to me that "How I Met My Spouse" stories are the perfect venue for the study of characterization. I'm going to use my own story of how I met my wife to display a dozen slightly unusual methods of characterization.

> Solitary people fall in love with couples, imagining their own lives transformed by such a union.

I met my wife—the writer Antonya Nelson—in 1983 during a fall semester of MFA study at the University of Arizona. Like the young couple described earlier, Toni and I met in a fiction workshop. Toni was the new, beautiful, and immensely talented first-year student, just twenty-two years old and radiant. Her skin actually gave off light. You could read by it. Meanwhile, I was twenty-nine, a third-year, not-so-promising student who had a checkered history in the girlfriend department and who lived in a tiny adobe shack to keep his ex-girlfriend from thinking she could move in. On the first day in that workshop when the teacher called her *Antonya*, I turned to her and said, "You go by Toni?"

These were my first words to my future wife, and it established a level of wit and intellectual banter that I have labored to maintain in the years since.

Early in the semester, I made a calculated play for her, a literary attempt to get her to have a drink with me. I was the president of a student organization that ran a contest, and Toni won the contest. (I was *not* the judge.) Serendipity had opened a door for me, and I was ready to plunge through. As part of the prize, Toni was to give a reading with Leslie Marmon Silko in the student union, and I had a plan for escorting the prize-winning beauty afterward in an official capacity to a local drinking establishment. When the time came for the reading to begin, we had to delay because Toni was not present. I looked all around the smallish room and could not find her. I told someone this, and Toni overheard me.

"I'm right here," she said. She was sitting at the table directly in front of me, but I had not been able to see her because she was with a man. That she might come with a dude was a possibility that the reptilian part of my brain refuted. I would subsequently discover that she was, in fact, living with this penis-lugging law student, and all my schemes and plans deflated like a penny balloon left too long in the light of day.

This kind of blindness is a means by which one may reveal character, as it has no physiological source—my eyesight was 20/20—but exists as a product of desire or some other equally revealing emotional or psychological state. In Eudora Welty's story "The Wide Net," William Wallace comes home after a night of drinking and discovers an empty house. His pregnant wife, Hazel, is nowhere to be seen. Welty writes, "He went through the house not believing his eyes, balancing with both hands out . . . he turned the kitchen inside out looking for her, but it did no good." Her disappearance leads him to put together a team to drag the river for her body. This is the main action of the story, an action of mythic proportions, but they fail to find Hazel.

Upon returning to the house, William Wallace hears someone call his name. It's Hazel, of course. He asks where she was that morning. And she tells him, ". . . you could have put out your hand and touched me, I was so close." The entire adventure is the product of his blindness. After spending the night drinking and being with the boys, he is unable to see his pregnant wife until after he has imagined her dead and has gone through the ritual of dragging the river. His blindness generates the story.

Productive blindness is often found in unreliable narrators, including those who have done unspeakable things they find impossible to examine, and, of course, you see it in people in love. Meaningful sensory deprivation is a writer's tool, and it is the first of the twelve methods of characterization.

Productive blindness is often found in unreliable narrators, including those who have done unspeakable things.

My failure to see Toni and the subsequent discovery that she was living with a guy could have been the end of us, but the fall semester in Tucson eventually includes the actual season of fall—though only after eight brutally hot weeks. During this season comes the holiday preferred by all creative writing graduate students everywhere: Halloween. Put a bunch of writers in costumes, and something lively is bound to happen—usually involving sex, alcohol, possibly drugs, occasionally motorized vehicles, almost always dancing, and probably another act or two from the remaining and various tribes of hilarity.

I had been to Central America the summer before that particular Halloween, and I'd participated in the fourth anniversary of the Sandinista revolution in Nicaragua, and I decided to come to the Halloween party as a revolutionary. My brother—a graduate student in sociology studying world revolutions—came to the party with me in identical garb. We called ourselves the Sandinettes and linked arms to kick Rockette-style while misquoting the Mexican revolutionary Emiliano Zapata: "We'd rather dance on our feet that live on our knees."

My current ex-girlfriend came as a sexy baseball player, which led to the predictable witless banter about getting to first base, swinging a big stick, et cetera. I'd like to remember us as droll bon vivants, but we were simply a crowd of twenty-somethings with cold beer in our mitts, sex on our minds, and occasional passing thoughts concerning point of view, aesthetic distance, and what costume you might wear if you were The Misfit.

The night developed an entertaining charge of malicious energy. One guest, reportedly a faculty member, came as a kazoo, and his body-length outfit entirely hid his defining human characteristics, the mouthpiece extending far above his head. Moreover, he (I think it was a *he*) refused to speak, igniting a storm of snooping, superstition, and indignation.

"Do we even know him?" someone asked. "He could be anybody."

"He just sits there," another noted. "I don't trust him."

"I detect an alien life force from within him," my brother, a *Star Trek* fan, announced.

"If he's not going to speak, he should *leave*," someone said. "He's creeping me out."

One fiction graduate student came as a drunk; he hadn't worn a costume and yet he was magnificently convincing. He routinely came to parties only to disparage his classmates, claiming that he could *write circles around any of you*. With a little luck, he'd pick a fight, which he would inevitably lose, as he would already be hopelessly smashed. His body was good at falling, and my brother had noted that it made a handsome human puddle.

"A great many people," my brother said, "are most appealing when unconscious."

That night, when Mr. Punch-Drunk let me know that he could write circles around me, I immediately and enthusiastically concurred but suggested that he should come up with a more illuminating metaphor. "What about saying you could write rhombuses around me?"

He took a swing at my chin.

My brother caught the roundhouse with his left hand, keeping his beer hand steady and dry. He advised Mr. Punch-Drunk not to mess with the Sandinettes. To me, he added, "Why joke with pathetic losers who only want to fight?"

I had no good answer. He was my younger brother, but he often offered good advice and was merely amused when I declined to take it, even when the results were disastrous. I already had a starter marriage under my belt, an advanced degree in a field I'd abandoned, a half dozen friends in prison, and the aforementioned penchant for taunting pathetic losers who only want to fight. My brother seemed to see my life as mediocre comic opera, badly written and often featuring marginally talented extras—that's on the one hand. On the other hand, he had front-row tickets.

With the mystery man in the kazoo outfit, we have our second method of characterization, and with Mr. Punch-Drunk, we have our third.

Method number two: the manner in which characters approach the inscrutable—especially an inscrutable person—tends to define them. The inscrutable person becomes a kind of mirror. This is the method employed by Alice Munro in "Friend of My Youth." In Munro's story, the narrator's mother insists that Flora Grieves is deeply distressed by losing her fiancée to Flora's sister, Ellie, even though Flora says she is not; following Ellie's death, the narrator's mother is absolutely outraged when Nurse Atkinson weds the same man, feeling that Flora has again been robbed of her chance at marriage and happiness. But throughout the story Flora is steady and does not feel persecuted and, yes, she appears happy. All the while, the mother's marriage is described as something like a prison. Flora Grieves is an inscrutable character and Munro uses her to define the other characters in the story.

Muriel Spark's short novel *The Prime of Miss Jean Brodie* shows a teacher with her students, and while it investigates the lives of the students, Miss Jean Brodie's life is mostly known through her dialogue and her students' speculations. In the paragraph that follows, the Brodie set—the name given to her favorite students—has heard that Miss Brodie might be applying to a progressive, or *crank*, school to avoid being fired: "[Miss Brodie] looked a mighty woman with her dark Roman profile in the sun. The Brodie set did not for a moment doubt that she would prevail. As soon expect Julius Caesar to apply for a job at a crank school as Miss Brodie. She would never resign. If the authorities wanted to get rid of her she would have to be assassinated."

While Miss Brodie's dialogue is often aphoristic and bold, the students exaggerate her, make her heroic, make her *knowable*.

But as James Wood points out in *How Fiction Works*, we know her mostly through her oft-repeated sayings, and when she is accused of being something other than our vision of her, we come to understand that our vision has been shaped not so much by her actions but by the perceptions of her students. This, then, is another strategy for making use of an inscrutable character: as an object of group misidentification, providing the writer with the opportunity to make dramatic and revealing corrections.

Method number three is pretty much the opposite approach. Characters like Mr. Punch-Drunk are defined by a single trait. You may recoil at the thought of such a reductive approach, but it is used repeatedly by one of our greatest writers, Flannery O'Connor. Think of the grandmother in "A Good Man Is Hard to Find," Julian in "Everything that Rises Must Converge," or Hulga in "Good Country People." These characters are not only defined by a dominant trait, each has the same dominant trait: hubris. They are not the same character because O'Connor inflects the trait, making Hulga an intellectual snob and the grandmother a class snob, while Julian is an intellectual snob who is hung up on his mother's class and race snobbery, but in each case they feel superior to others before coming to the painful realization that such feeling is an error. They do not seem like overly constricted characters because O'Connor does not let the trait be too narrowly defined, but each, I would argue, is defined by a single trait from which every significant act grows.

And perhaps there is a yet another method of characterization lingering here. By contrasting me with my brother, the reader gets a sense of both of us. Compare and contrast, then, comes in at method number four, and the typical manner in which it's used is maybe too obvious to go into, but here is a wonderful example from Edith Pearlman's story "Granski":

> My brother seemed to see my life as mediocre comic opera, badly written and often featuring marginally talented extras.

They were sixteen. During the school year, at home—she in Paris, he in Connecticut—each kept au courant with songs, the proper placement of studs, movies; of course they carried cell phones and knew where to buy weed. But here in Maine they could be their true selves. Their true selves were variously described by the family. Snooty agoutis, according to their younger siblings and cousins. Good sports, according to Gramp, a good sport himself. Too damned clever, said their mothers, who were sisters. The third sister, aunt to Toby and Angelica, complained that they breathed air rarefied even for this family, and we are already the most hyper-indulged characters on the face of the . . . Her statement dwindled as always. As for Gran—tall, crop-haired, pale-eyed Gran—whatever she thought of these particular grandchildren she didn't bother to say.

This lengthy description of the cousins serves to compare and contrast them with the other members of the family, and this single paragraph introduces and begins to define a slew of characters. It is a method that encourages compression, and many writers use it to great effect.

A variation of this method is distinct enough to merit its own number. So coming in at number five we have a type of compare/contrast that I'll call "the wheel." Barbara Pym is the author of *Quartet in Autumn*, a novel about four aging Brits. It was in this novel that I first noticed a simple but effective wheel strategy. Pym lets the reader know that the four main characters use the library but for different reasons, and she wheels through each character consecutively, giving you a sense of each in terms of his or her use of the library, how one may use it for shelter and another for human interaction, ending with Letty and the following: "Of the four only Letty used the library for her own pleasure and possible edification. She had always been an unashamed reader of novels, but if she hoped to find one which reflected her own sort of life she had come to realise that the position of an unmarried, unattached, ageing woman is of no interest whatever to the writer of modern fiction."

In this way, Pym also announces the intention of the novel.

To summarize the wheel, take some locale or activity and then wheel each of your characters through it, contrasting their uses of it. For example, have Character A at the dentist's office, and he is dealing with his anxiety by imagining how B and C routinely handle going to the dentist. A finds, though, that he cannot imagine how D would handle the visit, though he takes a few stabs at it. Fifty pages later we're with D and he's at the dentist. The reader will feel a specific little delight at this return, and D's behavior should surprise the reader in a revelatory manner—simultaneously revealing who D is and how A fails to understand him.

Dancing and drinking contests began, as well as heated conversations about who could and couldn't talk about Native American literature.

As the Halloween night deepened, the party began to roar. Dancing and drinking contests began, as well as heated conversations about who could and couldn't talk about Native American literature, whether one fiction professor was sexist, and whether that same professor was the kazoo. I dodged the chatter and danced. I had a good windmill style, mixed with some elaborate hopping, soulful grimacing, and the occasional shoulder rolling. None of my moves was especially good, but the combo had a kind of electroshock grace. My current ex-girlfriend and I danced, and she used the occasion to complain that I had been dancing with a number of other women. She then took me aside to tell me that if I left her, she would kill herself.

Given that I thought I'd already left her, it was a double bummer.
> or

My head began to whirl like a top quality center-spin reel, cast by an expert fisherman in a wide, fish-heavy river.
> or

My thoughts twisted like towels in a high-efficiency top-loading washer.
> or

I was struck dumb. Had no response. The tops of my shoes were covered with sand.

Method number six: point-of-view intimacy. Having an intimate point of view means that the sentences describing the thoughts and actions of the main character reveal something about the character's sensibility. Let me recount to you a neutral paragraph written by a nonexistent writer: "At the dinner table, Edie was allowed to drink champagne with her parents while her father served the food and her mother talked about her trip to Mexico, saying a few of the words in Spanish. Though the lasagna was overcooked, Edie told them she liked it. She wished she hadn't helped her father hide his mistakes. She wished she hadn't hidden her own. She was on the verge of saying something about all this, but she didn't want to spoil the dinner."

There's nothing wrong with this paragraph. It's perfectly functional, and one can easily imagine it appearing in a short story. However, what if the writer wants a more intimate point of view? She might do something like the following:

> At the dinner table, Edie was allowed to drink champagne with her parents while her father served the food and her mother prattled on about her trip, inserting occasional Spanish words, her mouth working so hard at forming them it was as if she were disgorging golf balls. Though the lasagna had scorched and was leathery, she complimented it a hundred times. Edie regretted helping her father hide his and her own messiness during her mother's absence. She wished the smell of smoke still lingered. She was on the verge of saying or asking something. She could feel her thoughts circling busily in her brain, crowded and confused, the champagne working like lubricant. But they were ugly things, her thoughts, like the many-legged insects that lived beneath rocks: you waited for them to scurry back into the darkness, out of sight. And her mother's eager face seemed directly

responsible. As she herself might put it, she was one of those people who made their companions sour with her sunniness.

Without adding any actions or additional insights, we nonetheless have a much stronger sense of the character through point-of-view intimacy, created in this case by imaginative verb choice, overstatement, dynamic specificity, exaggeration, evocative noun choice, and extended metaphor. It is a perfect example of how much a character can be revealed by means of such intimacy. The paragraph comes from a story called "Loaded Gun" by a writer I love—Antonya Nelson.

— ◆ —

I decided that I'd had enough dancing and just drank with my brother, who wanted to evaluate all of the costumes on a scale of zero to one hundred. Many of the men were, like the two of us, dressed as derring-do types—a cowboy, a warrior, an NBA player, a caveman, and so on. Weirdly, none of these guys, except for us, scored well. Many of the women were dressed as some type of sex object—a French maid, two Playboy bunnies, the aforementioned sexy baseball player, a Marilyn, and so on. These costumes scored surprisingly high.

During our costume perusal, my brother and I came across Mr. Punch-Drunk curled in the dirt in the backyard, his knees up to his chin in the preferred and endearing position of the ludicrously drunk worldwide; however, he'd added his own twist to the familiar pose: his pants were down around his knees.

My brother's evaluation: "Curious chap, this one."

Let us pause now while I make an awkward stretch to accommodate another method of characterization. If Mr. Punch-Drunk were the narrator of this evening, he would likely see the night as yet another tragic attempt to make the world recognize his genius, while the reader would, without doubt, be laughing at his futile gestures.

If you have a character whose experience of the narrative is tonally different from the reader's experience, you've created what I'm going to call tonal dissonance—and in the process, you've probably made the character memorable. Method number seven, then, is to employ tonal dissonance. If the character is exultant but the reader is sad, or you show a character going through hell and the reader is laughing, that character becomes powerfully memorable. In Mary Gaitskill's story "A Romantic Weekend," Beth has planned a getaway weekend with a married man. The story opens with her nervously waiting for him, only to spot him across the street, observing her:

> At the height of her anxiety she saw him through the glass wall of the pizza stand. She immediately noticed his gloating countenance. She recognized the coldly scornful element in his watching and waiting as opposed to greeting her. She suffered, but only for an instant; she was then smitten by

love. She smiled and crossed the street with a senseless confidence in the power of her smile.

"I was about to come over," he said. "I had to eat first. I was starving." He folded the last of his pizza in half and stuck it in his mouth.

She noticed a piece of bright orange pizza stuck between his teeth, and it endeared him to her.

The difference between the experience of the characters and the experience of the readers is enormous. Gaitskill's use of tonal dissonance makes the characters unforgettable by emphasizing the disparity between the world they inhabit and the world of the reader.

———— •◦• ————

Cutting to the chase: Toni showed up at the party some hours into the fray with no costume, but a short plaid skirt and light-colored blouse, those beautiful eyes, beautiful legs, her skin giving off light, no guy in arm or in sight. She approached me shortly after I'd had another unhappy encounter with my newly suicidal current ex-girlfriend, who'd said she wanted us to leave if I was just going to ignore her. I knew there was a logical problem in that formulation, but I couldn't quite find it. While I was looking for it, she stomped off and Toni

approached. She asked how I was doing.

I told her I was doing *okay*—a thoughtful, measured, and yet unpretentious response.

She replied, "You don't *look* okay."

At this point, I decided that I'd had more than enough personal criticism for the evening. I sighed, muttered something unintelligible, and wandered purposefully away.

I must pause to speak briefly about dialogue, method number eight on the hit list. We all know that what characters say reveals who they are (although playwrights often argue that characters speak not to reveal themselves but to *conceal* themselves). Dialogue is a vast subject, and I'm going to look at just one aspect of it, one very simple dialogue strategy: Put one character in your story who says precisely what most people know *not* to say.

Imagine, for example, that upon entering a crowded room, your protagonist, who has just had sex with his wife, is met by a character who says, "Hey man, you smell like you just had sex with your wife."

This kind of line creates opportunities for the writer, not the least of which being how the character is going to respond. He might deny it: "No, I was just . . ." What would you put in there? What does this character think might smell like sex and to which he would rather confess than admit to having had sex with his wife? Whatever he says will reveal him.

> I'd had another unhappy encounter with my newly suicidal current ex-girlfriend, who'd said she wanted us to leave.

Take a draft of a story that isn't yet working and add a character defined by a single trait—the knack for saying what should not be said—and see if that story doesn't get more lively, see if the main character doesn't suddenly take off.

Of course, my turning away wordlessly from Toni's statement reveals me, too, no doubt, but let's not analyze it in too much detail.

The party continued into the crooked hours of morning. My brother actually drove the mostly unconscious Mr. Punch-Drunk home, an act of generosity I found repugnant. I rode shot-gun and kept pointing out places where we could dump the body. I had avoided Toni for the remainder of the time that she stayed at the party.

That night, too, could have been the end of it between us, but the next week I ran into her at the university and she asked if she could visit the class I was teaching. She let me know that she hadn't meant anything rude by her Halloween comment. I told her that I was often a horse's ass. She laughed at this, evidently under the impression that I was joking.

I was in my fifth semester, and I'd finally been given a creative writing work-shop to teach. She had just started the program and was going to be teaching the same course in her second semester. I, of course, welcomed her to class, knowing that I could show her nothing about teach-ing but hoping that I might get off a few funny and/or charismatic lines that might convince her I was a worthy companion.

Later on, I would discover why Toni had developed an interest in me. (It was not my looks or sexual presence, so you know that I was disappointed.) A story I had submitted to workshop intrigued her. The story was one that I'd been working on for years. It was called "The Darkness of Love," and Toni fell for me while reading it. This may sound like an inci-dent so specific to writers as to defy generalization, but I find the opposite to be true. She fell for a *fiction* that she attributed to the other, and that is precisely what is necessary for love. We fall in love with a fictional version of the other that we think *they* have authored, fail-ing to see our own hand in the creation.

Method number nine is to investigate the fictions to which a character clings.

For example, let a character create or believe a fiction about another character, a fiction that others see through. The gap between what the character thinks and reality will be revealing. Or let the char-acter disbelieve a story that everyone else accepts. This may be as simple as one char-acter's evaluation of another's moral fiber. John Cheever uses variations of this

> We fall in love with a fictional version of the other that we think *they* have authored, failing to see our own hand in the creation.

strategy relentlessly. In his story "Goodbye, My Brother," the narrator says, "I was conscious of the tension between Lawrence and Mother, and I knew some of the history of it. Lawrence couldn't have been more than sixteen years old when he decided that Mother was frivolous, mischievous, destructive, and overly strong." The narrator does not agree with this evaluation of their mother, but the reader likely will while at the same time disapproving of Lawrence's behavior toward the woman. This convolution of feelings will make the reader deeply involved in this family, and all of the members of the family are characterized by their allegiances.

Toni visited my class. I have no memory at all of what went on in the classroom, but afterward I invited her to come out with me for drinks to discuss creative writing pedagogy. I took her to a nearby dive almost never frequented by MFA students. I was being cautious. After all, I had a maybe suicidal nearly ex-girlfriend, and Toni lived with a guy who was going to law school. I didn't want a scene or to get sued.

The bar was called The Buffet. We sat in a booth, talked about our lives, and drank beer. Later she would tell me what she thought during the conversation: *I could marry this guy*. My thoughts were more predictable and mundane: *This is the most beautiful woman on the planet*, I thought. Then realizing that this was as much a cliché as *writing circles around people*, I tried: *I would*

trade my soul to spend one night with her. This was not much better, and my soul had long ago been bartered for safety during a tight spot, enough gas to get home, a shot at the buzzer, or a cold beer in a nearly empty fridge. I didn't believe in God, but I'd brokered an unusual number of deals in the heat of many sizzling moments, and—calculating the usual depreciation—I figured the most I could hope for from Toni was a kiss on the cheek.

I didn't even get that.

Nonetheless, when I saw her the next day at school, I asked her out, and she said yes. On our first date, I took her to an obscure Mexican restaurant on the southwest side of Tucson called Karichimaka's—again, far from the MFA crowd. Over the next few weeks, during one clandestine meal or another, I found out that she had two other boyfriends besides the guy she was living with and me. She confessed that she used to be a big liar but now she had stopped. I discovered that even our workshop teacher was after her, as she wanted Toni to marry her son.

Over Thanksgiving break, Toni was driving to California to see one of her boyfriends, a former professor of hers just back from Europe, a cultured grown-up with a slender volume of poetry to his name. I figured my days were numbered. On the day she left, I chipped a bone in my throwing elbow while sliding headfirst into second base. When Toni called from the road, I told her I was in agony.

"I'm falling apart here without you," I said.

She turned around.

Ah, well, she had car trouble, but I prefer to think it was my painful ineptitude that made her steer her Maverick back in my direction.

This situation may be viewed as a forced choice. I had come to the MFA program from a counseling career, and I had administered forced-choice tests, which are used especially in personality inventories designed to reveal one's character (a task much like that of the fiction writer). These multiple-choice personality tests intentionally omit the answers that most people would choose in order to force the person to select an answer that pushes him out of his comfort range. The idea is that if you're forced, time after time, to make such a choice, a pattern will emerge, and that pattern will reveal you.

Imagine that you have to answer the following question:

When you have time on your hands, you tend to
>A. think about your mother.
>B. think about death.

In such a test, one wishes desperately for a *none of the above* option.

When I was studying to be a counselor, I had to take all of the tests before I could be certified to give them. After taking one particularly arduous forced-choice test, my teacher said that I scored in the normal range—more or less—in every category but one, the M/F scale.

What's the M/F scale? I asked.

Well, we no longer use it, he said. We no longer consider homosexuality a form of mental illness.

Say what?

Yes, my score on the M/F scale would have, at one time, made me clinically gay.

While I knew there was nothing wrong with being gay, I was a little surprised to find myself in that category. I did what no real patient ever gets to do: I looked over the questions that led to the score. I can remember one of the questions almost verbatim:

When you have time on your hands, would you rather
>A. read a magazine about
>   automotive mechanics.
>B. read poetry.

Okay, I thought, *so I'm gay*.

The forced choice is method number ten. In fiction, the forced choice is often presented in terms of a moral dilemma; the character must take action but all of the choices are unhappy ones.

Try it yourself. Put your character in a situation in which she must act but her choices are all disturbing. Or put her through a series of forced choices and see how quickly she is revealed.

———— ·•· ————

Toni chose to drive back to Tucson, and in December of 1983, we became a public couple. I told my ex-girlfriend that I really, really, really hoped she wouldn't kill herself, but I was in love. She guessed that it was Toni, which was not such a leap, given that every boy in the program was in love with her. I took Toni to meet my brother. "She's fantastic," my brother said, and then added, "Don't let her get to know you too quickly."

A month later, while standing with her in the living room of her rented house, I asked her to marry me. She said yes, and the radio immediately played "The Star-Spangled Banner" (the Jimi Hendrix version).

"The Star-Spangled Banner," in this scenario, is an objective correlative, which is method number eleven.

A practical way for a writer to think about the objective correlative: it's a means of avoiding some line that merely states a feeling. In my case, "The Star-Spangled Banner" kept me from having to say, *I felt like we were involved in something much larger than merely two people in love; it seemed enormous and of great national consequence.*

The objective correlative is an important means of characterization, and if you look for it, you'll find it in virtually every work of fiction.

— • —

To review: in January of 1984 Robert Boswell proposed marriage and Antonya Nelson accepted and "The Star-Spangled Banner" played. In the throes of my

I wasn't exactly an idiot, but there's no question that I had often lived my life as if I were.

elevated affection, I took Toni for a drive. I showed her the house where I'd lived with my first wife. Why this seemed the right thing to do, I'm not sure. I've heard that character is action, but I don't really want to know what this action reveals.

We didn't tell many people of our engagement, but of course I told my brother. "You'd be an idiot not to marry her," he said, but then he backtracked. "I didn't mean that the way it sounded." He paused to reconstruct. "What I meant to say was, whether or not you're an idiot, I'm glad you're marrying her."

I wasn't exactly an idiot, but there's no question that I had often lived my life as if I were. Method number twelve: Say the hardest thing about your characters. I lifted this advice from a book of writing hints that the poet Jon Anderson put together. By *saying the hardest thing*, I mean that you should push to get at the darkest or ugliest motivation you might honestly credit to your character's actions.

This final method is, I think, the most important on the list, as it has the power to turn ordinary characters into extraordinary ones. One of the attributes that makes Alice Munro's stories among the best ever written is that she will not let go of her characters until she has said the hardest thing. The following paragraph is from the end of "The Progress of Love." The character, who calls herself Fame, has had to admit that one of her memories is simply wrong—the recollection of her father looking on with approbation while her mother burns a great quantity of money:

> How hard it is for me to believe that I made that up. It seems so much the truth it is the truth; it's what I believe about them. I haven't stopped believing it. But I have stopped telling that story . . . I didn't stop just because it wasn't, strictly speaking, true. I stopped because I saw that I had to give up expecting people to see it the way I did. I had to give up expecting them to approve of any part of what was done. How could I even say that I approved of it myself? If I had been the sort of person who approved of that, who could do it, I wouldn't have done all I have done . . . I wouldn't be divorced. My father wouldn't have died in the county home. My hair would be white, as it has been naturally for years, instead of a color called Copper Sunrise. And not one of these things would I change, not really, if I could.

Fame has to admit that it is not merely people like the men in her life who lack the requisite seriousness that she associates with her parents; she, too, is lacking. And it is this kind of reckoning that elevates Munro's stories above those of her contemporaries.

Method number twelve: Say the hardest thing about your character.

———— ◆ ————

Toni and I were married in July 1984 at her family's summer home in Telluride, Colorado. Several of our friends played instruments, and they had gotten together to see what songs they all knew. Those songs became part of the wedding ceremony. They were "Route 66," "Our House," and "Twist and Shout." Meanwhile, we promised sickness and health, for better or worse, until the day that one or more of our hearts stopped beating.

My brother was there, of course, and he got the dancing started. We were in suits and nice dresses—costumes—and maybe it felt a little like that Halloween night when everything could have fallen apart but didn't. Mr. Punch-Drunk wasn't there, but several of my friends inadvertently did impersonations.

"You've got it made now," my brother told me, "so long as you do right by her for the remainder of your life."

I told him, as I had promised her, that I'd do my best.

And now we near the end of this public declaration—this tender, ridiculous, marginally grammatical, potentially humiliating public declaration. Do these dozen methods lead to the creation of memorable characters? I'll leave you to make that decision. What I can tell you is this: All these years later, Toni and I are still married, and I'm still amazed and baffled that she picked me. Our two kids are adults now and happy. We have dogs, a mortgage, a station wagon, a pickup truck, a ghost town—the whole bit.

We've published more than twenty books between us. Many of the people we knew back when are still our friends.

A few years ago, my brother died after a long illness. He could not talk in the end and had to use a computerized voice. He selected individual letters by means of a tiny device connected to his eyebrow, and sentences were arduous for him to create. On my last visit to see him, one of the final things he said to me was "love toni kids." Whether he was telling me about his own feelings or continuing his wise advice, I'll never know. 🔒

Kate Rutledge Jaffe

DWELLING

First you were a whirling in the stereo
        Wasn't she like starlight   you said   Why aren't I
made of boys   I wondered   Why can't I be a box
       a hare   a billion magnifying glasses
face down in the garden   the first bright sleeping animal
       But then the summer kicked out from
under us   lemonade in my hat

Couldn't you remember   the golden-brown moonlight
       its furious beaks   clacking
as we shook it   When I stared you
       down into the porch dust   a black blinked maybe-
world   and your face on mine   pushed to digging
       sounded like a horn for dinner
Special you called me   *Little*
       ready to fire upon the garden   exhausted
and drowning in this cigarette earth
       No buts you said   and played me off
back beneath the dark porch   into the banded arms
       of loose dirt   claystone colder than before

My glanced face   my lens-soaked eyes

        bent the dark stuff   swiftly into mother's pocket

You never amounted to much   Now do you see?

        It was just   a day   maybe

just a month   a cutting   a window

        onto which we   paged the sky

The Red Crown

Jon Raymond

He didn't know the exact name of the milk, he'd already forgotten that information, but he knew what color the carton was—bright yellow—and he knew the size she wanted, which was the normal size, not the narrow carton, or the giant plastic container with the built-in handle. She definitely didn't want whole milk, either, he knew that, too. She wanted 2% milk, but almost all the milk was 2% these days, wasn't it?

If there were any question about what kind of milk his wife wanted, she was now holding up the empty carton and asking him to please look at it closely and remember which one she was talking about because she didn't want to have to take it back, like last time.

"Please, Don," Karen said, almost pleadingly, holding the carton over the recycling bin, her waxy, raisined face pinched with concern, "just look at it. This one, okay? You can bring this with you if you want to. Just to compare."

"I know," Don said, still refusing to look at the carton, and leaving exactly what he knew under some question. They'd already been through this routine three times and he didn't want any more instructions. He preferred to stare at the hood of the stove behind Karen, noting the odd shape of the flanged metal. He wondered what ingenious human being had designed the contraption. That, he knew, was a thought that didn't lead to problems.

"I know you know," she was saying. "I mean, of course you know. But why not bring this along? What can it hurt?"

Don didn't answer, letting the yellow shape of the milk carton hover out of focus near Karen's shoulder as the sound of the grandchildren in the living room drifted in. They were fighting about a toy. He knew Karen was trying to be reasonable, but she also had to know that the idea of carrying an empty milk carton to the store so he could replace it with the exact same kind was humiliating. Who brought empty milk cartons to the store? No one. How many times had he gotten milk in his life? More than he could possibly count. And he was happy to do it again if she would just stop talking and let him put on his jacket and walk out the door. If only the zipper of his windbreaker wasn't so hard to get zipped he already would have left.

He tried and tried again, but he couldn't make the connection between the tongue thing and the clamp. The tooth was stripped, or possibly slightly bent. Tooth. Tongue. Maybe his fingers were the problem. They were too big and meaty. Why was the zipper so small?

He could feel Karen's eyes on him, and her watchfulness made him more self-conscious. He fumbled with the zipper worse than before, but he knew he had to remain calm. If he lost his temper now, the moment would go down as another episode of his decline, another entry in the document of his lapses and odd behaviors. He knew about the little journal Karen was keeping, her medical record for the eventual doctors of memory. Normally her vigilance didn't bother him that much; in a way, her escalating concern made his life easier. As her expectations of him diminished, his room to maneuver slightly grew, to the degree that he sometimes played up his problems to give himself an extra buffer of quiet and solitude. But in this case he didn't want to play them up.

> He tried and tried again, but he couldn't make the connection between the tongue thing and the clamp.

"Don . . ." she said. "Do you . . . ?"

"I'm fine," he said. "The zipper is stuck. I'm getting the milk."

"Are you sure you don't want . . . ?"

"No!"

Don felt guilty to be happier outside, away from his family, but the streets were so peaceful, so undemanding, he couldn't help it. The whole morning had been spent in some form of stress, hiding from his grandchildren and son to avoid the embarrassment of his infirmity. From the stillness of his office, he'd listened as they stormed around the house ripping pillows from the couch and scattering Legos on the floor. The one time he'd left the office, to go to the bathroom, he'd gotten entangled in a conversation with Bobby about Bobby's upcoming business trips, until it became obvious they'd had the same conversation very recently, and nothing had changed. And then, on his way back from the bathroom, he'd become trapped in a long conversation between Bobby and Karen about Bobby's coming birthday plans, a swirling exchange involving names and places and references he was sure he'd never heard of before, until eventually his own ignorance had become so physically palpable, so suffocating, he'd had to leave.

Away from the undertows of conversation, though, he could relax and sink into the spectacle of the springtime. There were so many blooming trees and opening buds to see. And then the gorgeous white cones of, what were they, horse chestnuts? He'd never learned the names of the plant life around his home, a great failing on his part, but on a day like this, what did it matter? The air was fragrant, the sky was radiant with clouds, and in silence, walking the road shoulder, he was able to feel if not strong at least calm, and lucid in his familiar cycle of thoughts.

As always, the spring trees astounded him—the way they rebuilt themselves after their harrowing passage through winter, their shocking explosion of green fireworks. He was so proud of the trees he wanted to salute them all. *Well done!* he thought. *You've pulled it off again!*

The next block was less lush, but the strip mall offered its own viewing pleasures. The signage, the mothers with their strollers, the brawny cars crawling around the parking lot, nudging into their places. Seeing all this human activity, all this polite enterprise, Don could convince himself that all must be well in the world. The scene was only one of many such scenes, an outcropping of a whole, pleasant, interconnected economy transpiring invisibly around the globe.

> He'd already forgotten the name of the brand Karen wanted but the block of yellow on the carton seemed like a familiar sensation.

Today, for some reason—maybe it was the temperature, or the angle of the light—the sight of the mall dislodged a cluster of memories in him, and with no effort on his part, vague images came floating to the surface of his mind. His old barber's name was John. He'd had a shop in the strip mall before the remodel. Don saw the shop's orange vinyl seats, the posters of the feather-haired studs, and the jar of blue antiseptic fluid stuffed with combs. He tried to dwell in the memory as long as he could, pulling it near, and caught some other lingering impressions: the scent of the hair product (called Roffler?); the soft, sturdy pressure of John's hands on his scalp. Don had gone there for forty years, every few months, for the same over-the-ears trim. But just as quickly as the memories formed, they faded away, without shape, without ending; he'd never exerted the will to make them into stories.

John the barber stayed in his mind, though—a blurry, resilient cipher. The name almost taunted him now. Don had gone to John for decades and yet when he thought about it, he realized he knew almost nothing about the man. He didn't know if he had children, if he fished, if he was a Republican or a Democrat. He didn't remember ever even having really talked to him. The main thing he knew about John was that he'd retired. Or had he? Maybe he'd only moved.

Two cars roared past over the wet road, gleaming in the sun. The world—the path to the store—was bursting with color, and yet numbingly familiar. The days changed but the signs for the bank and the nail salon were always the same. What kind of man didn't learn a single thing about his own barber in forty years' time?

The grocery store in the strip mall had everything he might need, but Don preferred the store that was a little farther down the road. It was cheaper, but mainly he liked it because over the years the owners had never altered the floor plan and had kept the labels for everything posted clearly in multiple spots. Walking through the whispering door, the fluorescent lights filling the corners, Don knew immediately where he was. He even believed he mildly recognized the faces of some of the cashiers, although maybe it was only the forest green of their aprons that gave him that feeling. A pedestal of six-packs displayed a pristine barbeque grill—a harbinger of summer—and a young man in the coffee aisle watched him with what looked like a kindly, even expectant, expression.

He was there for milk, he remembered, and before that could slip his mind he shuffled toward the back freezers, past the pizzas, the orange juice, the bagged vegetables, until he arrived at the dairy section—two entire refrigerator cases containing every size and consistency and purity level of milk on earth. There was skim, organic, half-and-half, liter and half liter, paper, plastic, and glass. He'd already forgotten the name of the brand Karen wanted, if he'd ever known it, but the block of yellow on the carton seemed like a familiar sensation. Yellow. Marigold. That was the name.

The glass fogged when he opened the door. He pulled out a half gallon, worried he was forgetting some other component of the decision, and closed the glass, enjoying the satisfying slurp of the rubber seal. When he turned to go he found the young man from the coffee aisle was now standing in front of the butter section, still with that kindly, expectant expression on his face. He seemed to be looking directly at Don. Don looked away, but the man didn't move, and eventually Don was obliged to look again. The man was slightly overweight, with a scurf of facial hair over his cheeks and neck and fine red veins detailing his nose. He wasn't as young as Don had thought, more like middle-aged, though to Don everyone was young. Young and basically indistinguishable from each other.

"Mr. Bowler?" the man said, and Don started. "I thought that was you! Wow. It's been a long time!"

Don pivoted slightly, offering up a noncommittal smile. He had no recognition of this person, and no idea of how to go about finding out who he was. He wished Karen were there. She was the one who loved this kind of chance encounter, the gossip and small talk in the aisles. On his own, his deficiencies were going to become obvious very quickly.

"Yes," Don said, holding the smile. "And how are you?"

"I'm fine," the man said. "It's so funny, I didn't know you guys still lived around here. I haven't seen you in, God, ages."

"We're still here, yes."

"Still in that same house then?"

"Oh yes," Don said, maintaining a cheerful front even as a brief stab of confusion lanced him. Had they moved? No. Absolutely not. His house was the same as it had always been. His house was his sanctuary.

"I drive by sometimes and I wonder," the man went on. "And how's Bobby doing? I was just thinking about him the other day. I haven't talked to him in way too long."

"He's just fine," Don said.

"I heard he has kids!"

"That's true."

"Boys? Is that right?"

"Two boys."

"Wow. What are their names?"

Don stared. A knot of shame tightened in his chest. He'd never been good with names. He'd always assumed he'd never see a person again when they met, that they'd forget him as soon as they parted, so why bother remembering them? Although certainly the names of his own grandchildren he knew. The older one was . . . Aaron? Adam? It was a bubble almost within grasp, but each time he tried to catch it, it popped. He didn't want to make a mistake, after all, nor did he want to show his confusion. But even as he pushed harder, reached deeper, he could feel a thick membrane congealing in his mind, a milky, opaque wall welling between himself and his life. His synapses felt padded with wool, his brain dampened by a thick blanket. He couldn't bring the names of his own grandchildren to his mouth.

A look of concern and disappointment settled onto the man's face, and in his mind Don lashed out at Karen. Why wasn't she with him? She should have been the one fielding this conversation, not him. She had all the answers for everything, she knew all the details. In fact, she knew so many details she'd practically crippled him with her knowledge. She'd made all their decisions. She'd done all their research. She'd taken such good care of him, protected him so completely, that she'd rendered him helpless.

The man still waited for an answer, his eyes soft with patience. A clerk walked briskly into view, scanning inventory. In the end Don resorted to a trick he'd been pulling sadly often of late.

"They're wonderful kids," Don said, pretending he'd misheard the question.

"I bet," the man said. "Well, hey, tell him hi for me, all right? From Scott."

"I will, Scott. He's traveling a lot these days. But I'll tell him."

> It was wonderful. For a moment, there was nothing he could do. His senses were completely filled.

Outside, the sky had darkened. A yellowish pall had overtaken the parking lot, and a few steps out the door rain began gushing. Don didn't want to go back in the store and have to talk to the young man again, he'd managed to withdraw fairly painlessly, nor did he want to get soaked on the way home, so to avoid both these outcomes, he altered course and hurried toward the wall of fir trees edging the lot off to the right.

In all the years he'd been making the trip to the store, the wall of fir trees had been there, a looming, dark barricade half hiding a neighborhood of dingy, mold-streaked little homes. The trees had never been inviting, but today the shaggy, ugly boughs offered a thick awning under which to wait out the shower.

Sure enough, the rain barely touched him. He stood and watched it fall on the parking lot, enjoying the smell of wet pavement, the warm, wonderful fragrance of the rubber washed from the asphalt. The rain crashed down, torrential, fuzzing around the hoods and rooftops of the parked cars, flowing in hard cataracts into the gutters, a wild, peaceful roar.

It was wonderful. For a moment, there was nothing he could do. His senses were completely filled.

Soon enough, though, the boughs were springing leaks, and cold droplets began falling onto his shoulders and head. The rain didn't seem to be letting up, so he decided to back a little deeper into the woods for better cover. He could see a darker area not too far away, which he figured meant a thicker canopy. Less drippage. Tucking the milk under his arm, he shuffled into the shadows, passing shabby houses and muddy, mossy lots surrounded by cyclone fences, wondering who would ever want to live in this dank world.

But the dark patch was a deception. The rain still spattered through the boughs, plonking on his head. He spotted another area ahead that looked even darker, and he aimed that way, but it wasn't as well-sheltered as he'd hoped, either. This happened two more times. Every time he thought he was approaching the perfect haven, the canopy parted slightly, and the rain poured through. In this way, edging from darkness to darkness, cradling the milk, he drifted ever deeper into the unfamiliar, wooded streets.

> He was lost, adrift. It would be frighteningly easy to slip off into nowhere at all.

Surely, he'd been on these streets before, he thought. They were only a few blocks from his home, and yet all the houses and yards seemed utterly strange. Occasionally, faint memories surfaced, only to sink back down in the fog. He had been here, yes, he had. Years ago, he'd brought Bobby to a playdate nearby, maybe many playdates. The parents, they'd had a sandwich shop. They'd always given away day-old sandwiches, shrink-wrapped and damp. He could taste their sandwiches, feel the gummy bread on his teeth, the shredded lettuce, the thick mayonnaise. Those were good sandwiches. Who were the people, though? He remembered a boy with a cleft chin. A girl crying behind a screen door. But the pictures were locked in shadow.

Even his pictures of Bobby in those years were locked in shadow. Who had he been? Don could barely find evidence they'd ever lived together. Every phase along the way had so neatly erased the phase before, so fully wiped away the tracks, and then at some point the whole path had dropped off a cliff. He could see Bobby in diapers, painting the sidewalk with water. He could see Bobby running hurdles. And then he was gone, a distant voice on the phone. He'd returned lately, his own children in tow, but he was always passing through, always distracted and exhausted, never able to sit with Don long enough to pierce the haze. He had no patience for the grown child his father had become. As perhaps Don himself had never had patience for a child.

Droplets tinkled on every side, shaking the fern fronds and sinking into the beds of fallen needles. The road was pocked with potholes and littered with rubble. The balmy air was rich with sap and rot. It was that time of year. There would be eight kinds of weather in an hour. It might hail in a second, or it might burst into sunlight.

He was lucky, and the sun came. The thrumming vibrations of the rain tapered off and a moment later the clouds parted, sending down sheets of scrubbed light. Beads of water sparkled on young green leaves. Getting home would be no problem now, he realized, except for the fact he didn't know where he was. Turning around, he discovered that the grocery store was no longer in sight. The potholed street led off into woodsy darkness and distant, intersecting streets of increasing obscurity. Clouds of steam were rising from the pavement, coiling fingers beckoning in every direction.

The street was all but deserted—only two cats slinking near fences and a person crouched in a garden. He saw a car far down the street, but it was already turning. He wandered over to the person through the roiling brightness, and it turned out to be a small woman in a pith helmet and enormous sunglasses, pawing like a badger with her muddy gloves. Beside her was a pile of wet weeds, and, drawing closer, Don saw she was Asian. He wondered if there was anything about Asians and gardening in the rain. Not that he knew of.

He stood near her gate waiting to be noticed. Eventually she said hello and he said hello back, and then he waited some more, watching her move the weeds to another pile in the far corner of the yard and return to her beds. She didn't seem bothered by his presence. Across the street someone walked outside, tossed a cup of coffee onto the lawn, and went back inside. He mentioned it was a nice day and she agreed. He waited a little longer before speaking again.

"You have a beautiful yard," he said.

"Thank you," she said, and kept digging, extracting the dirty tentacles of the weeds from the soupy earth.

"And you live right here? In this house?" he said.

"Yes," she said, smiling at the ground. She was an old woman and set in her movements. Her spadework was choppy, but well-practiced, second nature. She knew what the dirt needed.

"So you know where we are?" he asked.

"Where we are? What do you mean?" The woman turned and looked at him through her gigantic amber glasses, showing her wide, pleasant face, small chin, and tiny, friendly teeth.

"I mean, where am I," Don said. "Right now. I'm a little confused about that."

Don tried to make his question sound jolly, unworried, but in fact a sticky fear was rising in his throat. To hear himself ask these questions was to understand that something was deeply wrong. He was lost, adrift. It would be frighteningly easy to slip off into nowhere at all. One wrong turn, and another wrong turn, and Karen might never find him. He didn't have ID on him. He didn't have a phone. Like a child drifting into the deep end of a pool, suddenly sensing the terrifying depth beneath his feet, he panicked.

"You're on Bonita Road," the woman said, though he barely heard her.

"Okay."

"Just off Boones Ferry."

"Uh-huh."

The woman stood, clutching the weeds, or possibly greens. Maybe in Asia these weeds were greens. She asked him where he was going and again he could feel the white wall forming, the blankness spreading. He scoured his brain for his address, but the numbers didn't come up. He tried to summon a landmark, anything, but nothing came. He knew the rooms of his house, the arrangement of the furniture. He knew the whereabouts of the vacuum cleaner. But to place the house in space, that was impossible. He caught the sound of Bobby running in the hall, small feet slapping the warm pine. Or was it Bobby's sons running? When had that sound entered his catacomb?

She asked if he was all right, and he realized he was almost in tears, his mouth collapsing, his mind a hot, empty slate.

"I . . . I don't know," Don said.

"Why don't you just stay here," she said, peeling off her gloves. "I can call someone to help you. Is that all right?" He nodded. "Do you want tea or anything? Some water?"

He shook his head and watched her go inside. The door opened into homey darkness and closed, leaving him alone, still fearful, but relieved his fate had entered someone else's hands.

He waited a long time for the woman to come back. Long enough for a bird on a telephone pole to get bored and fly away. Long enough for the steam to thin and turn into mere wisps on the asphalt. The tracery was so delicate, so quiet, caressing the black ground. Her house was utterly still. Was that an Asian thing, too? Slow in emergencies?

He paced the edge of her fence, examining the tumble of plants. She had a beautiful yard. The plants came in so many shapes and sizes, with so many strange disks, stalks, and lattices, all with their inscrutable purposes, and their beautiful, unknown names. It was too late to learn the names now. For some reason, it had always seemed too late in his life. Too late to learn a language. Too late to play the piano. The life of knowledge and endeavor had always belonged to other people. His lot had been to watch.

He began to doubt the woman was coming back. Maybe there had been some misunderstanding. What had she said, exactly? He couldn't remember, and it made him a little angry. He'd been very clear. He had to get home. He had talked to a woman, hadn't he?

If he could just find the grocery store, he thought, he could make it home from there. He was almost positive the store was over to the right somewhere. He shuffled down the block to peer around the corner, still hoping the woman would emerge and call him back, but she didn't.

At the end of the block, he went ahead and walked another block, thinking he'd find the store, but at the end of that block it still wasn't in view. If anything, he seemed to be heading deeper into the woods again, deeper into unfamiliar territory. He'd been walking around in this forest for what seemed like days.

> For some reason, it had always seemed too late in his life. Too late to learn a language. Too late to play the piano.

The clouds were gathering again, dark gray and bloated with rain. He picked up the pace, hoping to find shelter before the next downpour, and his knee bumped the milk carton, causing him to drop it to the pebbly ground. He cursed himself. Now the carton was dented.

The sun was still shining when the rain hit again, the droplets and hail lit up like shrapnel. He arrived at a park and hurried over the grass to take shelter under the play structure, a wooden agglomeration of ladders and platforms, festooned with dangling chains and a single, blade-like slide. Under the bridge he found a decent spot to wait out the squall. It was reasonably dry, with a post to lean on, and a view of bark dust, some grass, a bushy red hedge, and, in the distance, bedraggled fir trees tossing in the wind.

The rain poured down, a chaos of water, flattening the grass under its attack. The sound became immense, and the bouncing spray fanned over him, coating his skin with fine dew. He tried to pull back farther, retract deeper into himself, but he couldn't escape, and eventually he simply gave up and watched, relinquishing himself to the world's flux of pictures. He stared at the rain spilling through the slats of the floppy bridge. The surface of the sidewalk clamoring with water. He saw his own old hands, flecked with bits of wet bark dust. Always before there had been bread crumbs of memory to hold on to, small, stray arrows leading back to his life, but now, here, he found almost nothing inside. Only the scene in his vision existed.

Rain soaked into his socks and pant legs, burrowed into his underwear. He tried to console himself by thinking about Bobby, but only the name, not the essence, throbbed in his brain. What did he know about Bobby? Bobby was a stranger now. Long ago he and his son had agreed to withdraw from each other, to retreat into their private worlds of indifference. They shared that same flaw in their blood—the same meekness, possibly even stupidity. It was a defect Don had spent his life trying to hide from the world, but somehow the world had discovered it over and over again. The world knew: he hadn't ever opened himself all the way; he hadn't ever truly allowed himself to be touched. And as punishment the world had consigned him to this purgatory. Not just now, but through his whole eventless life.

Don gazed out at the hammering rain, full of terror he might die in this spot, or simply freeze over and become a rock or a stump. To be lost, wet, and cold for eternity seemed wholly possible.

The rain couldn't hold its high power for long, and soon it was letting up, leaving the park in glassy, shocked silence. The trees dripped, the grass breathed, and a dark wall of purple clouds filled the horizon. The clouds continued shifting, and a bath of golden light flowed in from behind, collecting in a soft, luminous bowl. Don stared at the red hedge, which seemed to glow against the backdrop of the purple clouds, its spiky, shadowless leaves frozen with clarity. He didn't know the name of the hedge, but he knew he'd seen the kind before. It resembled laurel, but it wasn't laurel. He knew that every year the leaves grew in bright red and then faded to green. Every year, this plant put on a shaggy crimson coat and lost it.

He stared at the red leaves and felt a memory kindling in his darkness. It took a moment to ignite, but then, suddenly, it was there, entering him like a spirit. It was an old memory, full of texture, from a cloudy afternoon this very time of year. He could see himself standing in front of a hedge just like this one, holding not milk but the jar of pickled herring he'd been ordered to buy from the deli for his wife, who had just given birth to Bobby.

Vividly, the memory hovered in his mind. That bristling red hedge in the overcast light. The sound of traffic nearby. His shoulders uncontrollably heaving. He was weeping from relief, he remembered, because his wife and son were finally safe after hours of labor, and out of fear, too, because in a matter of days they would bring Bobby home, a terrifying prospect. He was weeping because he'd stepped from one life into another, and what was there to do but weep, and thank God? Thank you, God, he'd thought, for this great honor, this grand, awesome duty you've given, thank you, God. Thank you, God, for granting me this sacred responsibility, this ultimate labor. Thank you, God. Thank you, for this life to protect. For this body to cherish. Every year, the memory had returned, brought on by the red leaves, and every year a deep-lodged pearl of meaning had grown inside him by a single thin layer. But today, cracked open, the memory was as real and present as his own flesh. The moment of liquid joy before the red crown of leaves. Fire licking over his head. The day his child had come. The day Bobby was born.

In the sky, the wall of clouds was already breaking apart, and yellow sun clashed with purple masses and filigrees. The sunlight was getting harsher, and the hedge was losing its magic glow. He could hear the footsteps of a jogger on the sidewalk, the swish of wet tires somewhere not far away. What was he just thinking about, he wondered. Already, the past few moments were turning to mist.

The house glided into view in the police car's windshield, and then the car pulled into the driveway and came to a stop. From the backseat, Don could see Karen and Bobby in the living room window, their mouths moving with surprise and concern, busy formulating the million questions he wouldn't be able to answer. The whole drive home he'd been rehearsing the story about the young woman who'd rescued him, getting the details right. Her hair plastered to her cheek, her jogging clothes drenched. How she'd come closer, blurring through his tears, and paused for a moment to deliberate before bending and asking if he was all right. But now he wasn't sure if he would tell the story after all. The facts were getting fuzzy. Probably better to let the police handle the technical questions.

Don climbed out of the car, cradling the dented milk carton in his arms. His wet clothes were stuck to his skin and he shook his legs to release the clammy folds. The boys, both dressed like Spider-Man, had joined Karen and Bobby in the window, and all of them were watching him now. The boys seemed thrilled by the commotion and Don smiled and waved. The boys waved back, then scampered happily off into the living room's depths, followed by their dad. Don would go find them soon, he thought. He would read the boys a book. But first he had to get this carton of milk to the refrigerator. ⬢

PICNIC PICKS

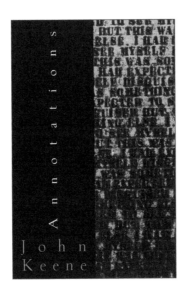

ON JOHN KEENE'S

Annotations

BY JEANNIE VANASCO

Dear Reader of 2113 (or thereabouts),

   Someone asked me recently, "What's the book that, a century from now, everyone will look down on us for not having praised enough?" I suspect you can confirm my answer: *Annotations,* by John Keene.

   But if, for some reason, it remains obscure, I am here to convince you to read *Annotations* and, should you recognize its genius, spread word so that it ranks among the great works in the English canon. If anyone can accomplish this, it is the owner of a century-old literary quarterly.

   Pulled from the slush pile at New Directions a few years after Keene graduated Harvard, and published by New Directions in 1995, *Annotations* reminds us that a human being is a process—here, the process is that of a boy developing into an artist.

   Born in the "summer of Malcolms and Seans, as Blacks were transforming the small nation of Watts into a graveyard of smoldering metal," the unnamed narrator traces his life as a black, gay child in St. Louis, living in his family's prefab in a working-class neighborhood: "Occasionally we heard shooting, but most often it was shouting, which a battle of fists or blades would readily resolve." This upbringing is set against the backdrop of a conflicted country: "Consider: images of Vietnam, the assassinations, and Watergate bear that fuzzy, bluish-white glimmer, since nearly all your recollections of that era's major events are but the residue of each evening's televised diversions."

Amid this violence, the narrator contemplates who he is by simultaneously reconstructing and speaking to the boy he was—a child entranced by language, who understands that words bear the reality of a thing, that they can be played with like toys or thrown like bombs. Language transforms his Catholic school playground into a battleground where his classmates taunt him: "Straight-A, Straight-A, nothing but a sissyboy who's scared to play." Their chant hurts and his masculinity crumples near the swing set, "like a raveling, forgotten husk-doll." It is proposed that he skip a grade, though the adults in his life fear "that might warp her emotional development." Keene's narrator's use of second-person and third-person, masculine and feminine, singular and plural pronouns to address himself throughout the book shows his struggle with his identity. Meanwhile, the relentless energy of Keene's language emphasizes its importance to his narrator: "Transforming the letters, nevertheless, into fully formed words was as important a confidence-builder as keeping the bike aloft on the graveled road or reaching the lake's mile marker. Thus he wrote but they professed to comprehend not a word, claiming the entire text unfolded like a riddle. Black pearls."

Even after his family moves from its single-family detached in the ghetto to "a ranch house in a suburb whose property values and lack of crime could boast of national renown," the narrator senses danger. The words of his world constantly invoke violence, even in the most innocent contexts: If he takes the long way to school, he passes a gas station where a man known as "Sarge" from his army days repairs cars. The other way offers a store that sells Bomb Pops on hot summer days.

And the past is always there to remind him that life is an endless war. Missouri soil rivaled Virginia's in number of Civil War battles, "yet this factlet often receives scant mention in the most authoritative studies of that conflict." His teachers acknowledge Missouri's Duden's Report, which led to tens of thousands of German immigrants settling there and fighting against slavery. But when the narrator presses his teachers to discuss the report's implications on the present time (think of the anti-German sentiment rampant in the United States as a result of World Wars I and II), they ignore him. How soon we forget, the narrator says: "what one century pens with the most illuminative articulation, the consequent one hundred years transform into an entirely new text, unrecognizable at first glance. There but for the great hoax go our eyes."

As the book nears its end, the narrator cites James Joyce as one of many influences, and *Annotations* does remind me of *A Portrait of the Artist as a Young Man*. Both works reject traditional narrative form in favor of internalized action, promiscuously employ pronouns, and cast other characters to show the development of the artist in relief against their lack of artistic awareness. On a class field trip to the Art Institute of Chicago, the narrator develops his appreciation of art, deciding that "appreciation becomes an effect rather than an immediate feeling of the picture, followed by a gradual perceptive glowing." Meanwhile, his classmates are most arrested by "the spectacle of the soldier grinding with the half-asleep young woman, which they watched through the undraped hotel window."

Just as Stephen Dedalus is considered Joyce's alter ego, it could be assumed that *Annotations*'s narrator is Keene. Keene is black, gay, and a writer and artist from St. Louis, both he and his narrator attended Harvard, and *Annotations* does move like a memoir between the innocence of outlook and experienced hindsight. A black-and-white photograph of a young boy, presumably the author, appears opposite the title page. The back cover sends us to the "fiction" shelves, though the jacket copy says that Keene "(re)creates his life story as a jazz fugue-in-words." So what do we call it?

A masterpiece.

Too often writers fall prey to the built-in curbs of genre and the imagination that a traditional prose style imposes. With its dense, impacted language, Keene's prose sounds like poetry: "Your tongue, but a bat in its cavern of reassurance, would take flight when you least expected it." How I read and reread that sentence! But the poetry of *Annotations* involves more than sound. Its lyricism consists in the presentation of ideas as themes repeated and developed. Only upon my most recent reading did I notice that "analysis" on page twenty-six "involves a subtler mode of seeing" and thirteen pages later "entails a subtler mode of seeing." Mystery, passion, and intelligence are there in equal proportion—there is nothing in the whole book that I want changed.

Annotations reminds me not only why I review books but also why I read them. Proust said, "Every reader finds himself. The writer's work is merely a kind of optical instrument that makes it possible for the reader to discern what, without this book, he would perhaps never have seen in himself." That a straight, white woman can see something of herself in this book is, hopefully, not an offense but rather a testament to its greatness. To borrow from page five, "the genius lies in the execution," and page twenty-two, "the genius lay in the execution," and page seventy-four, "the genius lies, in the execution." In his "execution" of *Annotations*, Keene reminds us that art, for the artist, is a battle, a matter of life and death.

Reader of 2013, I also wrote this for you.
All my best,
Jeannie

George Gissing
New Grub Street

OXFORD WORLD'S CLASSICS

ON GEORGE GISSING'S
New Grub Street

PAMELA ERENS

I credit the Victorian novelist George Gissing with curing me of a misunderstanding about the literary life. It always seemed to me that late-nineteenth-century England must have been the ideal time and place to be a novelist. George Eliot was revered. There was no television or Internet to siphon away the attention of the masses. Publishers did not need to make megabucks for corporate owners who also produced toasters or ran theme parks. The world was quieter then, and slower—seemingly good circumstances for the production of meaningful literature.

Then I read *New Grub Street*, Gissing's 1891 novel about this supposed golden age.

I came across the work of Gissing, whose name rang a distant bell, on the fifty-cent sale shelves at my local library. It was a different novel I discovered first: his wonderful *The Odd Women*, about turn-of-the-century English feminists. I was impressed that a book written by a man in 1893 could offer such a rich and sensitive account of what happens to women deprived of choices in love and work. After that, I knew I wanted more Gissing. So I found my way to *New Grub Street*, which I was able to obtain only secondhand, through an online bookseller.

New Grub Street is probably Gissing's best-known work today, although it's hard to find anyone who's read it, even lovers of Victorian literature. This a great shame, and surprising, too, for Gissing has Dickens's knack for comic caricature, Eliot's psychological insight, and Edith Wharton's understanding of class. If you're a writer who's ever felt sucky about your pitiful advances, the lack of reviews for your books, or your inability to place your literary work altogether, you will finish reading *New Grub Street* feeling much, much better. Because in the Golden Age of the Novel, things were actually much, much worse.

New Grub Street centers around two very different writers: Edwin Reardon, a talented writer of lyrical, psychological, rather plotless novels, and his friend Jasper Milvain, whose ambition is to become a sought-after and financially comfortable writer of reviews and articles about other people's books (he knows very well that fiction doesn't pay). The novel opens as it is dawning on Reardon that he has made a terrible mistake with his recent marriage. His first two novels were critical successes, but the income from them, enough to support him when he was on his own, will not stretch to keep a wife and young child fed and warm through the long, chilly London winters. His wife, Amy, doesn't understand why Reardon can't just write a potboiler and make a whole lot of money, and her disapproval and growing coldness deeply wound Reardon and eventually undermine his ability to write at all. The numerous, agonizingly detailed passages about Reardon's alternating writer's block and grim, forced attempts to write something the public will find "sensational" are some of the most frightening a fellow writer can read. Gissing recognized that for an artist the greatest terror is the fleeing of the muse or, as he puts it, the "outwearied imagination." Financial anxiety, he suggests, is one of the fastest routes to that exhaustion.

Meanwhile, his counterpart, Milvain, who enjoys boasting about how shallow and venal he is, is steadily rising in reputation. Milvain knows how the literary world really works. He understands that its mechanisms are primarily social, and so he has to court important editors and silly benefactresses and praise books he dislikes. As he explains it, even a good book "will more likely than not . . . be swamped in the flood of literature that pours forth week after week . . . If a writer has friends connected with the press, it is the plain duty of those friends to do their utmost to help him. What matter if they exaggerate, or even lie? The simple, sober truth has no chance whatever of being listened to." Milvain acknowledges that a "genius" may eventually be celebrated regardless, but *New Grub Street* is precisely a book about the problem of the nongenius writer, an effort to show what happens when the merely very talented make art in a thoroughly monetized culture.

Reardon's depression and escalating money troubles lead to the undoing of his marriage, conveyed with a dreadful intensity and inevitability that reminded me of two much more recent novels, Richard Yates's *Revolutionary Road* and Jonathan Franzen's *Freedom*. If Gissing has one point he wants to hammer home, it's that, in Reardon's words, "poverty degrades." It destroys love, work, and character. Otherwise decent, honest, and loving people become harsh and unprincipled for lack of money. Reardon grows withdrawn and frankly a bit unhinged; his similarly struggling colleagues torment their wives, turn to drink, commit suicide, or, if less devoted to their art, find solutions like Reardon's friend Whelpdale, who discovers he can make a bundle advising other people on how to write *their* novels. (*Tout ça change* . . .) The gentle and charming Biffen remains unmarried so as not to fall into the same difficulties as Reardon, then withers of loneliness. Always attentive to the particular problems of women, Gissing also shows, through the character of a grouchy critic's daughter, how sensitive and intelligent women writers were even less likely to make their way than their male peers.

Gissing knew the hardships of the writing life firsthand. While he seems in retrospect to be the success Reardon is not, publishing twenty-some novels before his early death at age forty-six, he did not experience himself as one. He was constantly strapped for money, given the draconian publishing arrangements of the time, under which writers sold the copyright to their works rather than earning royalties. Even when a book like *New Grub Street* went into extra printings, Gissing never saw a penny of the profit. His books received mixed reviews. He was under pressure, like Reardon, to write much and write quickly. His health was not good, and he had two terrible and distracting marriages.

While Gissing was resentful in life, he was generous as a novelist: Jasper Milvain, who could have been loathsome, has appeal and even his noble moments. It's clear that Gissing admired and even envied his character's vitality, optimism, and sheer instinct for survival. The ambiguity that animates every character makes *New Grub Street* not just a great, plotty read (there is also a love match beset by obstacles and a rich relative whose will offers surprises) but a novel of enduring interest. Gissing saw that men collude in their own failures and that the world needs its hustlers and finaglers as well as its oversensitive dreamers. Still, his message is unmistakable: there *are* no viable lives for the serious writer. Reading *New Grub Street* today, you can look at our culture of welfare benefits, free emergency-room visits, NEA grants, and MFA teaching jobs and say things are certainly better now. Or you can feel that the oppressive structures are still intact, the game is still rigged, failure still a near certainty, but that you've just spent several hours in the company of a writer and characters who *understand*. Either or both. I vote for both, which must be why I always close this dark, rather bitter novel feeling remarkably cheerful.

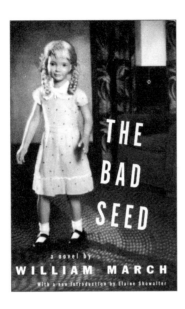

ON WILLIAM MARCH'S
The Bad Seed

SUSAN SCARF MERRELL

Ah, Rhoda Penmark. As much as I enjoyed reading your story, I hope never to meet anyone like you.

Like many writers, I'm tuned in to emotional nuance, to body language and tone of voice, the eye shift that reveals discomfort or the pause for calculation before a lie, and how that pause differs from the silence before a truthful revelation. For me, the sociopath is an alien form: to be utterly without conscience, so that one's evil is unreadable even to the vigilant, highly attuned observer—well, that's more unthinkable than any Borgesian creation. I'd like to believe that I would recognize pretty Rhoda Penmark, of William

March's 1954 novel, *The Bad Seed*, as the truly sociopathic little murderess she is, both remorseless and ladylike. But I suspect I wouldn't. Almost everyone, readers and fellow fictional characters alike, misreads her single-mindedness. She's not deceptive. She just is. And what she is makes *The Bad Seed* an extraordinary read.

With charming dimples, excellent manners, and neat brown braids "looped back into two thin hangman-nooses," Rhoda has to be one of the creepiest protagonists fiction has yet produced. Just eight years old, she is utterly pragmatic as she first drowns a little boy—he won a handwriting prize she felt she deserved—and then locks the handyman who suspects her of the crime into a basement room before calmly setting the place on fire. The previous year, when she was only seven, an old lady who had promised to bequeath to Rhoda a crystal ball with a gold ring in it "somehow fell down the spiral backstairs and broke her neck." Moments afterward, Rhoda says, "'She promised me the little glass ball when she died. It's mine now, isn't it?'"

Um, I guess so.

Rhoda's creator, William March, seems to have been as troubled as the perverse and violent characters he invented: hostile to children, obsessed with the sex lives of others, and given to spying on strangers having amorous encounters in remote sections of Central Park. The critic Elaine Showalter describes him as a "mysterious, disturbed and disturbing presence in literary New York." Born into poverty in rural Alabama, he was the second eldest of what would be eleven siblings. Lacking formal education, March became a highly decorated Marine and went on to produce six novels and three short-story collections, most to critical acclaim but lackluster sales. *The Bad Seed*, March's last book, changed all that: it sold more than one million copies, was turned into a film and a stage play, and was nominated for the National Book Award. Unfortunately, March never knew. He died of a heart attack just a month following the book's publication, at the age of sixty.

The world of *The Bad Seed* is serene on the surface, but violence is the main subject of its conversation, even in upper-crust dining rooms—killings and theft and sexual violence are on everybody's minds. In such a culture, perhaps someone should be astute enough to grasp little Rhoda for who she is. But it seems, at least at first, that no one is. She makes people uneasy, especially children, but they are too polite to allow themselves even to consider what she might be capable of doing. One of the most brilliant aspects of this strange little novel is the way that the most psychologically aware characters as well as those expert in true crime are alike unable to grasp Rhoda's unique brand of evil. How ironic it is when the self-satisfied crime writer Reginald Tasker pompously lectures Rhoda's mother: "Good people are rarely suspicious." He tells her that "some murderers, particularly the distinguished ones who were going to make great names for themselves, usually started in childhood; they showed their genius early, just

as outstanding poets, mathematicians and musicians did."

March immersed himself in Freudian psychology, and the denial-laced development of Rhoda's mother's understanding of her daughter's true nature—and her biological contribution to it—reveals how completely he understood the way our minds slowly become able to grasp such realities: "Then, overwhelmed with guilt so powerful that it was not bearable, she walked about the room in nervous panic, her damp hands pressed together, as though imploring some remote implacable power to give her peace once more." It is impossible not to have sympathy for poor Mrs. Penmark.

Is there anything more disturbing than suspecting a child of evil? I can still picture the glee with which I once saw a child lob a stone at the face of his mother, who was taking too long to say goodbye to other adults at a playground. I wonder who that child grew up to be. I think most children toy with the question of their own potentials to do bad, and to do so willfully. Perhaps this is a developmental need as innate as coming to terms with the idea of death. But the possibility of a fundamentally evil child—that unthinkable combination of the tabula rasa and the innate corruption—well, that's the most fascinating. Because the existence of that kind of child begs the question whether there's anything at all we can do to determine how our children grow up, any way at all to escape the destiny of DNA. The scientist Francis Galton first raised this question in the

Victorian era; no one has as yet answered it definitively, but Rhoda's creator leans persuasively to nature over nurture.

Reviewers of his era deemed March, as Alistair Cooke put it, "the unrecognized genius of our time." Despite—or, perhaps, because of—his own tormented nature, March is a compassionate and fluid stylist, as seen in this early passage about Rhoda's mother: "It seemed to her suddenly that violence was an inescapable factor of the heart, perhaps the most important factor of all—an ineradicable thing that lay, like a bad seed, behind kindness, behind compassion, behind the embrace of love itself."

I'd like to promise you a happy ending to this taut little novel, but instead I'll simply recommend you find out what happens to Rhoda for yourself. March's dark humor, his deep connection to the perversity that lies beneath the surface in all of us, and his inherent understanding of our blindness to it make *The Bad Seed* an achingly disturbing read.

The definitive study of Alfred Hitchcock by François Truffaut
Revised Edition

ON FRANÇOIS TRUFFAUT'S

Hitchcock

COLIN FLEMING

Having gotten out of college thinking, *Now it is time to be a writer*, I inevitably ended up working a number of shit jobs. The one that was supposed to be my big step up, after an inglorious stint as a doorman, during which I was urinated on a couple of times, was managing a vintage movie poster business in Boston's North End.

The North End is Italian mob territory. Or it was, anyway. The mail orders were seemingly never ending at this "store" that did not allow walk-in traffic, and I'd often be there in the middle of the night, packing up posters and film-related books. There was a weird vibe to the place, which I attributed to working at three in the morning. Then I learned, courtesy of a book on one of the store's shelves that had some lurid title like *Mob Executions of the 1970s*, that the place in which I sat had been a mob hangout/planning spot where people were whacked from time to time. I left that aisle in a hurry, in search of books more soothing, which is to say—for me, anyway—filmic.

And that's how I came by my copy of François Truffaut's *Hitchcock*, from 1966, which my employee discount landed me for five bucks. The proprietor of the store, who knew a scam or two in terms of defrauding the government, told me that he had been instrumental in getting Truffaut, Hitchcock, and their translator, Helen G. Scott, together for the series of long conversations that comprise the book. *Of course*, I thought, *okay, whatever, guy*, but provenance did not matter to me once I started reading what I still maintain is one of the three or four indispensable works of the cinematic literary canon.

The premise is simple: Truffaut engages Hitchcock on each of the latter's films to date, asking questions about casting, cinematography, intention, and his thoughts on the success, or lack thereof, of each venture. Truffaut was already a cinematic stud by this point, with *The 400 Blows*, *Shoot the Piano Player*, and *Jules and Jim* in his back catalog, films you wouldn't expect would appeal to a director like Hitchcock, who cared about reaching a general audience rather than just the art-house set—a set that nonetheless fell in line anyway, such was the artistry of Hitchcock's films. More importantly, as perhaps the most passionate of cinephiles and a former film critic to rival James Agee, Truffaut is conceivably

Hitchcock's ideal viewer, someone who understands the notion of pure, absolute cinema: an art form in which the camera's eye controls exactly what the viewer experiences, a sort of visual shorthand fired off into the heart of the human condition.

This idea might seem foreign today, in the CGI era and its penchant for clunky exposition, but that's why a book like this is vital not only to film history but also to understanding how an artist might target and reach an audience, regardless of medium. Both directors bemoan how cinematic storytelling seemed to get lazy with the advent of sound, once you could take the camera out of the mix and have Character A declare a bit of missing plot to Character B. Hitchcock never does this, as Truffaut points out in one impressively specific reference after another, as if he has near total recall of Hitchcock's films, whether one of the stone-cold classics like *Psycho* or an overlooked effort like *The Lodger*. You have the impression that Truffaut is going to stand up and start offering high fives as he talks about how the camera, in the space of seconds, establishes the entire backstory for Jimmy Stewart's central character in *Rear Window*. At the same time, Truffaut can come off as something of a prick if you just jump into the middle of the book to see what's said about your favorite Hitchcock film. Reading it all the way through, though, you eventually realize that these are two guys who don't speak the same language but who are totally at ease saying negative things about each other, from time to time, in this bonhomous way with zero hurt feelings. There's no ego anywhere here, only a dogged need to explicate what makes a piece of cinema work and what makes it fail.

Hitchcock can get somewhat pervy on occasion (he talks about several of his actresses as though he had ordered them up from a local madam) and you almost have the feeling he'd like some time alone. Better yet are the moments when Hitchcock gets miffed—or pretends to, anyway—and you sense that class conflict is about to ensue, with Truffaut on the side of the lofty experimental set and Hitchcock thick in the populist middle of things.

"It seems to me that you want me to work for the art houses," Hitchcock sniffs during a discussion of his 1956 film, *The Wrong Man*.

"Of course not. I hope you'll forgive my insistence on the point," Truffaut counters, but it's evident that Hitchcock likes being challenged, and likes viewing Truffaut as his audience, albeit in a context far removed from how, we learn, he tended to view audience: not as one person, but as a potentially massive demographic of people, each of whom will get something out of a movie at his or her own particular level. And so long as there is something in a picture for everyone, a work can be limitless in terms of who can relate to it. For Hitchcock, this is the key tenet of any legitimate work of art that is intended, and deserves, to last.

For all of the talk of process shots, spot-on casting decisions, continuous takes, and ingenious little flourishes—like lighting a glass of milk from the inside, in one instance, thereby highlighting a potential murder weapon—this is a book that likewise understands what makes "the public ask itself, 'What will happen next,'" as Hitchcock puts it. There may be nothing more central to pure cinema, pure reading, pure art, and pure humanity than that fundamental need to know, based on what has been thought and felt up to that point. But if that doesn't do it for you, there are a number of discourses on necrophilia that get Hitchcock going in a way that suggests to Truffaut that it's probably best just to indulge him, which is what I did every time my old boss told me, after running his latest scam, that this book wouldn't have existed without his efforts.

ON BRUNO SCHULZ'S

The Street of Crocodiles

TRIPP READE

I read Bruno Schulz's 1937 book, *Sanatorium Under the Sign of the Hourglass*, in a college literature class on magical realism. It was nothing like the science fiction and fantasy that was then my preferred literary diet. Where was the action? The plot? The dialogue? And that language: gorgeous and Latinate, frightening, superheated; breaking rules, boundaries, and sense. This fellow from Eastern Europe hadn't gotten the memo that language is supposed to serve the story, that it should never draw attention to itself. Instead, his sentences perform circus acts on the page or take strange turns into forbidding domains, such as when the narrator, working his way down through the loam of a figurative forest in *Sanatorium*, finds that "among all the stories that crowd at the roots of spring, there is one that long ago passed into the ownership of the night and settled down forever at the bottom of the firmament as an eternal accompaniment and background to the starry spaces." Even something as simple as drawing with crayons quickly leads to the sublime: "And when I reached for blue paint, the reflection of a cobalt spring fell on all the windows along the street; the panes trembled, one after the other, full of azure and heavenly fire." Any given paragraph zooms from normal to odd to LSD-weird and back. One reads Schulz in a constant state of "What the—?"

Years passed before I encountered Schulz again, this time via his 1934 book, *Cinnamon Shops*, which I read under the title by which it was published in the West, *The Street of Crocodiles*. As with *Sanatorium*, Celina Wieniewska's translation is excellent—any better and Schulz's fiction would have to be treated as a controlled substance. And as with *Sanatorium*, Schulz defies realism. The inanimate does not behave; there are numerous examples of sorcerer's apprentice moments, as in a section titled "The Gale," when "darkness began to degenerate and ferment wildly. There began the black parliaments of saucepans, those verbose and inconclusive meetings, those gurglings of bottles, those stammerings of flagons. Until one night the regiments of saucepans and bottles rose under the empty roofs and marched in a great bulging mass against the city." This time, more attuned to language, I lingered over the sentences, circling back to reexamine passages and taking as long to read these 160 pages as I would books triple the length.

But despite my careful reading, questions persisted: What, exactly, was going on in these pages? Was this a novel, a story collection, or some exotic species of memoir? If I focused only on the action, my summaries sounded like minimalist stage directions:

Narrator walks with mother to visit his aunt's house, where a cousin shows him erotic photographs.

Father gets out of bed at night, uses chamber pot, empties it out the window.

Hardly the glam stuff of page-turners, or even of page-lingerers. And yet I reread this book in wonder, always searching for the source of the enchantment. Something momentous seems to be happening in Schulz's fiction, but it's not evident in what the characters are doing or saying.

For example, the drabness of the world in his work seems a disguise to be flung aside at a moment's notice. As the narrator—a version of Schulz throughout the text—looks for the ineffable in the dreary shops and alleys of town, any person, creature, or object along the way can become grist for the search. A tramp becomes a woodland deity. A theater curtain, reimagined as a night sky, billows, and "the tremor sailing across the large area of that sky . . . revealed the illusory character of that firmament, caused that vibration of reality which, in metaphysical moments, we experience as the glimmer of revelation."

That vibration of reality. This echoes Schulz's 1936 *Ars Poetica*, titled "The Mythologizing of Reality," in which he writes, "We usually regard the word as the shadow of reality, its symbol. The reverse of this statement would be more correct: reality is the shadow of the word." This moves us closer to the heart of Schulz's project, which is to transform the world via language and so create a place that is more conducive to miracle. Here is the writer as demiurge, at the beginning of all things, inscribing nothingness with the Word.

I find in these pages paragraph after paragraph of pure cognitive music. The way Schulz deploys his words triggers something symphonic in the mind, lightning spiderwebs of associations that carry far beyond the text. At one point in a section titled "The Night of the Great Season," the narrator fuses his family's shop during a busy day of trading and a new biblical landscape: "The walls of the shop disappeared under the powerful formations of that cosmogony of cloth, under its mountain ranges that rose in imposing massifs . . . Against that backdrop my father wandered among the folds and valleys of a fantastic Canaan."

"Cosmogony of cloth" brings me to an enraptured, contemplative stop, out of which I slowly wake and move on. There are Baal worshippers, righteous heavenly anger, and desert plateaus, until it seems that a magician has pulled a tablecloth from beneath the reader, revealing another story entirely.

In Schulz's work, language doesn't serve the story; language *is* the story, an incantation that merges exterior and interior realities, and in doing so re-creates his small hometown of Drogobych, Poland (now in the Ukraine). To do this, Schulz employs metaphor and simile by the acre, synesthesia, and personification, until the subjective world of the narrator overgrows and permeates the little town and his family's boardinghouse and cloth goods shop, and the reader stops trying to separate the fantastic from the real. Schulz's alter ego documents, from a vantage point years in the future, the life of his town and family and especially his father's quixotic, demented struggle against the forces of the mundane, his interrogation of God. Again and again, the fantastic conjured by his father is diminished by the everyday, only to rise again in another scheme: a sudden aviary; a lecture on form versus matter delivered to an assemblage of tailor's dummies, shop employees, and servants; and, in a superb example of how Schulz can walk the difficult line between the horrific and the humorous, a scientific experiment in which an uncle is reduced to the function of doorbell and house alarm.

Threaded amid all this world-making are glimpses of what is recognizable as domestic realism: the narrator is attracted to, and frightened by, the sexuality of Adela the housemaid; resents his mother because he believes she doesn't love his father; and has relatives who fascinate and repel him. These glimpses are quickly swept up in the next clash between the fabulous and the pedestrian. Yet they're also reminders that this is an autobiographical work, that far down, at the foundation of this book, back in the waning years of the nineteenth century and just past the threshold of the twentieth, we find Schulz as a child, memorizing Drogobych and his family for later transmutation.

Schulz's literary output consists of only the two slim books, a novella (included at the end of *Crocodiles*), and a translation of Kafka's *The Trial*. He did not survive World War II, victim of one of those banal atrocities the Nazis perpetrated by the millions: shot twice in the head by a Nazi officer because Schulz's pen-and-ink drawings were admired by the officer's rival. So ended one of the most original voices in fiction. And yet in his ability to transform the world, on the page and subsequently in the reader's mind, he endures, patiently waiting for the next person to hear his music and sit blinking in wonder. For me, no other writer's words cast deeper, stranger shadows.

TORCH SONG: BORN AGAIN

And off I went into the heart

of the great american business

my father stood there waving

on the shore his face like lincoln's

on the penny inside my pocket

.

Hours I'm beneath the river

staring as I do into the necks

the collars of the straphangers

we say deliver us to our pay dirt

the black silos of our hours

TORCH SONG: O BEAUTIFUL

In the dunes you photograph

a woman her alabaster teeth

it's record of the marram grass

the taproots binding the last

stitch of land to her hostage sea

·

Or he steals home with the guns

the butter it's slung in a bindle

over his shoulder & she his white

horse she stands like an umpire

& yelling you're out in the dust

WRITE THE BOOK YOU
WANT TO READ

Parul Sehgal

A Conversation with Chimamanda Ngozi Adichie

Sinclair Lewis wrote that "every compulsion is put upon writers to become safe, polite, obedient, and sterile." Few writers have so flagrantly flouted these pressures as Chimamanda Ngozi Adichie, the celebrated Nigerian author of *Half of a Yellow Sun* and *The Thing Around Your Neck*. Her new book, *Americanah*, will be published in May by Knopf and, like its predecessors, it's a thrilling and risky piece of writing that takes on taboos, shatters pieties, and combines forthright prose, subversive humor, and a ripping good story.

The fifth of six children, Adichie grew up in Nsukka, a university town in Nigeria, in a house once occupied by the celebrated Nigerian novelist Chinua Achebe, who became a great influence on her.

"It was Achebe's fiction that made me realize my own story could be in a book," she said in an interview with the *New York Times*. "When I started to write, I was writing Enid Blyton stories, even though I had never been to England. I didn't think it was possible for people like me to be in books."

Adichie studied medicine briefly and moved to the United States at nineteen, eventually receiving an MFA from Johns Hopkins. Her first novel, *Purple Hibiscus* (2003), was well received; her second, *Half*

of a Yellow Sun, was a sensation. An unflinching look at the horrors of the Biafran War of the 1960s, it earned her an Orange Prize and comparisons to Achebe. In 2008, she was awarded a MacArthur "genius grant."

"Here is a new writer endowed with the gift of the ancient storytellers," Achebe praised her. "She is fearless."

In *Americanah*, Adichie fearlessly takes on what is so euphemistically called "American race relations." Our heroine, Ifemelu, a Nigerian transplant to the United States, writes a blog, the tartly titled "Raceteenth or Various Observations about American Blacks (Those Formerly Known as Negroes) by a Non-American Black," in which she scrutinizes Obamamania, white privilege, the politics of black hair care, interracial relationships, and the allure and savagery of America.

Adichie and I chatted over e-mail.

PARUL SEHGAL: I just finished the book and find myself moping and missing Ifemulu beyond all reason. She feels terribly real to me. Where did she come from? More broadly, how do your characters announce themselves? As a gesture? A voice? An argument?

CHIMAMANDA NGOZI ADICHIE: All of those, and more. Sometimes a character just forms in my head; other times a character is based on somebody real (although the character often ends up being quite different from the "real" person). Ifemelu is a more interesting version of me. Both Ifemelu and Obinze are me, really.

PS: How so?

CNA: I think I have Ifemelu's questioning nature, Obinze's longing. Like them, I'm always looking to learn. A bit of a romantic, but I hide it well.

PS: Ifemelu is the "Americanah" of the title, yes? Can you unpack this term a bit?

CNA: It's a Nigerian (actually, perhaps more regional than national, it's more often used in the southeast, where I am from) way of referring to a person who affects Americanness in speech or manner, or a person who is (genuinely) Americanized, or a person who insists on her Americanness. It's not exactly a polite word, but it isn't derogatory either. It's playful.

PS: Obinze and Ifemelu are that real literary rara avis: a happy couple. With romantic happiness so difficult to render on the page, I very much admired how you made them come to life. Did you have models, literary or otherwise, for their relationship?

CNA: Well, I had the old and grand tradition of the Mills and Boon romance novels that I read as a teenager! More seriously, my vision as a writer is dark. I am more drawn to the melancholy, the sad, the nostalgic. And so I wanted to do something a little different. I wanted to write a love story, a love story that would be both unapologetic *and* believable.

PS: Let's stay on love a moment more. Ifemelu writes on her blog that the solution to the problem of race in America is romantic love: "real deep romantic love, the kind that twists you and wrings you out and makes you breathe through the nostrils of your beloved. And because that real deep romantic love is so rare, and because American society is set up to make it even rarer between American Black and American White, the problem of race in America will never be solved." Now, I find Ifemelu utterly persuasive and charming and— sometimes, I must confess—a bit of a bully. For all these reasons, I'm inclined to agree with her. Do you?

I think that race, as it has been constructed in America, makes it almost impossible for people of different races to have a real conversation about race.

CNA: I have been told that I am a benevolent bully, so I suppose Ifemelu gets that from me. I do agree with her, very much. I completely believe in the power of love. I think that race, as it has been constructed in America, makes it almost impossible for people of different races to have a real conversation about race, let alone understand how the other person feels. Storytelling helps. Storytelling can be an entry point.

PS: But why are we at such an impasse?

CNA: Race is, I think, the subject that Americans are most uncomfortable with. (Gender, class, sexual orientation, ethnicity, religion are not as uncomfortable.) This is an American generation raised with the mantra: DO NOT OFFEND. And often honesty about race becomes synonymous with offending someone.

PS: As an outsider (albeit one who's lived in the U.S. on and off since you were nineteen), did it feel like a risky topic to take on?

CNA: In a way, it did. I am more or less expected, or maybe permitted, to write about African pathology, but I don't think

I am expected to write about American pathology. But in other ways, it isn't very risky because I *am* a foreigner. I am a bit removed and there is a certain privilege in that remove.

PS: And this extends, I suppose, into how Americans write (or, rather, don't write) about race. As one character, the formidable Shan, points out, "You can't write an honest novel about race in this country . . . if you're going to write about race you have to make sure it's so lyrical and subtle that the reader who doesn't read between the lines won't even know it's about race. You know, a Proustian meditation, all watery and fuzzy that at the end just leaves you feeling watery and fuzzy." *Americanah* is an incredibly blunt book about race. You go deep into colorism, debates about "good hair," all sorts of inter- and intra-ethnic prejudices, how racism enrages, yes, but also plain exhausts. Tell me about taking on this subject and your approach.

CNA: I wanted very much to write an honest book. I knew I could have done it differently, in a way that was safer. I know the tropes. I know how race is supposed to be

> I'm now happily black and now don't mind being called a sister, but I do think that there are many ways of being black.

addressed, but I just wanted to write the kind of novel about race that I wanted to read. I do realize that there is a certain privilege in my position as an outsider, a foreigner, somebody who is not an American. I am really looking in from the outside. I became fascinated by race when I came to the U.S. I still am. I am fascinated by the many permutations of race, especially of blackness, since that is the identity I was assigned in America.

PS: You give Ifemelu a similar line: "How many other people had become black in America?" Was it a specific moment for you? Did you resent it? Embrace it?

CNA: At first I resented it. A few weeks into my stay in the U.S., an African American man in Brooklyn called me "sister," and I recoiled. I did not want to be mistaken for African American. I hadn't been long in the U.S., but I had already bought into the stereotypes associated with blackness. I didn't want to be black. I didn't yet realize that I really didn't have a choice. Then my resentment turned to acceptance. I read a lot of African American history. And if I had to choose a group of people whose collective story I most admire today, then it would be African Americans. The resilience and grace that many African Americans brought to a brutal and dehumanizing history is very moving to me. Sometimes race enrages me, sometimes it amuses me, sometimes it puzzles me. I'm now happily black and now don't mind being called a sister, but I do think that there are many ways of being black. And when I am in Nigeria, I never think of myself as black.

PS: I was very moved by your TED talk on the "single story," in which you describe how dangerous it is for one narrative to be told about a people or place, and how pernicious, in particular, has been the single story about Africa ("a place of beautiful landscapes, beautiful animals, and incomprehensible people, fighting senseless wars, dying of poverty and AIDS, unable to speak for themselves and waiting to be saved by a kind, white foreigner"). Your books, diverse as they are, all seem intent on undermining the single story—about Africa, certainly, but also about war, childhood, fathers, love. *Americanah* homes in on and complicates the single story of the immigrant. Obinze, a Nigerian immigrant in London, notes that Westerners "all understood the fleeing from war, from the kind of poverty that crushed human souls, but they would not understand the need to escape from the ominous lethargy of choicelessness." What do you mean by "choicelessness"? What are its wages?

CNA: I don't start out writing to challenge stereotypes. I think that can be as dangerous as starting out to "prove" stereotypes. And I say "dangerous" because fiction that starts off that way often ends up being contrived, burdened by its mission. I do think that simply writing in an emotionally truthful way automatically challenges the single story because it humanizes and complicates. And my constant reminder to myself is to be truthful.

I grew up in a very comfortable, even relatively privileged family. Yet I experienced my reality as one of limited choices: go to university, become a doctor, specialize, practice, marry. And then there was the competing idea of "abroad" as a place of endless possibility. Abroad, you could be anything. And I think it's that idea that drives the need among middle-class Africans to leave.

PS: Were there aspects of this book that were especially challenging or pleasurable to write?

CNA: The whole book was challenging to write. I still stare at the manuscript, thrilled and amazed that I actually finished writing this. I loved writing about black hair. I'm mildly obsessed with natural black hair.

PS: Why?

CNA: I stopped straightening my hair with relaxers more than ten years ago. At first I was just tired of relaxers burning my scalp and then I started to really like my natural hair. I began to learn, and am still learning, how to take care of it. Because I didn't know how to. When I was growing up, straightened hair was admired; natural hair was not. I loved getting my hair straightened with a hot comb and, when I was a teenager, with a relaxer. So I had no idea what to do with my hair. It's almost absurd, how much I now enjoy trying new potions and products. So in the novel I had to restrain myself because I really just wanted to make the whole book about natural hair!

One day, in Lagos, I ran out of my hair products and decided to try honey and olive oil on my wet kinky hair, and it left me with really soft coils and then I thought: *I have to put this in the novel!* There's also a growing natural hair community that is very active on YouTube and when the writing was not going well, I would spend hours watching these women demonstrate how to get the perfect twist-out or how to use a new shea butter product. And of course, hair is quite political for black women. At least for a certain segment of the educated middle class. People make assumptions based on hair. Which can be very funny. Like a woman with dreadlocks is somehow more "conscious," even "soulful." Not always true, needless to say!

PS: The dangers of the single story! I'm fascinated by your rendering of your white characters. They're an exasperating bunch— so casually cruel and ignorant—and yet they're never just foils. Tell me about creating such ambiguous characters. Were you consciously trying to avoid the single story about racism/what a racist looks like?

CNA: I think one of the problems with the language of race in America is how singular it can be. So a racist, in the public imagination, can be only one thing: racist. Which is why people will often say, "Oh, she's not racist, she's kind and she gives money to charity" or something, as though a person cannot be racist *and* kind. I love Curt and Kimberly, both of whom are based on real people, and don't think of them as racist. The racist characters, I hope, are human, even if they appear briefly, like the carpet cleaner, because, well, racists are human.

PS: I've noticed that you find all sorts of ways to smuggle literary criticism into your novels, not least because your fiction has always been full of writers and writing workshops and writing professors. In *Americanah*, Ifemelu notes (with some disdain) that her boyfriend, Blaine, loves "novels written by young and youngish men packed with *things*, a fascinating, confounding accumulation of brands and music and comic books and icons, with emotions skimmed over, and each sentence stylishly aware of its own stylishness." It's hard not to read this as you playfully commenting on contemporary American fiction. Can you tell us a bit about what you're seeing in recent writing; are there trends you do and don't respond to?

CNA: I suppose I *was* playfully commenting on American fiction. I think of literature as

a big house with many rooms of the same size, but each decorated very differently. Some rooms do not appeal to me, even though I can see—in an objective sense—their value. I am quite old-fashioned in my literary tastes. As a lover of fiction, I am drawn to social realism, psychological depth, character, and emotion. I love fiction that has something to say and doesn't, as it were, "hide behind art." I love novels that feel true, that are not self-conscious experiments. I read a lot of contemporary American fiction and find the writing admirable but often it says nothing about American life, is more about style than it is about substance (style very much matters, but I struggle to finish a novel that is all style and has nothing to say).

PS: So who do you love? Is there a writer you like that you didn't expect to care for? How about an up-and-coming or little-known writer you'd recommend?

CNA: Ama Ata Aidoo and Chinua Achebe are very important to me. I admire many contemporary writers: Claire Messud, Sigrid Nunez, Lorrie Moore, Edward St. Aubyn, Jamaica Kincaid, Amit Chaudhuri. I didn't think I would much care for Sam Lipsyte's work, it didn't sound like my sort of thing, then I read his work and admired and enjoyed it very much. Up-and-coming writer I admire: Danielle Evans.

PS: A few novels conspicuously appear in *Americanah* and act as counterpoints, notably Graham Greene's *The End of the Affair* and *The Heart of the Matter*, his 1948 novel about an English couple settling in—and coming apart—in Sierra Leone. Does Greene have special significance to you?

CNA: I love both novels. *The Heart of the Matter* is close to my idea of a perfect novel. It is beautifully written and has a wonderful grave quality.

PS: Ifemelu writes a blog about race that has a vast and very engaged readership. You're read so widely and deeply here and in Nigeria, and I suspect you know something of what it's like to write for such an audience. What's it like?

CNA: It's wonderful to be read because that is the hope that drives writing—otherwise, why publish? Sometimes it's almost frightening as well. I haven't lost my sense of wonder. I once got on a plane in Nigeria and quite a few people on the flight were reading my novel and I was simply thrilled. But I don't think consciously of my audience when I write. I am very afraid of self-censorship, and I think it happens unconsciously when you become too aware of your audience. I also don't read reviews, because I am worried that I might "respond" to reviews when I write.

PS: It's fascinating to juxtapose *Americanah* with *Half of a Yellow Sun*, with its rigorous research into a suppressed history. By contrast, *Americanah* feels ruthlessly of this moment. You seem to be writing history as it happens (e.g., Obama's inauguration). Was this freeing? Terrifying? And are you one of those writers who writes to figure out how you feel about something or do you come to the page with your conclusions formed?

CNA: Both. (I love "ruthlessly of this moment.") I do know how I feel about race in a macro way, but I don't always know how I feel in a micro way, and writing fiction about it is my way of exploring, questioning, even learning.

PS: What are your days like now that this novel is complete? Do you plunge into a new project or do you rest?

CNA: I mope. I read—fashion magazines, in particular.

PS: What's coming down the pike?

CNA: Peplums are not going away, which I'm pleased about because I love peplums. And I notice some silly trends, like long shorts, that don't flatter anybody. I find women's magazines fascinating and very entertaining. I keep thinking: Do the women writing this actually believe themselves? What average woman wants to try neon orange eye shadow? ⚜

Camille Dungy

WHAT I KNOW I CANNOT SAY

We sailed to Angel Island, and for several hours
I did not think of you. When I couldn't stop myself, finally,
from thinking of you, it was not really you but the trees,
not really the trees but their strange little pods, blooming
for a little while longer, a bloom more like the final fringed fan
at the tip of a peacock's tail than anything I'd call a flower,
and so I was thinking about flowers and what we value
in a flower more than I was thinking of the island or its trees,
and much more than I was thinking of you. Recursive language
ties us together, linguists say. I am heading down this road.
I am heading down this road despite the caution signs
and the narrow shoulders. I am heading down the curvy road
despite the caution signs and the narrow shoulders
because that guy I fell in love with once lived somewhere near. Right there,
that is an example of recursive language. Every language,
nearly every language, in the world demands recursion.
Few things bring us together more than our need to spell out
our intentions, which helps explain the early 20th-century
Chinese prisoners who scratched poems into walls on Angel Island,
and why a Polish detainee wrote his mother's name in 1922. I was here,
they wanted to tell us, and by here they meant the island
and they also meant the world. And by the island, they meant
the world they knew, and they also meant the world they left
and the world they wanted to believe could be theirs, the world they knew
required passwords. Think of the Angel Island Immigration Station as purgatory,

the guide explained. He told tales of paper fathers, picture brides,
the fabrications of familiarity so many lives depended on. Inquiries
demanded consistency despite the complications of interpretation.
In English one would ask: How many windows were in your house
in the village? How many ducks did you keep? What is the shape
of the birthmark on your father's left cheek? In Japanese, Chinese,
Danish, Punjabi, the other answered. Then it all had to come back
to English. The ocean is wide and treacherous between one
home and the other. There can be no turning back, no correction
once what is said is said. Who can blame the Chinese detainees
who carved poems deep into the wood on Angel Island's walls.
Who can blame the Salvadoran who etched his village's name.
Few things tie us together more than our need to dig up the right words
to justify ourselves. Travelers and students, we sailed into the bay,
disembarked on Angel Island. I didn't think about you all day,
which is to say, the blue gum eucalyptus is considered a threat,
though we brought it across oceans to help us. Desired first for its timber,
because it grows quickly and so was expected to provide a practical fortune,
and when it did not, enlisted as a windbreak, desired still
because it is fast growing and practical, the blue gum has colonized
the California coastal forests, squeezing out native plants, dominating
the landscape, and increasing the danger of fires. I should hate
the blue gum eucalyptus, but from the well of their longing,
by which I mean to say from their pods, you know what I mean
I hope, their original homes, from the well of their longing
blooms explode like fireworks, and I love them for this. Do you hear me?
I absolve you. You are far too beautiful and singular to blame.

Trust

"We're just practicing," says Tina.

"We're just playing," says Rainey.

"We're just taking a walk."

"Yeah, but we're walking behind *them*," says Rainey. She and Tina have turned right about twenty feet behind a couple who lean into each other, slowly strolling, and here is something Rainey has noticed: couples don't attend to their surroundings the way solo walkers do. She wonders if the gun in her purse has a magnetic pull, if it wants to be near people.

"We're losing them," says Tina.

They're playing robber girls. Before they took the gun out for a walk, she and Tina were up in Rainey's room tying scarves around their heads to disguise their hair. They put on cheap lime green earrings from Fourteenth Street to take attention off their features, and T-shirts from Gordy's room to hide their own tops.

Dylan Landis

Gordy Vine lives in the West Tenth Street townhouse too, in the room next door to Rainey's. He is Rainey's father's best friend and a horn player, and he is as pale as the moon. His eyes are blue, but his hair is the color of milk. Gordy says shit like *You don't need to understand jazz. You are jazz.* The earrings and T-shirts will go in the trash right afterward, that's the idea.

Would go. They're just playing.

The man and the woman amble on through the purpling evening, walking single file past the trees that encroach on the sidewalk.

"Gordy didn't mind you going through his stuff, huh?" Tina's T-shirt says *Larry Coryell* on the front and *The Eleventh House* on the back. Rainey's says *Chick Corea.* Hers is signed.

Rainey regards Tina as they walk. She wonders if the question is loaded. Tina is the only person on earth whom Rainey has told about Gordy's night visits. But they are best friends. Tina must not mean anything. Plus, Rainey doesn't want to be what her father calls *those eggshell people.*

She says, guardedly, "If he figures it out, he'll be pissed. But he might not. I'm never in his room."

Ahead of them, the couple slows to look up at the window of a townhouse, and Rainey stalls by bending over to retie her sneaker lace.

Tina makes a little smirk-sound in her nose. "Yeah, why would you be," she says. "He gets into *your* room every night." Her face darkens. Her hand fastens to her mouth. "Oh, no," she says through her fingers. "I fucked up. It just came out. I'm sorry, Rain."

Inside Rainey's purse, the gun beats like a heart. Its workings are a mystery. She and Tina were afraid to check if it had bullets because of the little lever that looks like another trigger. Rainey thinks the round part might be called a *chamber*, which sounds romantic.

"It's okay," says Rainey, not breathing. What else is it her father says? *Fuck 'em if they can't take a joke.*

Through the darkness that drapes them all, she studies the woman who walks ahead of them. She's tucked her sleek hair into her collar, implying some magnificent length—*Like mine*, thinks Rainey—and she wears Frye boots, which make a lovely, horsey click on the sidewalk. It's not enough for this chick to hold the man's hand; she has to nestle both of their hands into the pocket of his leather jacket, a gesture that irritates Rainey and makes her think, bizarrely, of the airlessness of that pocket, of lying under her quilt at night, waiting to see if her door will open, and faking sleep.

How do you say no to an innocent back rub? She has asked Tina that.

"Do you *want* to say no?" Tina asked back, and Rainey wanted to sock her.

"It's not okay," says Tina. "I can read you. It was a shitty joke, Rain. It just came out. I don't know why."

As they walk on, Rainey can see what the man and woman stopped to admire: a red room hung floor to ceiling with paintings. "Really," says Rainey. "It's okay." She smiles sweetly at Tina. It isn't clear who's being punished by the sweetness.

What kills her is the woman's extraordinary cape. It flaps serenely around her calves like a manta ray.

"Swear it's okay," says Tina.

"I swear." She is still smiling and it is like smiling at Tina from across a long bridge. Rainey ought to get over it—seriously, fuck her if she can't take a joke.

> Inside Rainey's purse, the gun beats like a heart. Its workings are a mystery.

Tina exhales. "Okay." They both watch the couple for a moment. Then Tina says, "It's not like I need the money."

Rainey opens her mouth and closes it. She's tempted to make a crack but she holds it in. Tina goes on about her grandmother a lot—how she gets paid to live with her. How she can't bring anyone home because the grandmother doesn't like strangers. How the grandmother is blind. Best friends for five years and Tina has never invited Rainey home, so Rainey's not buying. She's never probed, though. Tina might detonate, or cry.

They've sped up, and now Rainey slows, partly so their footsteps won't be heard, but partly because she is pissed off and wants to consider the ramifications—that she *is* one of those eggshell people and fuck her because she cannot take this particular joke, and she suddenly has had it with the twenty-dollars-a-week grandmother story, because Tina has never had a twenty in her pocket once. A perverse urge to find the fuse in Tina rises up in her. And it would be so easy. Tina is like one of those sea corals they saw in a bio class movie that plant themselves any damn where they please, but close up tight as a fist when brushed by something they mistrust. In fact the only thing they do trust is this one fish called a clown fish. Rainey isn't anyone's goddamn clown fish.

She says, "I know, Tina. You get twenty dollars a week to live with your grandmother."

Tina looks at her slantwise and reaches deep into the bag on Rainey's shoulder—for the gun, Rainey thinks crazily, but it is only for the pack of Marlboros.

"Check out that cape," says Rainey. "That's mine."

"What's that supposed to mean, about my grandmother?" Tina lights a cigarette and drops the pack back in the bag.

Rainey wonders if she should be reeling Tina in right now, since they are playing robber girls. Besides, the grandmother is sacred territory. Rainey knows that without being told. Tina is tougher than Rainey but she is also easier to hurt. She knows *that* without being told. Rainey listens to the slow, steady hoofbeat of the Frye boots, satisfying as a pulse. Can you rob someone of her boots and cape? It's okay to think these things, because they are just playing. They will veer off any minute. The woman looks back, appraises them with a glance, and dismisses them.

> The man is handsome, his hair dark and thick, the shape of his head suggesting broad cheekbones that ride high.

"I asked you what it means about my grandmother," says Tina.

"It means your cup runneth over." Rainey uses her musical voice. "If you're getting twenty dollars a week."

"I don't have a cup." Tina's voice is low. "I have a savings account. I'm not supposed to touch it."

"You must be rolling."

Now Rainey too reaches for the cigarettes, which they jointly own, and lets her knuckles bump the gun. "What bank?" She's ultracasual. The gun is cold and bumpy and could shoot off her foot, but the weight of it feels good. Already she knows she will stash it at the bottom of her school backpack, with her picture of Saint Catherine of Bologna, patroness of artists.

"What *bank*? What is this, a fucking quiz? You don't believe me," says Tina. Reflexively, she passes over her cigarette so Rainey can light hers.

"I want that cape, Teen."

The couple turns left on Greenwich, walks a block, and crosses Barrow. Then they turn right on Morton. Rainey and Tina pick up their pace and fall back again, spooling out distance like kite string. It's perfect; they're all headed closer to the Hudson, where only true Villagers live and tourists rarely stray. Even from a half block back Rainey knows the man is handsome, his hair dark and thick, the shape of his head suggesting broad cheekbones that ride high. Rainey wants this man to desire her even as he looks at the gun and fears her. If she can make him desire her, she'll erase the feeling of Gordy's fingers where they don't belong, where he can still call it a back rub when he makes his night visits. Right now the feeling is like a dent at the edge of her left breast. It's a pressure along her neck where he starts stroking her long hair. She wants the cape, and she wants some other things that the man and the woman have. The money doesn't interest her.

"I have over a thousand dollars in Marine Midland Bank," says Tina.

"I'm going to take her cape," Rainey says. "You can have all their bread."

"If you don't believe me," says Tina, "I'm not taking another step."

"Oh?" says Rainey in the dangerously charming voice she saves for the final minutes with a victim in the girls' room. "Do you really live with your grandmother? Or do you just not want me to meet your family?"

Tina stops. *Let her*, thinks Rainey, *she won't stop long.* She keeps walking. By the time she makes half of Morton Street by herself she is trying not to trudge; she is missing Tina acutely, missing the way she bumps into her sometimes, the slight brushing of her jacket sleeve. Tina doesn't go in for hugging but she finds other ways to make contact, the affectionate shove, the French braiding of each other's hair, touching the hand that holds the match—anything that can't be called lezzy, which suits Rainey fine. At school there are teachers who insist they sit on opposite sides of the classroom, who make them play on separate teams: Rainey Royal and Tina Dial. When Rainey finally hears Tina approaching at a scuffing trot, she stops and waits, happy and faintly ashamed.

Tina says, "Gimme the goddamn bag, Rain."

Rainey passes it over. She waits to see if Tina is going to detonate and what that will look like. She waits to see if Tina can take a joke.

"I'm sorry, Teen."

Tina looks into the bag as she cradles it in front of her, and Rainey knows she is looking at the darkly radiant gun, a gun Rainey stole from her father's filing cabinet days earlier after one of his obnoxious sex talks. She's spent a lot of secret time in Howard Royal's room. She's excavated the postcards her mother sends from the ashram. She's stolen family photos from Howard's albums, one at a time. She's found boxes of Ramses and a pair of leopard-print underwear for men and the dispensers of birth-control pills from which Howard administers one pill every morning. *I know what girls your age are doing.* She hates those talks, Howard loosely strung across a brocade parlor chair while she's curled into her carapace to hide her breasts.

"I believe you," says Rainey. "I do."

In addition to the gun, Rainey stole her birth certificate from a file marked "Legal." *Rainey Ann Royal.* Who the fuck picked Ann, anyway? A girl named Ann would dance badly and her hip-huggers wouldn't hug. If anyone kissed her, she'd wonder where the noses go. In dodgeball, if you were feeling mean, Ann would be the girl whose anxious face you'd aim for.

Maybe *Ann* is the reason her mother left.

No one knows Rainey's middle name, not even Tina, and she knows every single other thing about Rainey. Tina knows it is a lie when Rainey says she plays jazz flute. She knows it is true that Rainey technically may have lost it to her father's best friend. She knows it is a lie that Rainey will move to the ashram when she is sixteen. She knows all this, and she doesn't judge.

Ahead, near the corner of Washington, the couple sits on a townhouse stoop. They kiss and lean into each other.

"She's blind," says Tina. It takes Rainey a second to realize they are still talking about the grandmother. "I *told* you." They are standing less than half a block from the couple, watching obliquely. The man lights two cigarettes and passes one to the woman. Maybe they are just playing too, playing at being robbed, Rainey thinks. The man glances up the sidewalk and watches Rainey and Tina, still in conference.

"I get it," says Rainey. "I believe you. I get it, Teen."

They resume a slow walk toward the townhouse stoop. Rainey could swear she hears Tina thinking hard in her direction. She could swear she hears something like *I'm lying, she's not blind. The twenty dollars, that's bullshit too,* and Rainey thinks back, *It's okay, Teen, I love you anyway, and we're going to just walk by these people, right?* and she hears Tina think, *Of course we are, we're just playing* when Tina drops her hand into the bag and says, "You don't get anything."

They are about a quarter block away. Less.

Alarmed, Rainey looks straight at the beautiful leonine man. "Don't do it," she says in a low voice. And then, because she knows it is too late, because it is not in her control and because she wants to do it too, she whispers, "Don't hurt anyone."

Now the woman looks up. In about fifteen steps, if they keep walking, Rainey and Tina will reach the man and the woman on the townhouse stoop.

They keep walking, slowly.

Tina whispers, "There a safety, right? That's what it's for, right?" Her elbow is cocked, it's obvious she's about to draw something out of the bag, and now they are right there, steps from the man and the woman sitting and smoking on the townhouse stoop, and Rainey has no idea if there's a safety or what a gun was doing in Howard's filing cabinet. She wants the man to look at her and lose all awareness of everything that is not Rainey, and he is, now, looking at her, but with the wrong expression. Quizzical. He looks quizzical, and the woman is checking his face to see what's changed. Tina stops. Rainey stops behind her. She has no idea what will happen if Tina steps any closer and the man twists her wrist so that the gun falls to the sidewalk and explodes, shooting someone in the ankle. She does want that softly gliding cape, which she will wear to school, inciting fabulous waves of jealousy.

She could go somewhere around the treetops and look down from there. It's a gift she has, one she likes to think her mother left her. The moment hurtles toward them. She has to decide fast. Tina faces the woman as if she were going to ask her directions. Her two hands shake around the gun, which is abruptly half out of the bag.

> She has no idea what will happen if Tina steps any closer and the man twists her wrist so that the gun falls to the sidewalk and explodes.

"This is a stickup," she says, trembling, her voice hoarse, and Rainey is far from the treetops, she is right there, feeling the concrete through her shoes.

The woman claps a hand over her mouth, stopping a laugh. "Central casting," she whispers from under her hand.

"The gun's real," says the man. "Shut up, Estelle." Rainey has no idea what *wuthering* means, but she thinks he must have that kind of face: brooding and gorgeous, from some dreamy old novel.

"Yeah, shut up, Estelle." Tina sounds like she does in the girls' room but with an undertow of fear. "You guys live here or what?" Rainey feels the approaching moment thundering right up to her. She feels like someone who can take any kind of joke, now. She can't wait to find out what her job will be.

The man and the woman say no and yes at the exact same moment. "Take our wallets," says the man. "You don't have to hurt anyone."

"Be nice," says Tina. "Invite us up."

"If you're going to do anything do it here," says the man. Estelle's hand remains plastered to her mouth, but her eyes are rounded

Rainey feels ravenous for what is about to happen. The sidewalk is pushing through her shoes now. "I'm feeling kind of antsy down here," she says in a voice that sounds like smoke and jazz. She has it down. "Take us upstairs, baby," she tells the man.

Tina walks up to the stoop and jabs the gun against Estelle's knee. Saint Tina of the Girls' Room—are they really in the same place, doing the same thing? Is it possible that Tina feels purification as she does this bad act?

Rainey's father's words unspool from her body as if she is expelling a magician's silk scarf: *They talk about this at school, don't they? How girls your age are approaching the height of their sexual powers?* She feels the nape of her neck sealing itself against Gordy's hand, and she looks at Estelle's neck with rising irritation.

"Okay okay okay okay okay," says Estelle, and gets up fast from the stoop.

"Hey, listen," says Rainey, batting Tina on the arm. She almost says her name but catches herself. "I totally believe you. I do. I had one crazy moment of doubt but it's over. I'm sorry." She watches as Tina closely scans her face as if she's not sure she's seen it before.

"You still think I'm bullshitting," says Tina, locking her gaze back onto the boyfriend and Estelle. "And you're still mad from what I said about Gordy."

Rainey is not afraid of Tina. She might be afraid of hurting Tina, though.

"I believe you to death," says Rainey. "And it's okay about Gordy. Come on. I'll prove it. Let's do something crazy."

"Oh my God," says Estelle. "Oh God oh God oh God."

> Tina holds the gun close to her own side, aimed at Estelle. "Oh, we can't wait to see your apartment," she says in a pretend-guest voice.

The brick building's entry hall is lit with bare bulbs and its stairs are thickly carpeted. Glossy black doors, greenish walls—Rainey feels like she is at the bottom of a fish tank. "Go," says Tina harshly, and the man looks at her jamming her purse, with the gun half in it, into Estelle's back. "Don't touch her," he says, and immediately starts up the stairs. Rainey listens for sounds from other tenants and hears none. "I'm aiming right at Estelle's spine," says Tina, and while it seems to Rainey that the man could lunge back down the stairs at them, it also seems that the word *spine* sounds menacingly like bone porcelain, and she is not afraid.

They climb, first him, then Estelle and Tina in a kind of lockstep, then Rainey, the shag carpeting hushing their progress, till the man stops at a door on the third floor and Estelle sags against it. She says, "You don't have to come in. You could just turn around. We'll give you everything."

Tina holds the gun close to her own side, aimed at Estelle. "Oh, we can't wait to see your apartment," she says in a pretend-guest voice.

Rainey holds her hand out for both sets of keys; she senses Estelle and the boyfriend trying not to touch her palm. It makes her powers grow, holding their keys and key chains: such intimate objects. She opens the shiny black door, feels for a switch, and turns on the light.

"You're not *kidding* we want to see it," she says.

The apartment, a large studio with two tall windows, is painted a deep violet, as if an intense twilight has settled. In contrast, the trim and furnishings—a bureau, a table with chairs, and a curvaceous bedframe—are painted bridal white. Rainey can't believe it. She walks down a violet hall into which a Pullman kitchen is notched, flicking on lights as she goes. At the end, she opens the door to a violet bath. She wants to steal all the walls.

Behind her, she hears Tina telling the boyfriend and Estelle to sit on the bed, and how far apart.

"What color is this?" she calls from the bathroom, where the white shower curtain manages to look like a wedding gown against the violet walls.

"I mixed it." Estelle is breathing hard. "I'm a set designer."

Rainey walks back down the hall into the main room and props herself against a white dining chair. Tina moves cautiously around the room, always watching Estelle and the boyfriend, lifting small objects off the mantel and nightstands and amassing a little pile of goods on the hearth. Rolls of coins. Earrings. The gun never wavers. Rainey asks Estelle, "Yeah, but what do you *call* it, this color?"

"Amethyst," says Estelle. "It's a glaze."

"It's incredible," says Rainey. "It's the most beautiful color I've ever seen."

Estelle hugs herself and shivers. "Please point that somewhere else," she asks Tina. "I swear I won't do anything."

"God, I love this place," says Rainey. "Would you light me a cigarette? And may I have your cape, please?"

Rainey watches Tina collect sixty-three dollars from the two wallets tossed on the table and a fistful of earrings from a bureau drawer. It takes Tina only a minute. The gun never wavers and she never stops watching Estelle and the boyfriend. She jams her prizes in the pocket of the boyfriend's leather jacket, which she is now wearing. Then she positions herself by the white marble hearth. Estelle and the boyfriend are not playing at being robbed. They sit on the edge of the bed about as far apart as they can while still holding hands—the holding hands was Tina's concession.

Glancing at Tina, Rainey catches sight of herself in the mirror over the hearth, luxuriant hair spilling out the back of the scarf. "Look at us," she says, giving Tina a light nudge. "Even with all this shit on, we're still cute. We should take a Polaroid. You got a Polaroid, Estelle?"

Tina keeps the gun aimed straight at Estelle as she turns quickly to look at herself in the mirror, then at Rainey. Her shoulders slump a little. She looks back at Estelle but says, "How can you tell it's still us?"

Rainey laughs. "You're tripping, right?" Tina shrugs. They both know she hasn't tried acid yet. "'Cause it looks like us," says Rainey. "Right?"

"I'm not sure," says Tina.

"You're on blotter," says Rainey, and waits for her to stop being spooky. Rainey once licked blotter off Gordy's palm and spent hours watching the walls quilt themselves exquisitely, kaleidoscopically.

"Who else would I think you are?" Rainey says. "Jimi Hendrix?"

"I know what Jimi Hendrix looks like. Don't move," she snaps at the boyfriend, who is edging closer to Estelle. "I *am* tripping," she says. "I don't recognize myself."

Rainey isn't sure she recognizes this Tina either, the one who sees a stranger in her own face. "Ever?"

"That would be retarded. I mean, with the scarf on."

It's Rainey's turn to *nosey around*, as her father would say. She takes her time. Tina's weirding her out. The nightstand alarm clock says they've been there only four minutes. Surely they can stay another four. She could swear that in the silence she can hear the clock whirr. The cape hangs heavy from her shoulders; it is too hot for the apartment but the weight feels terrific.

On a closet shelf she finds a stack of typed and handwritten letters rubber-banded in red. She takes it down and sets it aside on the bureau. "You don't want that," says Estelle, half rising. "It's old, it's just junk—"

"I don't always recognize people on TV, either," says Tina. "Or at school. You think there's something wrong with me?"

"Yes." Rainey goes back to the hallway Pullman kitchen for a pair of shears.

"Well, then fuck you," calls Tina.

"But there's plenty of shit wrong with me too," says Rainey, walking back in with the scissors.

Rainey snips buttons from Estelle's blouses, lace and ribbons from her nightgowns. She puts those on the bureau with the letters. "In winter?" says Tina. "When you put a hat on? I'm not a hundred percent sure it's you till you say something." She takes a deep breath and locks it up somewhere for awhile. "At least I always know my grandmother." She smiles; it's a private, knowing smile. Rainey could almost swear there's pride in it.

She bites her lip. She prowls the room more aggressively. She finds two photo albums at the foot of the hearth and begins robbing them of photographs. "Not my father," says Estelle, and starts to cry. "Not my grandfather."

"Who is this?" Rainey holds up a square color photo of a woman pretending to vamp in a one-piece bathing suit. Her smile is playful, as if she is somebody's mother who would never really, actually vamp. Mothers interest Rainey: their presence, their absence, the way they react to the heat waves her body gives off in the proximity of their husbands and sons.

"No one," says Estelle.

Rainey adds it to the stack. Estelle makes a high-pitched sound in her throat. Rainey, moving on, seizes two black journals from a nightstand drawer.

"Oh my God, no," says Estelle, but then she looks at Tina and the gun and closes her eyes.

> She finds two photo albums at the foot of the hearth and begins robbing them of photographs.

Rainey turns abruptly to face Tina. "Look," she says, "if you ever don't know who someone is, just ask me, okay?"

"Do you think I'm crazy?"

"Just ask me."

"Are we okay?"

Rainey sighs like of course they're okay, but she still hears it. *He gets into your room every night.*

"Do you think I have schizophrenia?"

"Just *ask* me," Rainey says.

She goes down the hall again, cape flapping behind her; she salvages a grocery bag from under the sink, unclips the receiver from the hallway wall phone and drops that in first. Then she drops in the letters, the cuttings, the photos, and the journals that she has piled on the bureau. The door lock, miraculously, requires a key on each side. She and Tina can actually lock these people in.

"Who's the woman in the photo?" demands Rainey.

Estelle, crying, just shakes her head.

"Take my watch," the boyfriend tells Tina. "Leave her papers and take my watch. You'll get fifty dollars for it, I swear."

"Thanks," says Tina, as if startled by his generosity. She makes him give it to Estelle, who holds it out, shrinking from the gun.

"The papers?" he says. But Tina's admiring the watch in quick glances, and Rainey's lost in a vision. She sees a tapestry made from scraps of handwriting and snippets of photos, tiny telegrams from the heart: patches of letters, strips of confessions, grainy faces of people who have, in one way or another, perhaps like her mother, split. She'll sew buttons at the intersections, layer in some lace. In Rainey's hands, such things will reassemble themselves into patterns as complex as snowflakes. She will start the tapestry tonight, in her pink room. What would Estelle do with this ephemera anyway, besides keep it closeted away?

"You have Paul's watch," whispers Estelle. "Can I have my papers?"

"Oh, it's Paul?" Rainey looks at the boyfriend. "I don't have Paul's watch." She swirls the cape and turns theatrically to Tina, who appears delicate in the leather jacket. "You have the watch, right?" Rainey sighs dramatically and runs her hands down the curves of her body, staring at Paul, who looks back at her with the directness of someone who respects the gun too much to move, but is not exactly afraid. This intrigues Rainey tremendously.

"I thought Paul would like me better, but *she* got the watch, so apparently not." She's just playing, but it seems to her that Tina looks at her sharply. "Listen," she says to Tina, "let's go. I'm great. I have every single thing I need."

She is surprised to see hurt flash across Tina's eyes.

"You're great?" says Tina. "Why are you great? What've you got that you need?"

Paul sits forward with interest.

"Shut up," says Tina, though he hasn't said anything.

"Don't," says Rainey. She is holding her grocery bag with one arm and has her left hand on the doorknob. "I said I believe you. Let's go." But Tina remains plastered to the hearth.

"What've you got that you need?" says Tina. When Rainey doesn't answer, she says, "What? You've got an albino freak who—" She stops, possibly because Rainey is staring her down, possibly out of restraint.

"An albino freak who *what*?" says Paul.

Rainey looks at Tina, flaming against the amethyst walls, radiant in her distress. She feels the gaze of Paul upon her, and she flushes. "I have everything I need *from this apartment*," she says, as if talking to someone from a distant land.

"Oh." Tina visibly relaxes, as if warm water were being poured through her. "I don't." She turns a slow, thoughtful quarter circle, looking around the room.

"Oh no," says Estelle. "Please go. Please please please go."

"Get those scissors, would you?" says Tina, taking a few steps toward Estelle.

Rainey picks them up off the nightstand, where she'd set them down after taking souvenir snippets from Estelle's clothes, and swings them from one finger. "What are you going to do, cut her hair?"

Tina smiles. "No, you are."

"Really? Seriously"—again she almost says Tina's name—"what are you planning to do with her *hair*?"

"Same thing I was going to do without it," says Tina.

Estelle lets go of Paul's hand and clamps both her hands around her hair. "For Christ's sake," says Paul.

Rainey wonders if the gun belongs to Tina now. Estelle's hair belongs to Estelle, that much is true. "No," she says. "This is between me and you."

"You said everything was okay," Tina says. "You said you believed me. You said, 'I'll prove it.'"

"I think she's proven quite a bit," says Paul.

"Whose boyfriend are you? Be quiet," says Tina.

Rainey sets the grocery bag on the floor and puts her face in the bowl of her hands, scissors still dangling, so she can think. Tina is telling the truth now. It's Rainey who's lying: she does not believe a word about the grandmother, and things are not okay. She looks through her fingers from Estelle, who has wrapped her long hair protectively around her fist, to Tina, who waits to see if trust can be restored.

She almost asks again about the woman in the picture. It's the right moment: she holds the scissors and Tina holds the gun. Instead she takes a deep breath of amethyst air. "Forgive me," she says, and for a moment, while neither Tina nor Estelle knows whose forgiveness she requires, she feels nearly free.

"Here," she says. She bends over quickly, so the tie-dye scarf falls forward and the violet room swings back, grabs a thick sheaf of her own long, dark hair, and cuts. 🛡

THE TWINS

You know those twins hanging on the corner,
      they look so much like me and my twin brother,
but like us when we were younger, in our twenties,
      the paler one like me, sickly, more uptight,
but weirdly aristocratic, more distant
      than the one like you, Tim, the one that if
you were him would put his arm around me
      with that casualness and gentleness
I've always craved between us, which we
      nearly lost in our twenties but got back
in our fifties now that death's in my face
      when I look at it at just the right angle:
then your smile's so open, Tim, that we go
      back even further, to when we were
boys listening on the stairs to our older
      brother telling us about girls, what
you could do with them, what they'd do
      with you . . . not much like our board games
when all we'd think about was rolling
      the dice and moving the metal dog or battleship
round and round the squares, counting out loud,
      intent on winning . . . but these past few days
your eyes keep confronting me in the mirror,
      your glance full of a goofball happiness!

And the wreath of poppies around your head
       grazes my forehead too, and like the dope
I used to shoot, the clear dose in the syringe
       lets me down into my body like I'm deep
inside your body, the two of us together
       fed by the same blood, waking, sleeping,
nestled next to each other, thumbs in our mouths—
       but it only lasts a little while, this feeling
of me inside you inside that liquid warmth
       up the back of my neck and down toward
my cock, the high moving at its own sweet will—
       Tim, I'll only belong to you forever
when the other brother, the pale and stern
       and faceless one who holds the needle still
when I slide it into the vein and smiles back
       my smile, I'll only belong to him too when he,
in some parody of an old rocker in a crowd
       of old rockers holding up lit cigarette lighters,
snaps shut that flickering: Oh sure,
       to sleep is good, to die is even better,
but the best is never to have been born.

THE CRAZE

What could I say, a laborer, to the overseas geniuses?
That my father fought their war against the Japanese?

That the leisure class I served I aspired to, so I could join
the high G of the cello floating off, slowly vanishing

in a *pianissimo fermata*? Then nothing more,
silence and night? But this was California,

and soon the heat pump and water filter
would strain the water to such a blueness and temperature

that acid-washed LA would go swimming night and day,
the blue havens built by alambristas, union bricklayers, unskilled juvies

teaching me the Faustian accounting
of my employer, Bob "Just Call Me a Genius" Harrington:

Screw 'em out of this, screw 'em out of that,
but sweep up your mess and you'll get

away with murder. Sucking up the slurry of cement
and sand, the hose pulsed in the pit

of the parvenu, the ingenue, the Hollywood producers
and Van Nuys GM bosses whose assembly line crews

riveted my beat-up Firebird's body, Wolfman Jack's XERB
taking *another little piece of my heart now, baby,*

as I sprayed gunite on rebar ribs and the air compressor
pounded like the other *Firebird*: Stravinsky taking his temperature

in West Hollywood, Schoenberg watering his lawn in Brentwood,
Mann perched above the waves in Pacific Palisades

had also perused catalogs weighing concrete vs. vinyl
as blast caps detonated in holes the demmies drilled

and ash sifted down over my face and shoulders
to postwar twelve tone assaulting my ears.

But while I and my transistor radio worked ten hour days,
my father dreamt our own little South Seas grotto:

every weekend we rose to the promise of chlorination
as he and "us boys" dug trenches for our water lines,

hacked away the hillside to make our ice plant grow,
and rented the monster backhoe,

digging out the pool pit to rim it with lava stone
against the mud. My father waved the baton

of his shovel to light the fuse to the chord
of dynamited stone: the cloud of our need

went up all over California
and rang in overtones all through me.

THE TRICK BAG

I bury my head in
It & everything tastes

Electric. The sky sings
Jigsawed. Cotton candy

Fills the hollows behind
My eyes. There's a thunder-

Burst in my gut. A crowd
Circles me, snickering.

One crows, *What's up,*
Mister Monster? Another

Calls me *Baghead*.
The oilcloth does not

Fit perfectly, but these
Hard times have proven

It—I can get used
To almost any shade

Of doom. My elastic socks
Droop-sag. Inhaling

The perfect dark, I am just
Born. Inhaling the perfect

Dark, I'm slumber. Inhaling,
I'm so old I might never again see

Tomorrow. Inhaling, I am
Moonshine. Inhaling, I inhale.

On the other side of the eye-
Holes, the day unravels. The

Taunters bully & rage. Ropes
Of light slip through

The swaying grass.
The ground quakes,

A pleasure that climbs
Me, settles in my chest.

Whirling, my insides tilt.
I am a ramshackle palace.

The brightness, the din,
Like a car crash. Around me,

It's beautiful stuff—the little
Oblivions smearing as I go.

AFTER THE WORLD DID NOT END

I'm a big jellyfish,
All grown-assed—I can

Admit it now: I am
A gelatinous head

Inside of a head
That smells of spit-

Up diamonds that's
Been jammed inside

Another head that,
Most certainly,

In oftentimes slats
Of moonlight, looks

As if a mustache
Has been Sharpied

Above its lip.
SO WHAT if the years

Haven't taught me
How to hold

Another's hand,
Tenderly, or drink

Orange smoothies
From the skulls

Of my enemies?
My ribs don't cradle

Me right & maybe
I like feeling as if

I'm slipping out
Of the enormous hand

That's puppeting me
Upright. But when the baby

Cries & tears jewel
His cheek's fat

Ledges, I fit into
Myself with the burn

Of a dislocated
Elbow being reset.

Watching him
Sleep today I'm on

Fire. I want to
Rip deep holes

In my body & umbrella
Over him—welcome

His shallow breaths
Into me as he rocks

A clockwise circle,
Eyelids tremoring

With white-hot dreams.

Beer Trip to Llandudno

It was a pig of a day, as hot as we'd had, and we were down to our T-shirts taking off from Lime Street. This was a sight to behold—we were all of us biggish lads. It was Real Ale Club's July outing, a Saturday, and we'd had word of several good houses to be found in Llandudno. I was double-jobbing for Ale Club that year. I was in charge of publications and outings both. Which was controversial.

"Rhyl . . . We'll pass Rhyl, won't we?"

This was Mo.

"We'd have come over to Rhyl as kids," said Mo. "Ferry and coach. I remember the roller coasters."

"Never past Prestatyn, me," said Tom Neresford.

Tom N.—so-called; there were three Toms in Ale Club—rubbed at his belly in a worried way. There was sympathy for that. We all knew stomach trouble for a bugger.

Kevin Barry

"Down on its luck'd be my guess," said Everett Bell. "All these old North Wales resorts have suffered dreadfully, haven't they? Whole mob's gone off to bloody Laos on packages. Bloody Cambodia, bucket and spade."

Everett wasn't inclined to take the happy view of things. Billy Stroud, the ex-Marxist, had nothing to offer about Llandudno. Billy was involved with his timetables.

"Two minutes and fifty seconds late taking off," he said, as the train skirted the Toxteth estates. "This thing hits Llandudno for 1:55 PM, I'm an exotic dancer."

Aigburth station offered a clutch of young girls in their summer skimpies. Oiled flesh, unscarred tummies, and it wasn't yet noon. We groaned under our breaths. We'd taken on a crate of Marston's Old Familiar for the journey, 3.9 percent to volume. Outside, the estuary sulked away in terrific heat and Birkenhead shimmered across the water. Which wasn't like Birkenhead. I opened my *AA Illustrated Guide to Britain's Coast* and read from its entry on Llandudno:

"'A major resort of the North Wales coastline, it owes its well-planned streets and promenade to one Edward Mostyn, who, in the mid-nineteenth century—'"

"Victorian effort," said John Mosely. "Thought as much."

If there was a dad figure among us, it was Big John, with his know-it-all interruptions.

"'Who, in the mid-nineteenth century,'" I repeated, "'laid out a new town on former marshland below . . .'"

"They've built it on a marsh, have they?" said Everett Bell.

"TB," said Billy Stroud. "Marshy environment was considered healthful."

"Says here there's waterskiing available from Llandudno jetty."

"That'll be me," said Mo, and we all laughed.

Hot as pigs, but companionable, and the train was in Cheshire quick enough. We had dark feelings about Cheshire that summer. At the North West Beer Festival, in the spring, the Cheshire crew had come over a shade cocky. Just because they were chocka with half-beam pubs in pretty villages. Warrington lads were fine. We could take the Salford lot, even. But the Cheshire boys were arrogant and we sniffed as we passed through their country.

"A bloody suburb, essentially," said Everett.

"Chester's a regular shithole," said Mo.

"But you'd have to allow Delamere Forest is a nice walk?" said Tom N.

Eyebrows raised at this, Tom N. not being an obvious forest walker.

"You been lately, Tom? Nice walk?"

Tom nodded, all somber.

"Was out for a Christmas tree, actually," he said.

This brought gales of laughter. It is strange what comes over as hilarious when hangovers are general. We had the windows open to circulate what breeze there was. Billy Stroud had an earpiece in for the radio news. He winced:

"They're saying it'll hit 36.5," he said. "Celsius."

We sighed. We sipped. We made Wales quick enough and we raised our Marston's to it. Better this than to be stuck in a garden listening to a missus. We meet as much as five nights of the week, more often six. There are those who'd call us a bunch of sots but we don't see ourselves like that. We see ourselves as hobbyists. The train pulled into Flint and Tom N. went on the platform to fetch in some beef 'n' gravies from the Pie-O-Matic.

> Aigburth station offered a clutch of young girls in their summer skimpies. Oiled flesh, unscarred tummies, and it wasn't yet noon.

"Just the thing," said Billy Stroud, as we sweated over our dripping punnets. "Cold stuff causes the body too much work, you feel worse. But a nice hot pie goes down a treat. Perverse, I know. But they're on the curries in Bombay, aren't they?"

"Mumbai," said Everett.

The train scooted along the fried coast. We made solid headway into the Marston's. Mo was down a testicle since the spring. We'd called in at the Royal the night of his operation. We'd stopped at the Ship and Mitre on the way—they'd a handsome bitter from Clitheroe on guest tap. We needed the fortification: when Real Ale Club boys parade down hospital wards, we tend to draw worried glances from the whitecoats. We are shaped like those chaps in the warning illustrations on cardiac charts. We gathered around Mo and breathed a nice fog of bitter over the lad and we joshed him but gently.

"Sounding a little high-pitched, Mo?"

"Other lad's going to be worked overtime."

"Diseased bugger you'll want in a glass jar, Mo. One for the mantelpiece."

Love is a strong word, but. We were family to Mo when he was up the Royal having the bollock out. We passed Flint Castle and Everett Bell piped up.

"Richard the Second," he said.

We raised eyebrows. We were no philistines at Ale Club, Merseyside branch. Everett nodded, pleased.

"This is where he was backed into a corner," he said. "By Bolingbroke."

"Boling who?"

"Bolingbroke, the usurper. Old Dick surrendered for a finish. At Flint Castle. Or that's how Shakespeare had it."

"There's a contrary view, Ev?"

> Ale Club outings were civilized events. They never got aggressive. Maudlin, yes, but never aggressive.

"Some say it was more likely Conwy but I'd be happy with the Bard's read," he said, narrowing his eyes, the matter closed.

"We'll pass Conwy Castle in a bit, won't we?"

I consulted my *AA Illustrated*.

"We'll not," I said. "But we may well catch a glimpse across the estuary from Llandudno Junction."

There was a holiday air at the stations. Families piled on, the dads with papers, the mams with lotion, the kids with phones. The beer ran out by Abergele and this was frowned upon: poor planning. We were reduced to buying train beer, Worthington's. Sourly we sipped and Everett came and had a go.

"Maybe if one man wasn't in charge of outings and publications," he said, "we wouldn't be running dry halfways to Llandudno."

"True, Everett," I said, calmly, though I could feel the color rising to my cheeks. "So if anyone cares to step up, I'll happily step aside. From either or."

"We need you on publications, kid," said John Mosely. "You're the man for the computers."

Publications lately was indeed largely Web-based. I maintained our site on a regular basis, posting beer-related news and links. I was also looking into online initiatives to attract the younger drinker.

"I'm happy on publications, John," I said. "The debacle with the newsletter aside."

Newsletter had been a disaster, I accepted that. The report on the Macclesfield outing had been printed upside down. Off-color remarks had been made about a landlady in Everton, which should never have got past an editor's eye, as the lady in question kept very fine pumps. It hadn't been for want of editorial meetings. We'd had several, mostly down at the Grapes of Wrath.

"So how's about outings then?" I said, as the train swept by Colwyn Bay. "Where's our volunteer there? Who's for the step-up?"

Everett showed a palm to placate me.

"There's nothin' personal in this, lad," he said.

"I know that, Ev."

Ale Club outings were civilized events. They never got aggressive. Maudlin, yes, but never aggressive. Rhos-on-Sea; the Penrhyn sands. We knew Everett had been through a hard time. His old dad passed on and there'd been sticky business with the will. Ev would turn a mournful eye on us, at the bar of the Lion, in the snug of the Ship, and he'd say:

"My brother got the house, my sister got the money, I got the manic depression."

Black as his moods could be, as sharp as his tongue, Everett was tender. Train came around Little Ormes Head and Billy Stroud went off on one about Ceaușescu.

"Longer it recedes in the mind's eye," he said, "the more like Romania seems the critical moment."

"Apropos of, Bill?"

"Apropos my arse. As for Liverpool? Myth was piled upon myth, wasn't it? They said Labour sent out termination notices to council workers by taxi. Never bloody happened! It was an anti-red smear!"

"Thatcher's sick and old, Billy," said John Mosely.

"Aye an' her spawn's all around us yet," said Billy, and he broke into a broad smile, his humors mysteriously righted, his fun returned.

Looming, then, the shadow of Great Ormes Head, and beneath it a crescent swath of bay, a beach, a prom, and terraces: here lay Llandudno.

"1:55 PM," said Everett. "On the nose."

"Where's our exotic dancer?" teased Mo.

Billy Stroud sadly raised his T-shirt above his man boobs. He put his arms above his head and gyrated slowly his vast belly and danced his way off the train. We lost weight in tears as we tumbled onto the platform.

"How much for a private session, miss?" called Tom N.

"Tenner for twenty minutes," said Billy. "Fiver, I'll stay the full half hour."

We walked out of Llandudno station and plumb into a headbutt of heat.

"Blood and tar!" I cried. "We'll be hittin' the lagers!"

"Wash your mouth out with soap and water," said John Mosely.

Big John rubbed his hands together and led the way—Big John was first over the top. He reminded us there was business on hand.

"We're going to need a decision," he said, "about the National Beer Scoring System."

Here was kerfuffle. The NBSS, by long tradition, ranked a beer from nought to five. Nought was take-back-able, a crime against the name of ale. One was barely drinkable, two so-so, three an eyebrow raised in mild appreciation. A four was an ale on top form, a good beer in proud nick. A five was angel's tears but a seasoned drinker would rarely dish out a five, would over the course of a lifetime's quaffing call no more than a handful of fives. Such was the NBSS, as was. However, Real Ale Club, Merseyside branch, had for some time felt that the system lacked subtlety. And one famous night, down Rigby's, we came up with our own system—we marked from nought to ten. Finer gradations of purity were thus allowed for. The nuances of a beer were more properly considered. A certain hoppy tang, redolent of summer hedgerows, might elevate a brew from a seven to an eight. The mellow back-note born of a good oak casking might lift an ale again, and to the rare peaks of the nines. Billy Stroud had argued for decimal breakdown, for 7.5s and 8.5s—Billy would—but we had to draw a line somewhere. The national organization responded badly. They sent stiff word down the e-mail but we continued to forward our beer reports with markings on a nought-to-ten scale. There was talk now of us losing the charter. These were heady days.

"Stuff them is my view," said Everett Bell.

"We'd lose a lot if we lost the charter," said Mo. "Think about the festival invites. Think about the history of the branch."

"Think about the bloody future!" cried Tom N. "We haven't come up with a new system to be awkward. We've done it for the ale drinkers. We've done it for the ale makers!"

I felt a lump in my throat and I daresay I wasn't alone.

"Ours is the better system," said Everett. "This much we know."

"You're right," said John Mosely, and this was the clincher, Big John's call. "I say we score nought to ten."

"If you lot are in, that's good enough for me," I said.

Six stout men linked arms on a hot Llandudno pavement. We rounded the turn onto the prom and our first port of call: the Heron Inn.

Which turned out to be an anticlimax. A nice house, lately refurbished, but mostly keg rubbish on the taps. The Heron did, however, do a Phoenix Tram Driver on cask, 3.8 percent, and we sat with six of same.

"I've had better Tram Drivers," opened Mo.

"I've had worse," countered Tom N.

"She has a nice delivery but I'd worry about her legs," said Billy Stroud, shrewdly.

"You wouldn't be having more than a couple," said John Mosely.

"*Not* a skinful beer," I concurred.

All eyes turned to Everett Bell. He held a hand aloft, wavered it.

"A five would be generous, a six insane," he said.

"Give her the five," said Big John, dismissively.

I made the note. This was as smoothly as a beer was ever scored. There had been some world-historical ructions in our day. There was the time Billy Stroud and Mo hadn't talked for a month over an eight handed out to a Belhaven Bombardier.

Alewards we followed our noses. We walked by the throng of the beach—the shrieks of the sun-crazed kids made our stomachs loop. We made towards the Prom View Hotel. We'd had word of a new landlord there an ale fancier. It was dogs-dying-in-parked-cars weather. The Prom View's ample lounge was a blessed reprieve. We had the place to ourselves, the rest of Llandudno apparently being content with summer, sea, and life. John Mosely nodded towards a smashing row of hand pumps for the casks. Low whistles sounded. The landlord, hot-faced and jovial, came through from the hotel's reception.

"Another tactic," he said, "would be stay home and have a nice sauna."

"Same difference," sighed John Mosely.

"Could be looking at 37.2 now," said the landlord, taking a flop of sweat from his brow.

Billy Stroud sensed a kindred spirit:

"Gone up again, has it?"

"And up," said the landlord. "My money's on a 38 before we're out."

"Record won't go," said Billy.

"Nobody's said record," said the landlord. "We're not going to see a 38.5, that's for sure."

"Brogdale in Kent," said Billy. "August 10, 2003."

"2:05 PM," said the landlord. "I wasn't five miles distant that same day."

Billy was beaten.

"Loading a van for a divorced sister," said the landlord, ramming home his advantage. "Lugging sofas in the piggin' heat. And wardrobes!"

We bowed our heads to the man.

"What'll I fetch you, gents?"

A round of Cornish Lightning was requested.

"Taking the sun?" inquired the landlord.

"Taking the ale."

"After me own heart," he said. "'Course 'round here, it's lagers they're after mostly. Bloody Welsh."

"Can't beat sense into them," said John Mosely.

"If I could, I would," said the landlord, and he danced as a young featherweight might, he raised his clammy dukes. Then he skipped and turned.

> He did so, and a lively blonde, familiar with her forties but nicely preserved, bounced through from reception.

"I'll pop along on my errands, boys," he said. "There are rows to hoe and socks for the wash. You'd go through pair after pair this weather."

He pinched his nostrils closed: what a pong.

"Soon as you're ready for more, ring that bell and my good wife will oblige. So adieu, adieu . . ."

He skipped away. We raised eyes. The shade of the lounge was pleasant, the Cornish Lightning in decent nick.

"Call it a six?" said Tom N.

Nervelessly we agreed. Talk was limited. We swallowed hungrily, quickly, and peered again towards the pumps.

"The Lancaster Bomber?"

"The Whitstable Mule?"

"How's about that Mangan's Organic?"

"I'd say the Lancaster, all told."

"Ring the bell, Everett."

He did so, and a lively blonde, familiar with her forties but nicely preserved, bounced through from reception. Our eyes went shyly down. She took a glass to shine as she waited our call. Type of lass who needs her hands occupied.

"Do you for, gents?"

Irish, her accent.

"Round of the Lancaster, wasn't it?" said Everett.

She squinted towards our table, counted the heads.

"Times six," confirmed Everett.

The landlady squinted harder. She dropped the glass. It smashed to pieces on the floor.

"Maurice?" she said.

It was Mo that froze, stared, softened.

"B-B-Barbara?" he said.

We watched as he rose and crossed to the bar. A man in a dream was Mo. We held our breaths as Mo and Barbara took each other's hands over the counter. They were wordless for some moments, and then felt ten eyes on them, for they giggled, and Barbara set blushing to the Lancasters. She must have spilled half again down the slops gully as she poured. I joined Everett to carry the ales to our table. Mo and Barbara went into a huddle down the far end of the counter. They were rapt.

Real Ale Club would not have marked Mo for a romancer.

"The quiet ones you watch," said Tom N. "Maurice?"

"Mo? With a piece?" whispered Everett Bell.

"Could be they're old family friends," tried innocent Billy. "Or relations?"

Barbara was now slowly stroking Mo's wrist.

"Four buggerin' fishwives I'm sat with," said John Mosely. "What are we to make of these Lancasters?"

We talked ale but were distracted. Our glances cut down the length of the bar. Mo and Barbara talked lowly, quickly, excitedly down there. She was moved by Mo, we could see that plain enough. Again and again she ran her fingers through her hair. Mo was gazing at her, all dreamy, and suddenly he'd got a thumb hooked in the belt loop of his denims—Mr. Suave. He didn't so much as touch his ale.

Next, of course, the jaunty landlord arrived back on the scene.

"Oh, Alvie!" she cried. "You'll never guess!"

"Oh?" said the landlord, all the jauntiness instantly gone from him.

"This is *Maurice!*"

"Maurice?" he said. "You're joking . . ."

It was polite handshakes then, and feigned interest in Mo on the landlord's part, and a wee fat hand he slipped around the small of his wife's back.

"We'll be suppin' up," said John Mosely, sternly.

Mo had a last, whispered word with Barbara but her smile was fixed now and the landlord remained in close attendance. As we left, Mo looked back and raised his voice a note too loud. Desperate, he was.

"Barbara?"

We dragged him along. We'd had word of notable pork scratchings up the Mangy Otter.

"Do tell, Maurice," said Tom N.

"Leave him be," said John Mosely.

"An ex, that's all," said Mo.

And Llandudno was infernal. Families raged in the heat. All of the kids wept. The Otter was busy-ish when we sludged in. We settled on a round of St. Austell Tributes from a meager selection. Word had not been wrong on the quality of the scratchings. And the St. Austell turned out to be in top form.

"I'd be thinking in terms of a seven," said Everett Bell.

"Or a shade past that?" said John Mosely.

"You could be right on higher than sevens," said Billy Stroud. "But surely we're not calling it an eight?"

"Here we go," I said.

"Now this," said Billy Stroud, "is where your 7.5s would come in."

"We've heard this song, Billy," said John Mosely.

"He may not be wrong, John," said Everett.

"Give him a 7.5," said John Mosely, "and he'll be wanting his 6.3s, his 8.6s. There'd be no bloody end to it!"

"Tell you what," said Mo. "How about I catch up with you all a bit later? Where's next on the list?"

We stared at the carpet. It had diamonds on and crisps ground into it.

"Next up is the Crippled Ox on Burton Square," I read from my print-out. "Then it's Henderson's on Old Parade."

"See you at one or the other," said Mo.

He threw back the dregs of his St. Austell and was gone.

We decided on another at the Otter. There was a Whitstable Silver Star, 6.2 percent to volume, a regular stingo to settle our nerves.

"What's the best you've ever had?" asked Tom N.

It's a conversation that comes up again and again but it was a lifesaver just then: it took our minds off Mo.

"Put a gun to my head," said Big John, "and I don't think I could look past the draught Bass I had with me dad in Peter Kavanagh's. Sixteen years of age, Friday teatime, first wage slip in my arse pocket."

"But was it the beer or the occasion, John?"

"How can you separate the two?" he said, and we all sighed.

"For depth? Legs? Back-note?" said Everett Bell. "I'd do well to ever best the Swain's Anthem I downed a November Tuesday in Stockton-on-Tees:

19 and 87. Four point two percent to volume. I was still in haulage at that time."

"I've had an Anthem," said Billy Stroud of this famously hard-to-find brew, "and I'd have to say I found it an unexceptional ale."

Everett made a face.

"So what'd be your all-time, Billy?"

The ex-Marxist knitted his fingers atop the happy mound of his belly.

"Ridiculous question," he said. "There is so much wonderful ale on this island. How is a sane man to separate a Pelham High Anglican from a Warburton's Saxon Fiend? And we haven't even mentioned the great Belgian tradition. Your Duvel's hardly a dishwater. Then there's the Czechs, the Poles, the Germans . . ."

"Gassy pop!" cried Big John, no fan of a German brew, of a German anything.

"Nonsense," said Billy. "A Paulaner Weissbier is a sensational sup on its day."

> We settled on a round of St. Austell Tributes from a meager selection. Word had not been wrong on the quality of the scratchings.

"Where'd you think Mo's headed?" Tom N. cut in.

Everett groaned: "He'll be away down the Prom View, won't he? Big ape."

"Mo a lady-killer?" said Tom. "There's one for breaking news."

"No harm if it meant he smartened himself up a bit," said John.

"He has let himself go," said Billy. "Since the testicle."

"You'd plant spuds in those ears," I said.

The Whitstables had us in fighting form. We were away up the Crippled Ox. We found there a Miner's Slattern on cask. TV news showed sardine beaches and motorway chaos. There was an Internet machine on the wall, a pound for ten minutes, and Billy Stroud went to consult the meteorological satellites. The Slattern set me pensive.

Strange, I thought, how I myself had wound up a Real Ale Club stalwart. Nineteen ninety-five, October, I'd found myself in motorway services outside Ormskirk having a screaming barny with the missus. We were moving back to her folks' place in Northern Ireland. From dratted Leicester. We were heading for the ferry at Stranraer. At services, missus told me I was an idle lard-arse who had made her life hell and she never wanted to see me again. We'd only stopped off to fill the tires. She gets in, slams the door, puts her foot down. Give her ten minutes, I thought, she'll calm down and turn back for me. Two hours later, I'm sat in an empty Chinese in services, weeping, and eating Szechuan beef. I call a taxi. Taxi comes. I says where are we, exactly? Bloke looks at me. He says Ormskirk direction. I says what's the nearest city of any size? Drop you in Liverpool for twenty quid, he says. He leaves me off downtown and I look for a pub. Spot the Ship and Mitre and in I go. I find a stunning row of pumps. I call a Beaver Mild out of Devon.

> The hot nights were certainly a torment. Lying there with a sheet stuck to your belly. Thoughts coming loose, beer fumes rising, a manky arse.

"I wouldn't," says a bloke with a beard down the bar.

"Oh?"

"Try a Marston's Old Familiar," he says, and it turns out he's Billy Stroud.

The same Billy turned from the Internet machine at the Ox in Llandudno.

"Thirty-seven point nine," he said. "Bristol Airport, a shade after three. Flights delayed, tarmac melting."

"Pig heat," said Tom N.

"We won't suffer much longer," said Billy. "There's a change due."

"Might get a night's sleep," said Everett.

The hot nights were certainly a torment. Lying there with a sheet stuck to your belly. Thoughts coming loose, beer fumes rising, a manky arse. The city beyond the flat throbbing with summer. Usually I'd get up and have a cup of tea, watch some telly. Astrophysics on Beeb Two at four in the morning, news from the galaxies, and light already in the eastern sky. I'd dial the number in Northern Ireland and then hang up before they could answer.

Mo arrived into the Ox like the ghost of Banquo. There were terrible scratch marks down his left cheek.

"A Slattern will set you right, kid," said John Mosely, discreetly, and he maneuvered his big bones barwards.

Poor Mo was wordless as he stared into the ale that was put before him. Billy Stroud sneaked a time-out signal to Big John.

"We'd nearly give Henderson's a miss," agreed John.

"As well get back to known terrain," said Everett.

We climbed the hot streets towards the station. We stocked up with some Cumberland Pedigrees, 3.4 percent to volume, always an easeful drop. The train was busy with day-trippers heading back. We sipped quietly. Mo looked half dead as he slumped there but now and then he'd come up for a mouthful of his Pedigree.

"How's it tasting, kiddo?" chanced Everett.

"Like a ten," said Mo, and we all laughed.

The flicker of his old humor reassured us. The sun descended on Colwyn Bay and there was young life everywhere. I'd spoken to her only once since Ormskirk. We had details to finalize, and she was happy to let it slip about her new bloke. Some twat called Stan.

"He's emotionally spectacular," she said.

"I'm sorry to hear it, love," I said. "Given you've been through the wringer with me."

"I mean in a good way!" she barked. "I mean in a calm way!"

We'd a bit of fun coming up the Dee Estuary with the Welsh place names.

"Fy . . . feen . . . no. Fiiiif . . . non . . . fyff . . . non . . . growy?"

This was Tom N.

"Foy. Nonn. Grewey?"

This was Everett's approximation.

"Ffynnongroew," said Billy Stroud, lilting it perfectly. "Simple. And this one coming up? Llannerch-y-mor."

Pedigree came out my nose I laughed that hard.

"Young girl, beautiful," said Mo. "Turn around and she's forty bloody three."

"Leave it, Mo," said Big John.

But he could not.

"She's come over early in '86. She's living up top of the Central Line, Theydon Bois. She's working in a pub there, live-in, and ringing me from a phone box. In Galway I'm in a phone box too—we have to arrange the times, eight o'clock on Tuesday, ten o'clock on Friday. It's physical fucking pain she's not in town anymore. I'll follow in the summer is the plan and I get there, Victoria Coach Station, six in the morning, eighty quid in my pocket. And she's waiting for me there. We have an absolute dream of a month. We're lying in the park. There's a song out and we make it our song. 'Oh to be in England, in the summertime, with my love, close to the edge.'"

"Art of Noise," said Billy Stroud.

"Shut up, Billy!"

"Of course the next thing the summer's over and I've a start with BT up here and she's to follow on, October is the plan. We're ringing from phone boxes again, Tuesdays and Fridays, but the second Friday the phone doesn't ring. Next time I see her she's forty bloody three."

Flint station we passed through, and then Connah's Quay.

"Built up, this," said Tom N. "There's a supermarket, an Aldi? And that's a new school, is it?"

"Which means you want to be keeping a good two hundred yards back," said Big John.

We were horrified. Through a miscarriage of justice, plain as, Tom N. had earlier in the year been placed on a sex register. Oh the world is mad! Tom N. is a placid, placid man. We were all six of us quiet as the grave on the evening train then. It grew and built, it was horrible, the silence. It was Everett at last that broke it; we were coming in for Helsby. Fair dues to Everett.

"Not like you, John," he said.

Big John nodded.

"I don't know where that came from, Tom," he said. "A bloody stupid thing to say."

Tom N. raised a palm in peace but there was no disguising the hurt that had gone in. I pulled away into myself. The turns the world takes— Tom dragged through the courts, Everett half mad, Mo all scratched up and one-balled, Big John jobless for eighteen months. Billy Stroud was content, I suppose, in Billy's own way. And there was me, shipwrecked in Liverpool. Funny, for a while, to see "Penny Lane" flagged up on the buses, but it wears off.

And then it was before us in a haze. Terrace rows we passed, out Speke way, with cookouts on the patios. Tiny pockets of glassy laughter we heard through the open windows of the carriage. Families and what-have-you. We had the black hole of the night before us—it wanted filling. My grimmest duty as publications officer was the obits page of the newsletter. Too many had passed on at forty-four, at forty-six.

"I'm off outings," I announced. "And I'm off bloody publications as well."

"You did volunteer on both counts," reminded Big John.

"It would leave us in an unfortunate position," said Tom N.

"For my money, it's been a very pleasant outing," said Billy Stroud.

"We've supped some quality ale," concurred Big John.

"We've had some cracking weather," said Tom N.

"Llandudno is quite nice, really," said Mo.

Around his scratch marks an angry bruising had seeped. We all looked at him with tremendous fondness.

"'Tis nice," said Everett Bell. "If you don't run into a she-wolf."

"If you haven't gone ten rounds with Edward bloody Scissorhands," said John Mosely.

We came along the shabby grandeurs of the city. The look on Mo's face then couldn't be read as anything but happiness.

"Maurice," teased Big John, "is thinking of the rather interesting day he's had."

Mo shook his head.

"Thinking of days I had years back," he said.

It has this effect, Liverpool. You're not back in the place five minutes and you go sentimental as a famine ship. We piled off at Lime Street. There we go: six big blokes in the evening sun.

"There's the Lion Tavern?" suggested Tom N.

"There's always the Lion," I agreed.

"They've a couple of Manx ales guesting at Rigby's," said Everett Bell.

"Let's hope they're an improvement on previous Manx efforts," said Billy Stroud.

"There's the Grapes?" tried Big John.

"There's always the Grapes," I agreed.

And alewards we went about the familiar streets. The town was in carnival: Tropic of Lancashire in a July swelter. It would not last. There was rain due in off the Irish Sea, and not for the first time. 🛡

THE TALENT

*For unto every one that hath shall be given, and he shall have abundance: but
from him that hath not shall be taken away even that which he hath. And cast
ye the unprofitable servant into outer darkness.*

—MATTHEW 25:29–30

The man in the pig suit is back,
standing outside the gates
of the state capitol, holding a sign
that reads LAWYERS ARE SWINE,
his bitter face only just visible
inside the soiled pink vinyl,
his outrage clambering over
the westbound traffic on Eleventh.
It's so heavy, believing
there is a story in every moment, every
person, all those spots you press
to find they're rotted straight through,
all those ropes of thickened scar tissue—
the divorce gone bad, the drunk driver
gone free—it's always complicated,
even when the message is *fuck you.*
He makes me think of Susan,
beginning to cry, asking, *Who do you think
Jesus will come to first if not the insane
and the depraved?* And, see, that

was a complicated moment for me,
as my envy of Susan's faith
was exactly equal to my envy
of the depraved to whom Jesus
would come. The light stays red
long after I expect it to turn green,
so I have the pleasure of watching
the cars as they begin to turn south
on Congress, as they begin to go on
with their lives. In the backseat,
the baby is silent. No words
yet, not a single word, only sounds.
She is pure of story, sitting, facing
backward, looking up, maybe,
to the rotunda, where the great
woman of Texas stands all day and night
in her robe with her arm extended
elegantly toward heaven, holding one
giant star above her head. Strange
woman. I read somewhere that
to make her recognizable from this far
her features had to be exaggerated
beyond recognition and that close up,
she looks like a monster.

PRAYER (5)

When I said I wanted to work harder than
everyone, I didn't mean work harder. I didn't
mean that I wanted to answer more e-mails
and forget to eat lunch. I meant sweat.
And I didn't mean sweat, of course, but light.
I guess I meant I wanted to shine brighter
than everyone. And that's where I've gone
wrong again and again. With or without
God, this moment continues to end and end.
With or without virtue. What is virtue, anyway,
if not a discussion between the self
and the self, a way not to stop the end
from coming, but to feel it, at least, as it passes.
In the park yesterday, sitting on the lawn
with the baby, I watched a boy and his younger sister
walk to the pool. He was carrying a bag
with their towels, she was wearing green floaties
pushed very high up on her arms. Once
they'd passed, the boy turned to face the girl
and yelled *STOP IT!* into her round face,
and the girl smiled hugely at having worn him
down and then assured him that she would
stop, and though I'd been watching them
and continued to watch them, I could not perceive
what it was she'd stopped doing.

MY OWN PRIVATE
BYRON

Miciah Bay Gault

Alas! Poor Yorick. Your Skull's a Bong.

Wheeler Cemetery in northern Vermont is small and surrounded on three sides by long, glossy fields of corn. Bluish hills rise in the distance, and a quaint red barn squats down the way. I park my car on the side of the road and enter through a gate. A white picket fence encloses the cemetery, and the grass inside is speckled with clover and tiny purple flowers. I wander from grave to grave, the only person here.

On one side of the cemetery the stones are old, cracked, mossy, the inscriptions mostly worn off, though I can still make out a few: *Rest dearest rest. From care and sorrow free / peaceful be thy quiet slumber / peaceful in the grave so low / thine be pleasures without number.* The people buried here in the 1800s had names like Josiah, Franny, Prudence, Owlif.

On the other side are newer graves. These tombstones are fancier, engraved with stars and flowers and kittens, but definitely less romantic. On this side people have planted miniature gardens at their loved ones' graves. There are lilies, and lots of flags. There are plastic butterflies on sticks.

And then I find what I have come to see: an aboveground tomb, huge and

gray and granite, with a four-inch slab on top. It's the size of a very large dining room table, but more important looking. It reminds me of the big stone table Aslan died on in *The Lion, the Witch and the Wardrobe*.

The man whose name is engraved in this stone was laid to rest in 2002. He was woken from his *quiet slumber* three years later, when a seventeen-year-old boy broke into the tomb and made off with the man's head.

Nicholas comes to class wearing torn-up jeans, a gauzy shirt, and a cowboy hat. He has sharp, high cheekbones, sensual lips, pale eyelashes, an elegant jaw. He is exquisite, despite strange adolescent proportions—his giant galloping Adam's apple, his slender neck. His body is all angles, all bones and muscles close to the surface. Something else is close to the surface as well: impatience, a restless vibration.

This is English composition at the community college. The classroom is long and bare, and Nicholas is a mass of heat and color and frenetic energy. He's lovely. He looks like some sort of luminous, androgynous underwear model. He's the kind of boy gods fall in love with when they catch sight of him from their seats on Mt. Olympus. I want to keep staring at him, but I'm the teacher and I have to teach.

After class I ask him where he grew up, where he went to high school, and he tells me. "But I didn't graduate," he says.

In the days that follow, I tell a lot of people that one of my students went to jail for grave robbing.

"Because I went to jail for two years. Jail and prison."

"Oh wow," I say. "What for?"

"I made a bong out of a human skull," he tells me.

"So you went to jail for . . . ?"

"Grave robbing," he says.

Walking home I hear the words in my head: *grave robbing*. I can't wait to tell my husband. All through the neighborhood insects buzz and other clandestine creatures snuffle low to the ground. It seems to me that something else is afoot in the dark, something more than the usual skunks and moths.

In the days that follow, I tell a lot of people that one of my students went to jail for grave robbing. I expect them to be as intrigued as I am, but they're not. What they are is seriously grossed out.

"That is *disturbing*," one friend says. "I wish you hadn't told me."

Of course it's disturbing, I think. And now my fascination seems disturbing too, and I try to recalibrate, but I can't. Just thinking the words *grave robbing* gets my heart going. I feel grateful that something so wonderfully creepy can exist in my world.

I look up the story on the Internet, and it's all true. After being tipped off to a disturbance in Wheeler Cemetery on April 8, 2005, police found that an aboveground crypt had been broken into. The coffin was open, the corpse inside decapitated, and the head nowhere in sight. "Yes, indeed," Police Chief Richard Keith said. "We found remains and they had been disturbed." Later, near Nicholas's house, investigators discovered the gardening tools he used to break into the crypt, along with the deceased's head, bow tie, and glasses.

Nicholas agrees to tell me his story, and we meet at a coffee shop/music venue where he sometimes works as a bouncer. The place is dim and comfortable, and Tom Waits growls from the speakers, accompanied by the hiss of the milk steamer, the clinking of spoons against mugs, and the murmur of conversation from other tables. I ask Nicholas about his family, his friends, his experience at school.

"I wasn't very popular," he says, "partially because I was so peculiar."

In addition, he tells me, he didn't hit puberty until he was seventeen.

"So I was tiny, *tiny*," Nicholas says.

"Scrawny?"

It wasn't just that, he says. It was that he was still a little kid. He had no hair on his body. His voice hadn't changed. "For all intents and purposes, physiologically, I was prepubescent," he says.

We happen to be listening to Tom Waits's raspy, wonderful frog-cry of a song "I Don't Wanna Grow Up." *How do you move in a world of fog . . . Makes me wish that I could be a dog.* At twenty-one, Nicholas is so unflinchingly sexual that I'm having trouble imagining him four years ago with the voice and body of a little boy. Also, I'm having trouble reconciling this young man and his fussy vocabulary with the boy who thought it was a good idea to raid a crypt.

Nicholas first told the police he intended to use the skull to make a bong. He tells me a different story. At first, he says, he thought of grave robbing as a lucrative venture. Gold wedding ring! Gold pocket watch! He would get rich off the man's jewelry, then clean the skull, bleach it in the sun, and give it to his friends—his only real friends at the time as a wedding present.

He was disappointed when he realized that there was nothing of value in the crypt. "The guy didn't even have any shoes on," he says incredulously. "It'd be pretty cool to wear a dead guy's shoes."

"Was it hard work?" I ask him.

"Smashing open the vault itself was easy. But then—caskets are locked, as it turns out, so I just had to keep smashing the top of it with a maul. And then getting the head itself off was like—well, the saw had broken, so I did it just with my hands, just like tore pieces out of it, and spun it around—I mean there's a lot of stuff still holding it on. You'd be surprised. That stuff seems to last."

> Nicholas first told the police he intended to use the skull to make a bong. He tells me a different story.

"So was it, like, *gross?*"

"I don't know. Not really. It didn't smell bad."

"Did it smell like anything?"

"No," he says. Then he spends some time trying to find the right word to describe the lack of smell.

"Odorless?" I suggest. "Odor-neutral?"

"I feel like there's a more apt term," he says.

He stands on the grave's edge with the freshly turned dirt all around him. The rich, rotten smell rises up. This isn't Nicholas. I'm thinking of someone else now.

"Whose grave's this, sirrah?" says Hamlet.

"Mine, sir," says the clown/grave digger.

"I think it be thine, indeed; for thou liest in't."

This scene is best known for what comes next: Hamlet holds Yorick's skull and realizes that someday (he has no idea how soon it's coming) he too will be nothing but bones. But it's the comedy on the edge of a grave that reminds me most of Nicholas; it's that grave digger's puns, his linguistic precision.

"What man dost thou dig it for?" Hamlet tries.

"For no man, sir."

"What woman, then?"

"For none, neither."

"Who is to be buried in't?"

"One that was a woman, sir; but, rest her soul, she's dead."

"How absolute the knave is!" Hamlet exclaims.

For me, Nicholas's story isn't the memento mori that Yorick's skull is for Hamlet. It's maybe the opposite: a refusal to connect the idea of bones with the inevitability of my own death, or the deaths of the people I love.

"So it wasn't gross to you," I say. "You were just focused. Would it have been gross to *me?*"

"I would imagine. It was like—the epidermal layer was grayish green. I know the perfect word for it," he says, trying to remember. "Something I learned in *Lolita*. It was . . . having a lightish blue gray color . . . or a yellowish green color. Something that lends a frosted appearance that often wipes away."

The word he's searching for I realize later must be *glaucous*. I still remember the words *I* learned from reading *Lolita* back in college: *hirsute, crenulated, paroxysm, diaphanous*. I'm grateful for, but also kind of appalled by, this small similarity between Nicholas and me. My brain says, *A most diaphanous nymphet.*

"Basically," he says, "it was this filmy goo that would wipe away. And then the dermal layer, or whatever. The next layer of skin. You know like if you go out and get chicken? Like if you get fried chicken? And you reheat it in the microwave? The texture of the actual meat of the chicken?"

"Under the skin?"

"Well, it's still the skin, but it's under the first layer of skin. Stringy? And, like, hard? And he didn't have any ears, all that was left of them was this outer rim, really dark brown and pressed against his head. And his hair was all kind of essentially gone. It had been absorbed by the massy goo of the head."

"So did it look like a person?"

"Yeah, it looked like a person. It looked like a pretty unhealthy person."

"Facial features, though?"

"Eyes were closed. I never actually got to look at the eyes too clearly. Yeah, I mean, he had a nose, still had eyelashes."

"Were you surprised by it? Was it what you'd imagined?"

"I don't like to assume anything. I don't like to make suppositions. I took him as he was. I was accepting of him. This is how you are."

In Ray Bradbury's story "Skeleton," a man is terrified of his *own* skeleton and can't endure the thought that this symbol of Halloween creepiness lurks under his skin. "He raged for hours," Bradbury writes. "And the skeleton, ever the frail and solemn philosopher, hung quietly inside, saying not a word, suspended like a delicate insect within a chrysalis, waiting and waiting."

Nicholas shrugs and sips his tea. The music plays, and parents play board games with their children at nearby tables. A plate clatters to the floor, and someone says, "Thank you, thank you very much!" and everyone in the place kind of chuckles.

Nicholas is definitely not the first teenager to get in trouble for grave robbing. When I start looking into it, I discover that in 2008, three teens were arrested outside Houston, Texas, for digging up a grave and making—what else?—a bong out of a human skull, this one belonging to an eleven-year-old boy who died in 1921.

In 2004, according to the *Times*, two teenagers in Scotland were arrested for robbing a grave and stealing the skull. They showed it to some girls who were hanging out drinking in the graveyard that night. "It looked a bit stringy," a fourteen-year-old girl told police. "It looked like it had been covered in coffee stains or nicotine. I didn't think it was real, but it was a dead head. He had it by the neck. He wrapped his sleeve around his fist and then put his fist in the neck. He then passed it around. It was scary. Its mouth was all shriveled up. It had no eyes. He started using it as a puppet."

But it's not just teenagers looking for thrills. Apparently, people rob graves for all kinds of reasons. A man in Waterbury, Connecticut, was arrested a few years ago for looting graves and stealing a gold ring and two sets of gold dentures. In England, at a guinea pig farm, animal rights activists desecrated the bones of a worker's mother-in-law. A nineteen-year-old Floridian told police he'd taken a skeleton from its grave to help him measure the coffin he was building; he tried to return the bones, but the grave had already been filled in. In Newark, New Jersey, practitioners of Palo Mayombe, a religion with Caribbean roots, were charged with robbing graves and using human skulls in their ceremonies and rituals.

A woman in Athens, Georgia, dug up her boyfriend's ashes because she'd been excluded from his funeral; in Wisconsin, another woman unearthed an old boyfriend's ashes from a cemetery plot and, ostensibly to spite his family, drank the beer that had been buried with him.

In 2006 in Madison, Wisconsin, three men dug up the corpse of a twenty-year-old woman recently killed in a motorcycle crash so one of the men could have sex with the body.

I read about Burke and Hare, the infamous "resurrection men" of nineteenth-century Edinburgh, who sold corpses to doctors and medical students for research. The hundreds of newspaper articles I find announcing missing corpses throughout the United States in the nineteenth and early twentieth centuries somehow create a romantic impression: dark graveyards, sweet-smelling grass, rich earth, moonlight illuminating a shovel, daring medical students looking for their next autopsy. I think of Hannah Tinti's great adventure *The Good Thief*, originally titled *Resurrection Men*. I have a sense of those late-night resurrections as swashbuckling fun, but I know there was surely both a stench and a sadness to it, that it was filthy, frightening work.

The new Byron biography by Edna O'Brien comes out, and I read it, thinking about Nicholas. Lord Byron, too, had morbid tendencies. He once gave human bones as a wedding present. He mounted skulls on silver bases to use as drinking cups.

> He loves words the way a lot of young men love girls; he wants to master them, make them his.

When his friend Shelley died, Byron, standing in the light of the funeral pyre, asked if he could have the skull.

Byron, like Nicholas, was the object of admiration and speculation and grotesque fascination. Byron was beautiful but flawed, with a clubfoot that only added to his desirability. Women everywhere longed to master Byron's "under-look," which I picture as moody, brooding, dangerous, disdainful.

In class, Nicholas is aggressive, his gaze challenging. He loves words the way a lot of young men love girls; he wants to master them, make them his. He has an appetite for books, reads lustily, Don Juan looking for his next conquest in the dictionary. He signs his e-mails *anon*. But he's not your usual logophile; he has other ways of expressing himself. He carries a huge knife in his bag beside his copies of *Lolita* and *Anna Karenina*, and I can see scars up and down his arms.

I have to wonder if there's some major lack in me, something missing. Why else would I respond to Nicholas with curiosity and, let's face it, delight? As with any deficiency, I must crave what I don't have. I'm full of *life*—literally: I'm eight months pregnant as I write this. But on some level I must want something darker. Nicholas and his grave robbing are sharp and exciting, a surprising minor chord, a little bit of perversion in an otherwise maddeningly pleasant existence.

Maybe I've been bitten—forgive me—by the vampire bug, and that explains my fascination with Nicholas and his casual manner with the bones of others. Obviously, vampire love is bigger and more pervasive now than ever. Edward Cullen has been dead of Spanish influenza since 1918, and I know a *lot* of college girls who consider him the perfect guy. And he's just one of several new undead dreamboats.

But here's the thing: death isn't sexy. At least, not the deaths I've witnessed. My uncle Tim died of AIDS in 1989. In the weeks leading up to his death, his wasted body was not sexy lying on my grandmother's guest room bed. The smell of the gardenias floating in bowls on his bedside table was otherworldly, but not sexy. My uncle Joe shot himself. His young daughter's voice over the phone that night saying, *Why, why, why did he do it?* as if I knew the answer to this impossible question: not sexy. Even my beautiful friend Cara who overdosed on heroin was sexy only in life. In death she was serious looking in her coffin: puffy and pasty and made up with a strange maiden-aunt hairstyle.

I know that death isn't sexy, but still I love Nicholas's story. And I like Lord Byron, underlook and all. And I like vampires and werewolves. I like those bad boys. Maybe there's a death force as strong as the life force, wrestling for control over our sexual impulses, the joy of arousal ending always with *les petites morts*.

Puberty arrived while Nicholas was in jail. He shot up. He kept outgrowing his clothes.

Impetuous Dante Gabriel Rossetti threw a bundle of unpublished poems into the grave with his beloved wife—and model—Lizzie Siddal after she overdosed on laudanum. Later, he regretted it and dug up her coffin to retrieve the poems. They say that when the coffin was pried open, her hair, the russet locks for which she'd been famous in life, was still flaming bright on either side of her bare skull.

Siddal was the model for John Everett Millais's famous painting of the beautiful drowned girl, her voluminous dress waterlogged, long red hair floating about her face, one pale hand still clutching a drenched bouquet, probably rosemary for remembrance, and pansies for thoughts, and fennel and columbine, and rue and daisies and withered violets: Ophelia, whose suicide is the reason the grave digger must turn over poor Yorick's grave—to make room for one more corpse.

Back in the coffee shop, Nicholas shakes his head as he remembers the dead man's ears and nose and eyelashes. "Also made me decide," he says, "I will never ever be preserved and put in a fucking casket in the ground. I really wish you could just be buried. Just your naked-ass body."

My uncle Tim's body was cremated. That someone's body could be reduced to three tins of grit and bone chips was surprising to me. I was thirteen and couldn't conceive of my own body as *matter*, mere substance, like his. If I were to die, it seemed my body would have to go with me. There was no separating my*self* and my body.

I ask Nicholas if he had friends in jail. He says everyone there really liked him. They thought he was funny because they'd seen some coverage of his crime on TV.

"So they knew what you were in for?"

"Yeah, and I was also like this little kid. I had absolutely no facial hair, no armpit hair, vestigial pubic hair . . . or, no, *nascent*, nascent pubic hair."

Puberty arrived while Nicholas was in jail. He shot up. He kept outgrowing his clothes. "I constantly had to get new pants in jail," he says. Hair grew on his body, but it bothered him, and he shaved it off—shaved even his legs. Also, he started cutting himself, and he would get in trouble for that.

"So what happened when you got in trouble?"

"You would go to the hole."

The hole was a room with only a bed and a toilet. "No books, no pencil, no paper," Nicholas says. "You're allowed to pace up and down a hallway for an hour a day, that's it." The longest stretch of time he spent in the hole was forty days.

"Did you go crazy?"

"No, you just sleep all the time. And eating! Eating becomes so wonderful, because it's the only . . ."

"Stimulation."

"Exactly."

I picture him alone in *the hole*. A bare room and this teenage body, the limbs shaved smooth. Stripped down somehow to the essentials. A mind, a body. Muscles. Skin.

"So meanwhile," I say, "you're going through puberty, and you're in jail, and there are no girls around."

He was released early from jail into a mental health facility, where he promptly started sleeping with a counselor ten years older. They were discovered, she was fired, and then she killed herself. Nicholas went back to jail.

For Halloween the year I was twelve, I dressed as the goddess Persephone.

My costume involved layers of tulle in pale, pretty colors, a mask with fake violets glued on, and a pomegranate, that sexy blood-red fruit, the fruit of the underworld, the fruit the young goddess eats—six seeds, only six—that seals her fate as part-time queen of the dead.

"Now what in the world are you, a fairy?" kind ladies said from their doorways as they held out brimming bowls of candy.

In answer I held out the pomegranate.

"What's that, an apple?" they said.

No one knew about Persephone. But I bet they knew how it felt to be twelve years old, a child picking flowers in the meadow one moment, an almost-woman and object of desire the next. I'm sure they knew what it felt like to long for your mother and your home while simultaneously longing for something forbidden: the blood-red fruit.

I am lucky, because I was raised to feel fine—proud, even—about my sexuality. Sex was an adventure. My first experiences with sex were *innocent*, if that makes any sense, and sweet, and exciting, and even wholesome, like some fresh natural thing you take from a garden. Sex that grows from a seed, a natural consequence of water and sunlight.

In marriage, though, I find myself in the kind of safe haven I haven't known since childhood. I'm part of a family again. I've got someone looking out for me, helping me make decisions. How strange that now—a wife, a mother—I've somehow become the girl picking flowers in the meadow again: safe, cosseted. And again, as in adolescence, I dream of what's under the earth. As in adolescence, *exhumation* becomes a necessary curiosity.

So here I am, at this wooden table with Nicholas, listening to his story.

And then later alone, with the computer on my knees, digging up the words. And using those words as tools to try to unearth something even deeper.

I ask about the widow. I haven't thought much about her through all this, how she certainly would have had a hard time separating her husband's body from his *self*. The beloved from the body of the beloved.

"I don't know," Nicholas says. "I wrote her an apology note the other day. I thought it was a very well-worded and meaningful letter. But the victim's advocate made me change it to the point where it was just this very standard *I'm sorry, I did bad, ohhh, I hope you don't feel too bad*. I had no connection with it anymore."

"So what did it say? Like, did you feel bad?"

"It's hard for me to understand how I feel about it. I certainly wish I hadn't done it. Empathy comes really hard for me. And it comes at really odd times. Just like shows up out of nowhere for seemingly no reason. But I certainly wish I hadn't done it."

"For her sake?"

"Yeah. More than just for me. It's hard for me to put myself in her shoes, but it's like I still understand how hard it is for her and I wish I hadn't done it."

I say goodbye to Nicholas and walk home from the coffee shop.

I think about Nicholas for a few minutes, and then there's no more time for that. I have to continue with my day. It's time to pick up Lily from school. Time to get dinner started. Time to load the dishwasher, the washing machine. Time for flies to buzz at the window. Time for dust to gather on the windowsill. Time for the basil plant to turn its leaves toward the sun. Time for crackers, and juice. And the ring of the telephone, and the dog barking across the street, and all the smells and tastes and sounds of this sensory life.

A few months after English composition class ends, Nicholas gets the lead in a local production of *The Rocky Horror Picture Show*. Not drippy Brad, but Dr. Frank-N-Furter himself. He's glorious. He wears three-inch platform heels and red and black lingerie. His mouth is red. His thighs are long and pale. His jaw makes a beautiful shape on the stage. *Appetite* radiates off him. He makes love to Janet. He makes love to Brad. His minions swarm around him. I watch from the audience as he weeps at the end, and his makeup runs down his cheeks. I watch him sing tenderly, and fall to his knees, and then die.

I want you to see Nicholas as I see him. Tall. Young. Filthy. Gorgeous. A body constructed of elegant angles, all bones and muscles close to the surface. Not on stage in his lingerie and wig. Not the way he looks in the coffee shop drinking tea.

Picture him that night, with the wind and the moon. So much blood pumping from his young heart. The flesh under his fingernails, flesh in the whorls of his fingertips. His muscles working to move that stone slab.

I think of the Bradbury character frightened of his own bones. There's something terrifying under Nicholas's golden skin, too. And under my skin, I guess. Some fucked-up tangle of desires and obsessions. But what am I supposed to do with all that, dig it up? Or let it stay where it is, comfortably buried. ⬠

Mark Wagenaar

A LITTLE DREAMBOOK OF LAST DAYS

One vision has the world as the back of a turtle

                                                   adrift on an endless sea.

Another as one of a handful of petals thrown from heaven.

If there's a sound to end the world,

                             whatever it is—

peach pit in space or the dream of a horse in a meadow—

it's a train horn, it's shofar call sounding

                                     the dark through all things

in Denton, the 12:21 northbound

to middle-of-the-night Oklahoma City.

If you've seen the maps of social network connections

       plotted as shimmering arcs—

or airline flights between cities, between continents—

you've traced the paths of modern-day slaves.

Gravity might only be a billion coincidences,

an immanent God gone begging,

                              pulling all things toward each other

(which is to say Himself) but there's some thread

                                     that runs through us all,

though it might resemble the copperhead-bright

arthritic pain coiled through my father's knees,
my mother's shoulder, my brother's back.

Past midnight, late autumn. The little torches
                                        of the marigolds
lose their flames a spark at a time,
until only the cold has enough light to find its way,
                                        the coming cold,
which would have us believe it's the last
                                        in a long line of gods
who have recast the world in their own image:
a via negativa of the whole hemisphere.

If there's a scent on earth we won't find in heaven
                    if there's a heaven to follow
it's the sickly sweet smell of overripe pears,
a hornet hollowing one,
    turning like a star in its own nova
(coronaed by pear flesh, its own little heaven),
turning in its death,
just enough light for the cold to see.

THE EGGPLANT, THE GOAT
THE MOUSSAKA

Jennifer Gilmore

It's all Greek to me!

It's the end of June and my husband and I will be leaving Naxos for New York soon. The days before we leave the island are always frantic; these are the last moments my mother-in-law has to feed her son before he returns to his life of American food filled with, Voula believes, chemicals and preservatives and butter, each with the power to kill him. Today, Voula and I are on a journey for eggplant, so she can prepare the moussaka that she has been talking about making for most of June. Moussaka takes a good deal of time; it requires many ingredients that need to be procured throughout the island, and therefore moussaka is special. Moussaka equals love.

We have been searching for a particular farm for an hour.

"There it is." Voula points toward the mountains in the hazy distance. "That is the place."

I don't see it. The Aegean gleams below the mountains. The island of Paros is at the horizon, and the stark whitewashed buildings of town rise in the middle distance.

"It's farther," I say. I think of the crude map my husband drew, which I accidentally left on the kitchen table by the pots of honey and tahini.

My mother-in-law folds her arms over her chest. "Come on! I remember. It was right here."

This farm is the only place where Voula will buy vegetables, because there are no pesticides used, which is unusual for the local farms, whose crops compete with cheaper ones from Athens. This summer she has cooked dolmades from her own grape leaves, the vines of which snake along the whitewashed walls of her yard. She has made countless salads of fresh lettuces and peppers from her garden, with olives and tangy chunks of feta nestled on top. She has stuffed zucchini and baked lamb and pilafed rice and roasted *gavros* with the famous potatoes of Naxos, which are sweet and flavorful, deep yellow in color, utterly distinct. But Pedro and I are leaving, and there has yet to be moussaka.

The beef filet—part of a butchered cow from her friend's farm in the mountains—is ready for grinding. The Naxos potatoes are washed and set on the wooden table in her kitchen, along with the eggs from a neighbor's farm, trembling in a wooden bowl. The glass bottle of organic milk chills in the fridge. Everything is ready but the eggplant.

Voula grew up on Naxos, in Potamia, a village in a fertile valley with a natural spring running through it, coveted on the water-deprived island. Pedro and I had the rehearsal dinner for our wedding on Naxos, at a taverna across from the Church of St. John. Our niece and nephew were baptized at that church, the boy, dripping with oil, held up to the golden icons. At our rehearsal dinner, Voula served goat on a spit, and for the vegetarians she offered rooster. That was nine years ago, the year of the Athens Olympics, relative boom times for Greece.

Voula has lived all over the world, but before she left with her Spanish beau—who arrived on Naxos to do geological work and found her scrubbing floors in the monastery cut into the cliffs—she knew little of anywhere else. I imagine her in her twenties, leaving on the boat Pedro and I arrive on.

Pulling into Naxos always takes my breath away. To the left of the harbor, with its piers and moored boats, and at the top of a raised peninsula, are the remains of the Temple of Demeter, where Ariadne is said to have been left sleeping by Theseus, before Dionysus found her. The old city, with its Venetian castle, sits atop a hill, overlooking the port and the stores and cafés on the main street along the harbor, usually crowded with people enjoying life. This year, however, the cafés were nearly empty when we walked off the boat to see Voula in her dark glasses, waving her arms.

Now she is back on Naxos for good; her husband, the father-in-law I have never met, lives halfway around the world. He is not a topic we discuss. Despite her familiarity with the island, she has absolutely no idea where this farm that has the only usable eggplant on an island of eggplant, in a country of eggplant, is located.

Everything good comes from the mountains, says Voula, like the honey, which arrives in August: you can taste the clover and lavender the bees have feasted on all summer. Lambs and cows must roam free to achieve maximum nutritional benefits, and the same goes for the sheep and goats whose milk makes the *kefalotyri* she would smuggle in her suitcase when she used to visit us in New York. Now she stays put; her garden, she claims, needs her in every season.

Voula's garden is filled with an orchard of lemons and winter orange trees, but the best summer oranges—for the juice she squeezes every morning—come from a man on a bike who sings below her window on his way to town. Occasionally he brings *vissino* cherries. One summer I pitted three kilos with a hairpin for preserves; when I was finished, the kitchen, streaked with the deep red stain of cherry juice, looked like the scene of a murder.

The restaurants on the main street and in the old city, Voula insists, serve food made only with ingredients shipped in from Athens and are, therefore, verboten. I have learned over time that "Athens" is code for pesticides or pollution or terrible crime, depending on the context. The only term worse than "Athens" is "New York City."

Despite the mandate, Pedro and I often sneak off in the evening to an *ouzeria* for grilled octopus and squid and a Plomari ouzo, served in a narrow glass with a single ice cube. *Of course we didn't eat a thing*, we tell Voula as we enter the house and she stands close, to smell our breath. When I first started coming to Naxos, it was booze and cigarettes we tried to hide, but now, just the smell of the zesty yogurt sauce from a late-night gyro can put her in a panic until morning.

"Wait!" Voula screeches. "Stop!" It is difficult to turn on these small crumbling roads. Privately, I curse my husband, who refused his mother this trip, as he feels it's unnecessary and uses way too much overpriced petrol. Also, he insisted, the trip would surely involve other errands and could be half a day's journey; it could lead anywhere, he said. Trying to quell her burgeoning fears that we would not eat properly before leaving, I offered my services. Now I see that one wrong move will take us tumbling over the cliff.

> One summer I pitted three kilos with a hairpin for preserves; when I was finished, the kitchen, streaked with the deep red stain of cherry juice.

I remember Pedro's map, its sketched waves to the road's right, and so I turn away from the ocean, choppy, glinting. The mountains, dotted with olive trees, rise before us. Dill as tall as children has grown wild along both sides of the dusty road, and I can smell the flavor—touched with anise—and the sweet wildflowers through the open windows.

The next thing that happens stuns me: Voula gets out of the car while it is still in motion. Her feet drag along the tarmac and I jerk to a stop. She marches over to what I now see are goats roaming in a field, not an unusual sight. I breathe heavily, recovering from almost killing my husband's mother. *She just got out!* I imagine telling Pedro when I arrive home, alone. *I did* NOT *push her!*

"See?" Voula leans toward a goat that seems to understand he is being admired and stands still. She squints into the sun as she points to the goat's leg. "Look at these legs!" she says. "My goodness, I want to bring him home and cook him for my son."

I know she doesn't mean as a pet and I distract myself fleetingly by thinking of the delectable goat in parchment I've eaten several times at Axiotisa, the only restaurant Voula will patronize. It's just off Kastraki, near the beach where Voula and her cousins own a small patch of land. The mountains, where the soil is the richest, used to be the coveted land, but the tourists like the beach, and the tourists, now declining in number, have all the money. Voula's portion of land is too small to build on, given new laws, and she won't sell to her cousins, nor they to her,

Voula's Moussaka

(as explained/interpreted by her daughter-in-law, Patricia)

3 pounds Yukon Gold potatoes, peeled,
  thinly sliced

4 medium-sized eggplants, cut into
  ¼-inch slices

½ pound ground beef (unless you want to
  grind it yourself!)

½ pound ground lamb (same as above)

1 large onion, chopped

2 cloves garlic, minced

¼ teaspoon sage

¼ teaspoon oregano

¼ teaspoon thyme

1 bay leaf (optional)

Chopped parsley to taste

3 tomatoes, chopped

Salt and pepper to taste

For the Béchamel sauce

½ gallon milk

10 heaping tablespoons flour

2 yolks, lightly beaten

¼ teaspoon sweet paprika

¾ cup kefalotyri cheese

Vegetable Preparation

(This can be done the night before.)
Lightly brush the eggplant with olive
oil on both sides and roast at 400
degrees for fifteen minutes, until soft in
the middle. Then add a bit of salt and
pepper. If you'd rather, you can fry the
eggplant, just don't crowd the pan. You
can drain the oil in a colander over night.

While the eggplant is roasting, thinly
slice the potatoes and fry in olive oil
until tender and golden brown. Let
drain on a paper towel.

As the potatoes are cooking, prepare
the meat.

Meat Preparation

Brown the meat for about three
minutes or so, until the pink color
disappears. Add the chopped onion and
sauté with the meat until translucent.
Add the oregano, sage, thyme, and
garlic. Finish with salt, pepper, parsley,
and the chopped tomatoes.

Béchamel

Warm the milk over medium heat and
slowly add in the flour, beating the
mixture as you go until the mixture
comes to a boil and thickens. Then
take the pan off the heat and slowly
add the egg yolks, then salt and pepper,
and the grated kefalotyri. Finish with
sweet paprika.

Assembling

In a lasagna pan, layer half the potatoes,
then the eggplant, then the meat, and
then the remaining potatoes. Pour the
béchamel over the top. Place in an oven
preheated to 375 degrees and cook for
forty minutes to an hour, until the top is
golden brown. Sprinkle with paprika.

Serve with a salad of your choice,
preferably Greek.

so the plot is empty but for some weeds, a wild rosemary bush, a thread of bougainvillea woven through the fenced barrier.

Axiotisa is unusual for its creative use of traditional ingredients. The Greek salad is served with *xinomizithra*—a fresh, sour goat cheese sprinkled with oregano—spooned over rocket greens and tomato; the goat, boiled with herbs from the garden below the restaurant's terrace, is surprisingly tender. The *keftedes*—croquettes made from everything from tomato to zucchini to beets—are gorgeous, light and flecked with fresh dill. The last time the three of us ate at Axiotisa, Voula chastised me—not for the first or second second time—about not having a washing machine in our home. *The germs!* she said, as she dipped a pita into the fava spread topped with olive oil. *Washing the cloths with all the other people!* She looked at her son. *I feel sorry for you,* she said, pushing the dish toward him and nodding at it.

Now I shout out the window at my mother-in-law, who is crouching in a field by a goat. "Please get back in the car, Voula!" I say.

She shuffles back in—without the goat—and slams the car door. "That was a beautiful goat and I must feed my son." She looks me up and down, her nose scrunched, as if she smells something rotten. "Someone has to."

Here it is! Voula has told me at each turn. *Turn down here!* We passed a ruin I wanted to stop to see. *Go! Go!* she said. Because what can be gained from only looking? Life is about good nutrition. After nearly two hours we reach the farm, a mere twelve kilometers from Voula's home. It turns out to be an unremarkable greenhouse. I try to hide my disappointment—I wanted crops! I wanted donkeys!—as a couple moves about, tying up beans. *They were once professors!* Voula screams, and I close my eyes and nod, smile when they arrive and my mother-in-law speaks with them in the Greek I can understand perhaps three words of. We take our eggplant, which fills a sack heavy enough to kill a man, and before we are out the door we turn back for enough tomatoes to keep her in Greek salad through winter.

"I think the *tyropita* place is still open," Voula says when we are again in the now sweltering car, the vegetables nestled in the backseat.

I knock the back of my head against my seat; my husband was correct that the journey would involve more than just eggplant. And she does not mean the bakery on the main street, which serves frozen and reheated cheese-and-spinach pies to tourists, but the place tucked away on a hidden corner on a street not suited for cars; often she cannot find it. The tyropitas at

> Before we are out the door we turn back for enough tomatoes to keep her in Greek salad through winter.

Anekamma are handmade by two Naxian women. How I love those pies. Every visit I long for a zucchini-and-feta pie, *kolokithopita*, but the locals usually buy up the pies by noon and we are always too late.

How I love those pies. My first summer on Naxos, the three of us drove high into the mountains, to the village of Aperanthos. It was twilight, the island turning on for the night, the sun dipping into the sea as we ascended into the mountains, and we sat at a restaurant overlooking the steep valley beneath. Voula plucked a green walnut from a tree whose branches stretched over us. *So fresh!* she said, waving the air around her face in steady circles as if she were savoring a fine wine. No pollution like you have in New York, she'd said to me.

We ordered several meze, as is the Greek way, and when the tyropita arrived, Voula cut in to the crisp phyllo and she served it to us both. "Oh my GOD!" I said when I tasted the oozing graviera, rich and buttery and sweet. "This is amazing!"

"Shhh!" Voula hissed. "Be quiet!"

I looked at Pedro in disbelief, as I had many times that first summer in my mother-in-law's house. He usually met my gaze with an eye roll or a shrug, but this time he raised his eyebrows. "You really should be quiet. They will think we don't feed you," he said. "You're not," he said, "*starving.*"

Every year I asked to return there, but this year, Voula shook her index finger at me.

"No good. The son? Drugs. All the money goes into making him stop the drugs."

"Really!" I said, because I have never been above gossip.

I learned later, though, that he'd gone bankrupt. It was true, Yanni, who owns the sweet shop Voula and other older people of the island frequent, told Pedro that no one was going to the restaurant. *The Americans don't come, then the Europeans don't come. And now?* he had said, cutting off pieces of baklava, so much honey dripping between the folds of phyllo it looked practically sexual, *now even the Greeks stay home.*

Voula and I leave the farm and drive slowly back down the hill toward town, the afternoon light casting a scrim-like filter over the water. In town, we drive through the maze of streets—more suitable for walking or for donkeys than for this old Volkswagen—and finally, we find the hidden bakery.

A wooden sign dangles from the door. "Clisto," it says. Closed.

"Fish?" Voula doesn't miss a beat. It's as if tomorrow she will not do a version of this over again with her son.

"But aren't you going to make moussaka?" I ask. Fish, I don't mention, is extremely expensive.

I can tell this decision is tremendous. Moussaka takes time—the hoisting of the circa 1955 meat grinder from the depth of the pantry could take an entire morning. There could be a nutritious branzino or a dorado available today. Fish is an afternoon activity; it involves waiting for the fisherman to come in with the catch. It is another journey entirely, a different side of island life. And the goat with the fine legs, I know, has not left her thoughts for a moment. I realize her desire to feed Pedro is not just about the moussaka—soon Pedro and I will be gone and she'll have to walk to town or call her cousin for a ride, and he will make her wait. She will be at the will of the man on the bike, singing below her window, for most everything from the mountains. And her son will be gone until the following June.

"The moussaka!" She has chosen. "Quick, quick, home."

I struggle to reverse out of the cobble-stoned alley that my husband navigates with ease, but that, for me, is like moving a car through a vise.

"Quickly!" she says. "Please!"

It has become an emergency. I can hear the gears strip, and then, finally, we are out and up the main street, through the green gate: home. "Hurry!" she says. It is the second time today Voula has left the car before it has stopped moving.

Pedro greets us at the door, tapping a pretend watch, grinning. It's been nearly three hours since we left on a twenty-minute journey. I refuse to look at him as I remove the two heavy paper sacks from the backseat. Voula has already run into the house and is washing her hands and slamming around the small chaotic kitchen that I have not once been allowed to cook in, not even to fry a mountain egg or squeeze a magical orange.

In the living room the news is on. All I can make out is a bit about stolen pensions and hand grenades on the streets of Athens.

"It sounds dire," I say to Voula as I set the packages on the floor as I have been taught, so as not to bring in the germs and dust from the car to the table.

"It's a mess," Pedro begins. "Mama, we need to talk about your money. Where it's kept," he says. "What we are going to do."

"That is Athens!" I hear a pan crash down on a stove. "Greece is fine!" she screams. She comes out of the kitchen, her expression not unlike the one she wore earlier, in that open field, squinting into the sun. "Look all we have? Look at my trees. Soon there will be oranges. I am going now to pick my lettuces." She slips into her clogs by the door.

"I'll do it, " I say, trying to calm her. I enjoy gathering the leaves, carefully removing the outside leaves to reveal the tender ones growing beneath.

"Here we have everything! We have cucumbers, zucchinis," she says as she heads out the door. She doesn't seem to have heard me. "No chemicals on Naxos. Everything fresh fresh. Soon, I tell you, there will be eggplants!"

I can hear her clomping down the stairs. I look at my husband. "Naxos is beautiful," she says. Her footfalls stop; she is in her garden. "No pesticides, no chemicals. Everything is safe here. How," I hear her ask, "could you ever leave?" 🛡

DISNEYLAND

Katie Arnold-Ratliff

Don't count on this Monte Cristo.

We were a family obsessed. Every spring until I was fifteen, my parents minivanned me and my two siblings from the Bay Area to Anaheim, where we would hole up in a motel and visit Disneyland for a solid week. We never went anywhere else on vacation. I could find my way from Splash Mountain to It's a Small World even if I were in a coma. I know the fragrance of Pirates of the Caribbean (dank cave, with a singed soupçon of wood smoke), the exact intonation of the Matterhorn's safety message ("Permanecer sentados, por favor"), and the taste of every dish at every restaurant—because I have eaten it all, twice.

The park's food was as much an attraction for me as any of the rides. I lived for the churros, the mint juleps, the

Mickey-shaped pancakes, the massive turkey legs. But above all, I cherished our annual lunch reservation at Blue Bayou café, where I would order the hallowed Monte Cristo sandwich: an overstuffed turkey, ham, and Swiss creation that gets battered, deep-fried, and dusted with powdered sugar. This greasy love child of croque-monsieur and French toast was, to me, the highlight of the trip.

The glory of the park's food is what brings me to Disneyland today: I am in LA on vacation and have detoured to Disneyland to revisit the dining options that held my preadolescent self in thrall.

This is the day I will learn that memory is a form of self-deceit.

When I arrive at the Mickey and Friends parking structure with my friend Laura—a foodie of similar enthusiasm, sentimentality, and caloric recklessness—attendants direct us to level "Goofy." We're nearly thirty, highly caffeinated, and genuinely excited. We can appreciate irony, sure, but neither of us is too cool for sincere delight. The day before, we'd gone to what Laura called "Secret Breakfast," which turned out to be a diner hidden inside the Los Angeles Police Academy. As rounds were fired in the shooting range out back, we walked through the lush Spanish-style courtyard and then dispatched our eggs while gazing at photos of fresh-faced cadets from the '30s and '40s. It was like we were eating in *L.A. Confidential*. As Laura and I enter

Disneyland, I realize we've come here for a similar reason: to be transported.

This is Disneyland's objective, and food is key to its mission. You return to the quaint Main Street of your small-town childhood (whether you had one or not) via an ice-cream sundae; to the Old West by way of a rack of ribs; or to the pastel splendor of Disney's animated films with a Technicolor Mickey lollipop. Disney understands that a transcendental experience requires absolute consistency. You won't see a Haunted Mansion cast member in antebellum dress walking through Critter Country on her way to a smoke break. The illusion must be carried through—visually, musically, olfactorily (the urban legend that they pipe in the scent of waffle cones on Main Street is indeed true), and edibly.

"It's surprising how good the food is here," I tell Laura. We're eating churros while in line for Indiana Jones Adventure; it's 10:30 AM. "The Plaza Inn on Main Street has the *best* fried chicken, and this place"—I point to nearby Bengal Barbecue—"does awesome meat skewers."

"Ooh, fried chicken," she says.

We do the Jungle Cruise, Enchanted Tiki Room, Haunted Mansion, and Big Thunder Mountain Railroad, and then our lunch reservation at Blue Bayou—which is located inside Pirates of the Caribbean—is upon us. We'd gotten coffee and pastries in LA and we ate churros an hour later. We're full, but forget that. It's Disneyland.

My Le Special de Monte Cristo ($25) turns out to be embarrassingly huge, and also just embarrassing: I have a sudden understanding of how dated, how patently midcentury, this dish really is. I see Laura squinting at it, and I feel kind of dumb. Moments earlier, when Laura ordered the jambalaya ($32), the waitress warned it was "a little spicy." As I discover that my sandwich is still saturated with the grease in which it was fried, Laura starts sweating. Then panting. Then she drains her iced tea. Meanwhile, I get through three bites of my food before I must stop. It's not that I'm full. It's that I was *already* full, and now I've ingested a few tablespoons of warm vegetable oil. Laura has politely pushed her plate aside, and I try to reconcile the me who offers up restaurant tips, who gamely orders for the group, who makes a big chunk of her living writing and thinking about food with the me who just led an old friend seriously astray.

"You want to do Star Tours next?" Laura asks weakly.

"Sure," I chirp. We're engaged in a game of indigestion chicken: neither of us wants to be the one who says, "I'm concerned this ride might cause me to shit my pants." We shuffle grimly to Tomorrowland.

By the time C3PO has taken us at warp speed to Tatooine—which involves 3-D glasses and merciless jostling—I've already planned my apology to the people in the row ahead of me, on whom I'm about to vomit. Laura is deathly pale, her red hair shellacked to her forehead. "Let's get a soda," she says.

At the intersection of Tomorrowland and the Swiss Alps, we sip a shared four-dollar Sprite as if it's God's nectar. And then, like magic, we're mostly okay. We walk very slowly to Alice in Wonderland, the floaty Peter Pan ride, and Toontown's roller coaster. Eventually, we feel normal enough for the whiplash factory that is Space Mountain. While we wait in line, Laura tracks down the Kogi truck on Twitter. It's 6:00 PM, and, being food dweebs freshly cured of gastric distress, we're on to dinner.

She looks up from her phone. "Or should we eat here? That's what we came for, right?"

"Oh," I say. "Right."

All day I've been sneaking glances at sweaty chicken fingers in Frontierland, congealed pizza in Tomorrowland, a syrupy brew called Blue Raspberry Drink at the base of the Matterhorn. The realization I've been battling—that I was dead wrong about Disneyland's food—now feels undeniable. The churro was great, I reason. But then, it's a churro. I'm forced to admit that the sandwich I'd loved—call it the Monstrosity Cristo—has leveled me in more ways than one. I have a kind of nausea of the soul.

I see it all so clearly now: the food was never good. I was just a kid who loved Disneyland.

Maybe it's this epiphany, or the grease in my gut, or the confusing reality that I've eaten very little in eight hours of walking and sun and yet I am hideously full—but Space Mountain finishes the job Star Tours started. I'm so ill when I disembark I can barely stand. "I never realized that ride went upside down," I groan. "It doesn't," Laura says. This is when I notice that Tomorrowland is spinning. This place has literally made me sick.

I begin to glean what else lurks behind the park's slavish consistency. You'll never see futuristic Dippin' Dots ice cream carts anywhere besides Tomorrowland because if one were parked between the parasol vendor and the mint julep stand in New Orleans Square, your subconscious might shudder with cognitive dissonance. This is Disneyland's chief enemy. The illusion cannot be broken lest you see the place for what it is: 400 percent Markup Land. Laura and I have dropped a total of seventy dollars just on food and gotten what? Excellent churros and an admittedly miraculous Sprite, but also a sandwich so physically and psychically shattering I'm already determined to try to make it at home—its datedness be damned!—to redeem this bitter day as best I can. It's not a small thing to me. Disneyland was my family's religion, and it's slipping through my fingers and my bowels.

"I just realized I'm starving," Laura says, apparently ignorant of the day's tragedy. "Let's get fried chicken!"

At the Plaza Inn, the golden-brown breasts and thighs piled at the buffet look

> The illusion cannot be broken lest you see the place for what it is: 400 percent Markup Land.

PHOTO © MIKE SAECHANG

gorgeously crisp but fill me with disgust. I've never reacted to food this way. I worry I'm one of those women who doesn't know she's pregnant. Then I worry I won't want to have children if pregnancy makes me dislike fried chicken.

"I have to get out of here," I say. It'll be a few days and one negative pregnancy test before I understand why: I couldn't bear to watch one more beloved thing turn out to be crap.

At Bengal Barbecue, I order a Chieftain Chicken ($3.89) and a Banyan Beef ($4.29). Not surprisingly, I've romanticized the skewers, too: the former is coated in a ketchup-based gak, and the latter

tastes solely like black pepper. But Laura's Outback Vegetable kebab ($3.79) features a plump potato, a wheel of zucchini, a hunk of bell pepper. It's appealingly charred. She exclaims over it. I cling to this minor deliverance as we head toward the exit, stopping to watch the fireworks over Sleeping Beauty's Castle.

Everyone on Main Street is smiling at the sky. The air is warm and still. I don't feel sick—I just feel glad to be back. I always had such a nice time here. Laura's face is pink and yellow and green as the lights burst above us, and this kid who was just slapping his mother is transfixed. He's eating ice cream. Everybody's eating ice cream. I think about how if I batter just the bread, not the whole Monte Cristo, it could work. I think that if I really am pregnant, I could bring my theoretical child to Disneyland. He could eat his first ribs here, like I did, and his first turkey leg. And if he grew up and decided Disneyland is bullshit, maybe it would at least have shown him the joy of inhabiting someone's fully realized vision. Maybe he'd find that useful if he ever did something creative—if he became, say, a writer. Maybe Disneyland wouldn't serve him his greatest meal, but maybe it would impart the bittersweet and valuable truth that even if something you love doesn't change, you do. And maybe it would teach him that it's his right to stubbornly love it anyway. 🏰

The Monte Cristo Sandwich, Redeemed

(serves one)

2 slices good white bread
2 slices Comté cheese
3 slices cooked bacon
2 slices deli turkey
1 extra large egg
1 tablespoon milk
1 tablespoon butter
Salt and pepper to taste
Powdered sugar, for dusting
Dijon mustard, for dipping

Over medium heat, melt butter in a sauté pan.

Whisk eggs, milk, salt, and pepper in a shallow dish until combined.

Dip both sides of bread in egg mixture until bread is lightly soaked. Place in sauté pan. Cook one side of each slice of bread until golden brown.

In the pan, turn one of the slices of bread so the browned side faces up. Layer cheese, bacon, and turkey on bread and top with the other slice so the browned sides are facing in and touching the sandwich filling.

Continue cooking until the cheese is melted, turning once so that both of the outer sides of the bread are browned.

Remove from heat, dust with powdered sugar, and serve with mustard.

Jodi Angel's first collection of short stories, *The History of Vegas*, was published in 2005 and was named as a *San Francisco Chronicle* "Best Book of 2005." Her work has appeared in *Tin House*, *Zoetrope: All-Story*, *Esquire*, *One Story*, and the *Sycamore Review*, among other publications and anthologies. Her second collection, *You Only Get Letters from Jail*, is forthcoming from Tin House. She grew up in a small town in Northern California—in a family of girls.

Katie Arnold-Ratliff is the author of the novel *Bright Before Us*. Her fiction and non-fiction have appeared in such publications as *Time*, *Slate*, and *Salon*, as well as *O, the Oprah Magazine*, where she is a Senior Editor.

Kevin Barry is the author of the story collections, *Dark Lies The Island* and *There Are Little Kingdoms*, and the novel, *City of Bohane*. His story in this issue, "Beer Trip To Llandudno," won the Sunday Times EFG Short Story Award. He has also won the European Union Prize for Literature and the Rooney Prize for Irish Literature. He also works as a playwright and screenwriter. He lives in a swamp in County Sligo, Ireland.

Ellen Bass's poetry books include *The Human Line* and *Mules of Love*. Among her awards are the Lambda Literary Award,

New Letters Poetry Prize, the Larry Levis Prize from *Missouri Review*, and the Pablo Neruda Prize from *Nimrod*. She teaches in the MFA poetry program at Pacific University.

Sophie Cabot Black is the author of two previous poetry collections, *The Descent*, winner of the Connecticut Book Award, and *The Misunderstanding of Nature*, winner of the Norma Farber First Book Award. Her third, *The Exchange*, is forthcoming this year. She lives in New England.

Robert Boswell's new novel is *Tumbledown*, published by Graywolf Press in August 2013. He is the author of seven novels, three story collections, a play, a cyberpunk novel, and two books of nonfiction. He is married to Antonya Nelson. They share the Cullen Distinguished Chair in Creative Writing at the University of Houston.

Kimberly Bruss is an MFA candidate at the University of Houston and poetry editor at Gulf Coast Literary Journal. She is originally from Wisconsin. This is her first national publication.

Camille T. Dungy is the author of *Smith Blue*, *Suck on the Marrow*, and *What to Eat, What to Drink, What to Leave for Poison*. She edited *Black Nature: Four Centuries of African American Nature*

Poetry, and co-edited the *From the Fishouse* poetry anthology. Her honors include an American Book Award, two Northern California Book Awards, a California Book Award silver medal, and a fellowship from the NEA. Dungy is a Professor in the Creative Writing department at San Francisco State University.

Laura Eve Engel's work has appeared or is forthcoming in *Boston Review*, *Crazyhorse*, the *Southern Review*, and elsewhere. She was the 2011-2012 Jay C. and Ruth Halls Poetry Fellow at the Wisconsin Institute for Creative Writing.

Pamela Erens's second novel, *The Virgins*, will be published by Tin House Books in August 2013. Her debut novel, *The Understory*, was a finalist for both the *Los Angeles Times* Book Prize and the William Saroyan International Prize for Writing. She was formerly an editor at *Glamour* magazine, and her criticism has been published in the *Millions*, *Los Angeles Review of Books*, and *Gently Read Literature*, among others.

Colin Fleming writes for the *Atlantic*, *Rolling Stone*, and ESPN *The Magazine*, and his fiction appears in *Black Clock*, *The Iowa Review*, and *Boulevard*. His first book, *Between Cloud and Horizon: A Relationship Casebook in Stories* is forthcoming, with another, *Dark March: Stories for When the Rest of the World is Asleep* to follow. He's wrapping up a novel called *The Freeze Tag Sessions*, about a piano prodigy.

Carrie Fountain's poems have appeared in *American Poetry Review*, *Crazyhorse*, AGNI, and *Southwestern American Literature*, among others. Her debut collection, *Burn Lake*, was a winner of a 2009 National Poetry Series Award and was published by Penguin in 2010. She lives in Austin, Texas and teaches at St. Edward's University.

Miciah Bay Gault is the editor of *Hunger Mountain* at Vermont College of Fine Arts. Her fiction and essays have appeared in AGNI, *The Sun Magazine*, and other journals. She lives in Montpelier, Vermont, where she's recently finished her first novel and had her first baby.

Jennifer Gilmore's most recent novel, *The Mothers*, was recently published in April 2013 by Scribner. She is also the author of the novels *Golden Country* and *Something Red*. Her work has appeared in magazines and journals including *Allure*, *Bomb*, *BookForum*, the *Los Angeles Times*, the *New York Times*, the *New York Times Book Review*, *Salon*, *Vogue*, and the *Washington Post*. Currently she teaches at Princeton University and lives in Brooklyn.

Kate Rutledge Jaffe's poetry and fiction have appeared in the *Believer*, the *Missouri Review*, *Narrative Magazine*, and elsewhere, and received the Matt Clark Prize in Poetry and the Fulton Prize in Short Fiction. She's a graduate of the University of Montana's MFA in Creative Writing program, where she edited

CutBank. Originally from the Pacific Northwest, she now lives in Missoula, Montana.

Stephen King's latest novel is *Joyland*. In September Scribner will publish *Doctor Sleep*, a sequel to *The Shining*. This summer CBS begins broadcasting a television series based on his 2009 novel, *Under the Dome*. In addition to his many fiction bestsellers, he's the author of *On Writing: A Memoir of the Craft*. In 2003 he was honored as the recipient of the National Book Foundation Medal for Distinguished Contribution to American Letters.

Dylan Landis is the author of *Normal People Don't Live Like This*, a novel-in-stories that made *Newsday*'s Ten Best Books of 2009. She received a 2010 fellowship from the National Endowment for the Arts and lives in New York City. This is her third story in *Tin House*.

Alex Lemon is the author of *Happy: A Memoir* and three collections of poetry: *Mosquito*, *Hallelujah Blackout*, and *Fancy Beasts*. A fourth collection is forthcoming from Milkweed Editions. He lives in Ft. Worth, Texas, and teaches at TCU.

Susan Scarf Merrell teaches in the MFA in Creative Writing and Literature at Stony Brook Southampton, and is Fiction Editor of *TSR: The Southampton Review*. Her literary thriller set at Bennington College in the 1960s, narrated by a young woman who moves with her professor husband into the home of novelist Shirley Jackson and Jackson's husband, Stanley Edgar Hyman, is forthcoming from blue rider/ Penguin in 2014.

Liz Moore is the author of the novels *The Words of Every Song* and *Heft*, along with works of short fiction and creative nonfiction that have been published in print and online. She is also a professor of writing at Holy Family University in Philadelphia, where she lives. Her third novel is forthcoming from W.W. Norton.

Allyson Paty is the author of the chapbook *The Further Away* ([Sic], 2012). Her poems have appeared in *Best New Poets 2012*, *DIAGRAM*, and *Harpur Palate*, among other places. *Torch Songs* is a collaboration with Danniel Schoonebeek.

Jon Raymond is the author of the novels *The Half-Life* and *Rain Dragon*, and the short-story collection *Livability*, winner of the 2009 Ken Kesey Award for Fiction. He is the writer of several films, including *Wendy and Lucy* and *Meek's Cutoff*, and co-writer of the Emmy-nominated screenplay for the HBO miniseries *Mildred Pierce*. His writing has appeared in *Bookforum*, *Artforum*, *Tin House*, the *Village Voice*, and other publications. He lives in Portland, Oregon, with his family.

Tripp Reade lives in Durham, North Carolina, where he tries to make the words come out right.

Elissa Schappell is the author of *Blueprints for Building Better Girls* and *Use Me*. She is a contributing editor and the Hot Type book columnist at *Vanity Fair*, a former senior editor of *The Paris Review*, and co-founder and now editor-at-large of *Tin House* magazine. She lives in Brooklyn with her family.

Danniel Schoonebeek's work has appeared in *Boston Review*, *Fence*, *Crazyhorse*, *Kenyon Review*, *Verse Daily*, *Colorado Review*, *The Rumpus*, and elsewhere. Recent poems from *Torch Songs* appear in *Denver Quarterly*, *Colorado Review*, and *Gulf Coast*. *Torch Songs* is a collaboration with Allyson Paty. Allyson and Danniel have each previously appeared in *Tin House* as New Voices in Poetry.

Parul Sehgal is an editor at the *New York Times Book Review*. She is the recipient of the National Book Critics Circle Balakian Citation for Excellence in Reviewing.

Tom Sleigh's many books of poetry include *Army Cats*, which won the Updike Award from the American Academy of Arts and Letters, and *Space Walk*, winner of the Kingsley Tufts Award. He's received the Shelley Prize, an American Academy in Berlin fellowship, grants from the Lila Wallace Fund, the Guggenheim Foundation, NEA, and many others. He teaches in Hunter College's MFA Program.

Rich Smith was raised in Belton, Missouri. He holds an MA in Poetry from Ohio University and is currently enrolled in the MFA program at the University of Washington. His poems have been published in *Guernica*, *Bellingham Review*, and *Southeast Review*.

Jeannie Vanasco enjoys freelancing in her railroad apartment all the livelong day. Her writing has appeared in the *Believer*, the *Times Literary Supplement*, the *New Yorker*'s Page-Turner blog, *Coffin Factory*, and elsewhere. With the support of a Hertog Fellowship, she is currently writing a memoir that concerns necronyms, mental illness, and an artificial eye.

Mark Wagenaar is the 2012 winner of the Pollak Prize, for his debut collection *Voodoo Inverso*, now available from the University of Wisconsin Press. A past winner of the contests of *Fugue*, *Phoebe*, *Columbia: A Journal of Art & Literature*, and several others, his poems have appeared most recently in the *North American Review* and the *Southeast Review*. He and his wife, fellow poet Chelsea Wagenaar, are doctoral fellows at the University of North Texas.

CREDITS:

Page 12: Photos © Christmas w/a K, David Holt London, EBRPD Public Affairs, El Caganer, Florida Keys—Public Libraries, Kim Scarborough, Seattle Municipal Archives, Travis Isaacs, UF Digital Collections, and Waka Jawaka

Page 63: "Firm and Good," by Jodi Angel is from the collection, *You Only Get Letters from Jail*, to be published in July 2013 by Tin House Books.

COVER:

Divers, 2010, 3-color silkscreen on toned paper, 14½ x 11 inches, ©Kim Sielbeck, www.kimsielbeck.com

© TOM MARKS / CORBIS

time	space	support
3 years	*Austin*	*$25,000 per year*

MFA IN WRITING

THE MICHENER CENTER FOR WRITERS
The University of Texas at Austin

www.utexas.edu/academic/mcw
512-471-1601

TEXAS STATE UNIVERSITY
The rising STAR of Texas

MFA

FINE ARTS

with a major in
CREATIVE WRITING
and specializations in
FICTION OR POETRY

We now offer classes in creative nonfiction.

In the Texas Hill Country right next door to Austin

THE ENDOWED CHAIR IN CREATIVE WRITING
2012–2014 Cristina Garcia
Tim O'Brien, Professor of Creative Writing

FACULTY

Cyrus Cassells, Poetry
Doug Dorst, Fiction
Tom Grimes, Fiction

Ogaga Ifowodo, Poetry
Roger Jones, Poetry
Debra Monroe, Fiction

Kathleen Peirce, Poetry
Nelly Rosario, Fiction
Steve Wilson, Poetry

ADJUNCT THESIS FACULTY

Lee K. Abbott
Catherine Barnett
Rick Bass
Ron Carlson
Charles D'Ambrosio
John Dufresne
Carolyn Forché
James Galvin
Amelia Gray
Saskia Hamilton
Shelby Hearon
Bret Anthony Johnston

Hettie Jones
Patricia Spears Jones
Li-Young Lee
Philip Levine
Carole Maso
Elizabeth McCracken
Heather McHugh
Jane Mead
W.S. Merwin
David Mura
Naomi Shihab Nye
Jayne Anne Phillips

Alberto Ríos
Pattiann Rogers
Nicholas Samaras
Elissa Schappell
Richard Siken
Gerald Stern
Rosmarie Waldrop
Sharon Oard Warner
Eleanor Wilner
Mark Wunderlich

RECENT VISITING WRITERS

Kevin Brockmeirer
Olga Broumas
Michael Dickman
Louise Erdrich
Nick Flynn
Richard Ford

S.C. Gwynne
Yiyun Li
Thomas Lux
Mihaela Moscaliuc
Karen Russell
George Saunders

Charles Simic
Robert Stone
Justin Torres
Wells Tower

Visit *Front Porch*, our literary journal:
www.frontporchjournal.com

$60,000 W. Morgan & Lou Claire Rose Fellowship
for an incoming writing student

Additional scholarships and teaching assistantships are available.

Tom Grimes, MFA Director
Department of English
Texas State University
601 University Drive
San Marcos, TX 78666-4684

Phone **512.245.7681**
Fax 512.245.8546
www.mfatxstate.com
mfinearts@txstate.edu

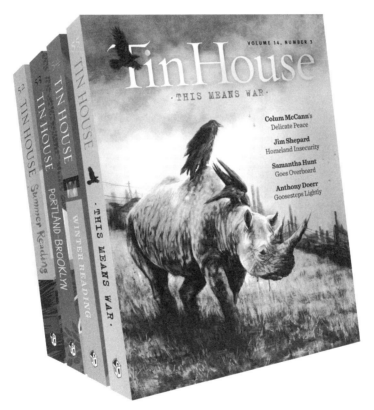

ABOUT THE COVER

Kim Sielbeck inherited her love of the sea from her father, an oceanographer with the coast guard. As a child, her family relocated frequently, "but always to places along the coast." Like much of her work, this issue's cover art, *Divers*, uses ocean imagery to evoke themes of exploration and place.

"*Divers* was a piece that came together the summer after I graduated college," she says, "I'd read an article about people diving for sunken treasure, and how dangerous and exciting it is. This was also the summer that tons of people were getting violently attacked by sharks on the East Coast." Sielbeck's art often holds a dark whimsy. Passed-out musicians and Tom Waits–inspired ice-cream men populate her landscapes, as do Williamsburg skateboarders and cats in T-shirts. In *Divers*, the line quality recalls the covers of vintage adventure magazines. The transparent ink of the water lends an almost delicate sense of depth and texture. The sharks, shaped from negative space, are both ethereal and menacing.

Based in Brooklyn, Sielbeck is a multi-disciplinary artist, skilled in printmaking, illustration, lettering, and other media. By day, she's a textile designer. In conversation, she references artists from the Golden Age of illustration—Shore, Pyle, and Wyeth—models of craft and design. These influences are clear in her solid use of composition and narrative, and though her art has a decidedly contemporary feel, Sielbeck prefers traditional techniques: "At the root of all of my pieces is a real drawing. For me, I guess it's the experience of creating a drawing that I like the most."

More of Sielbeck's work can be found at: www.kimsielbeck.com

Written by *Tin House* designer Jakob Vala, based on an interview with the artist.